Christmas 2010

Dear Friends,

Merry Christmas! As [...] s kind of girl. And I can [...] than one in Cedar Cove. That's why I wrote *A Cedar Cove Christmas*, which was published as a small hardcover a couple of years ago. In it, I introduced the character of Mary Jo Wyse. Mary Jo comes to Cedar Cove on Christmas Eve, pregnant and unmarried and looking for a hotel room. I also introduced her irrepressible brothers, the three Wyse men. By now, I'm sure it's obvious that I was retelling the original Christmas story. I had a lot of fun with that, right down to the little drummer boy—but I'm getting ahead of myself. If you haven't read the story yet, I don't want to spoil it for you. And if you have, you'll see that I've included extra content in the form of a prologue. Time doesn't stand still in Cedar Cove!

Soon after *A Cedar Cove Christmas* was published, my readers asked if the story would ever come out in paperback. The answer is yes—here it is—but as you probably know, I want you to think of me as a value-added author. So I wanted to give you something more…. *5-B Poppy Lane* was part of an anthology published four years ago. Again, I've written a prologue and also an epilogue to frame the story and offer a bit of Christmas spirit. I wrote this in honor of my father, who was a POW during World War II. *5-B Poppy Lane* is, of course, an address in Cedar Cove; it's also a story of romance and adventure, and I'm confident you'll enjoy it.

I'm delighted that you're joining me in my favorite town at my favorite time of year!

As always, I love getting your comments. You can reach me at P.O. Box 1458, Port Orchard, WA 98366 or via my website at www.DebbieMacomber.com. May your Christmas be filled with the warmth and joy of the season.

Debbie Macomber

DEBBIE MACOMBER

CHRISTMAS IN CEDAR COVE

MIRA®

MIRA®

PLEASE RECYCLE • THIS PRODUCT IS RECYCLABLE

Recycling programs for this product may not exist in your area.

ISBN-13: 978-0-7783-2822-3

CHRISTMAS IN CEDAR COVE

Copyright © 2010 by MIRA Books.

The publisher acknowledges the copyright holder of the individual works as follows:

5-B POPPY LANE
Copyright © 2006 by Debbie Macomber

A CEDAR COVE CHRISTMAS
Copyright © 2008 by Debbie Macomber

For questions and comments about the quality of this book please contact us at Customer_eCare@Harlequin.ca.

www.MIRABooks.com

Printed in U.S.A.

Also by Debbie Macomber

CAST OF CHARACTERS

Some of the Residents of Cedar Cove, Washington

Charlotte Jefferson Rhodes: Mother of **Olivia** and of **Will Jefferson.** Now married to widower **Ben Rhodes,** who has two sons, **David** and **Steven,** neither of whom lives in Cedar Cove. Charlotte and Ben live on Eagle Crest Avenue.

Olivia Lockhart Griffin: Family Court judge. Mother of **Justine** and of **James** (who lives in San Diego). Married to **Jack Griffin,** editor of the *Cedar Cove Chronicle.* Their home is at 16 Lighthouse Road.

Justine (Lockhart) Gunderson: Daughter of Olivia. Mother of **Leif.** Married to **Seth Gunderson.** Their home is 6 Rainier Drive.

Will Jefferson: Olivia's brother, Charlotte's son. Formerly of Atlanta. Divorced, retired and back in Cedar Cove, where he has recently bought the local art gallery.

Grace Sherman Harding: Olivia's lifelong best friend. Librarian. Widow of **Dan Sherman.** Mother of **Maryellen Bowman** and **Kelly Jordan.** Married to **Cliff Harding,** a horse breeder living in Olalla, near Cedar Cove. Cliff has a married daughter, **Lisa.**

Maryellen Bowman: Oldest daughter of Grace and Dan Sherman. Mother of **Katie** and **Drake.** Married to **Jon Bowman,** photographer.

Bob and Peggy Beldon: Retired. Own the Thyme and Tide B & B at 44 Cranberry Point.

Roy McAfee: Private investigator, retired from Seattle police force. Three adult children—**Mack, Linnette** and **Gloria.** Married to **Corrie,** who works as his office manager. The McAfees live at 50 Harbor Street.

Linnette McAfee: Daughter of Roy and Corrie. A physician assistant, she now lives in North Dakota.

Mack McAfee: Son of Roy and Corrie, brother of Linnette. Fireman and EMT in Cedar Cove.

Gloria Ashton: Deputy in Cedar Cove Sheriff's Department. Daughter of Roy and Corrie, born prior to their marriage and adopted by the Ashton family of California as a newborn.

Troy Davis: Sheriff of Cedar Cove.

Pastor Dave Flemming: Local Methodist minister. He and his wife, **Emily,** are the parents of **Matthew** and **Mark.**

Shirley Bliss: Widow and fabric artist, mother of Tannith (**Tanni**) Bliss.

Shaw Wilson: Friend of Tanni's. Works at Mocha Mama, a local coffee shop.

Helen Shelton: Widow and friend of Charlotte Rhodes. Helen lives at 5-B Poppy Lane.

CONTENTS

5-B POPPY LANE

To my parents
Ted and Connie Adler
who married July 25, 1942,
before my father
headed off to war

Prologue

It was early afternoon, Christmas Eve. Snow was falling lightly, adding to the festive atmosphere inside and out. Helen Shelton fussed with the decorations in her small Cedar Cove duplex, making sure everything was in place. The tree, a real one, featured the ornaments she'd started acquiring when she'd married Sam in 1946. He'd bought her many of these, and as she hung them carefully on the branches she'd relived their history, hers and Sam's. He'd died almost thirty years ago but she remembered every Christmas they'd spent together.

The Nativity pieces were arranged on her coffee table with the Infant Jesus nestled in the manger, surrounded by the other familiar figurines. A large evergreen wreath hung on her front door. The house was redolent with the scents of spruce and spice—ready for Christmas.

Helen wanted everything perfect when her only granddaughter and her husband arrived. In preparation she'd mulled cider and baked Ruth's favorite Christmas cookies from an old gingerbread recipe; they'd first made it together when Ruth was a child. Even now, after all these years, Helen remembered the thrill she'd felt when her granddaughter was born. Oh, she loved her grandsons, but for a grandmother there was something special about a girl.

The doorbell chimed and Helen peeked outside to see her dear friend Charlotte Rhodes standing on the porch. Delighted, she opened the door and quickly ushered Charlotte inside. They were both getting on in years, and Helen suspected neither of them had many Christmases left. She didn't have a fatalistic view of life by any means, but she was a practical woman. Helen knew what it was to face death. She had no fear of dying.

"Merry Christmas," Charlotte said, unwrapping a hand-knit lace scarf from around her neck. Her friend was the most exquisite knitter. Many a time she'd assisted Helen with her knitting projects. She gave her the confidence to try new things. Why, with Charlotte's help a few years back, Helen had completed a complicated Fair Isle sweater. She still felt a bit of pride whenever she wore that sweater. She was a competent knitter in her own right; she didn't mean to discount her skills. But Charlotte had such an encouraging way about her, and not just when it came to knitting. Helen had confided in Charlotte about what had happened to her during the war, and Charlotte had urged her to share it with her family. Eventually, she had...

"Merry Christmas," Helen said, taking Charlotte's coat and scarf and hanging them up. She led her friend into the kitchen. "This is such a pleasant surprise."

"I knew your granddaughter and her husband were stopping by, so I brought some of my green tomato mincemeat." She removed two beribboned jars from her ever-present knitting bag.

"Oh, Charlotte, *thank* you." Helen accepted the jars and put them on the counter to admire. Charlotte was well aware that Helen had a weakness for her homemade green tomato mincemeat.

"Consider this a small Christmas gift," Charlotte said, looking pleased at Helen's reaction.

"Didn't you say it was too much work this year?" Helen could swear Charlotte had claimed she was finished with canning. And who would blame her?

"I did say that, and then I took a look at all those green tomatoes and I couldn't help myself. Besides, Ben swears mincemeat is his favorite pie."

"I thought your peach pie was his favorite."

Charlotte actually blushed. Those two had been married for several years now but they still behaved like newlyweds. It always made Helen smile.

"Ben says that about all my pies."

"Well, I'm very happy to get these. I'll make a pie for tonight's dessert." Helen automatically set the teakettle on the burner, dropping teabags in her best china pot.

"What time is your granddaughter getting here?"

Helen glanced at the kitchen clock. "Not for several hours. Around five."

Charlotte pulled out a chair and sat down, reaching into her voluminous bag for her knitting. Socks again. Charlotte was never without her knitting, and these days it was usually socks. Helen had recently made socks, too, but not ones you'd wear. She'd knit both Ruth and Paul Christmas stockings to hang by the fireplace. Because of the intricate pattern, it had taken her the better part of three months. She planned to give them their made-with-love Christmas stockings when they exchanged gifts that evening.

It wasn't long before the tea was ready and the two of them sat across the table from each other, a plate of the gingerbread cookies between them.

"I've met your granddaughter, haven't I?" Charlotte asked, picking up her teacup and frowning slightly.

"Yes, don't you recall? Ruth certainly remembers you."

"She does?"

"It was a few years ago. She was in quite a state when she came by to visit. She was absolutely beside herself because she wasn't sure what to do about Paul."

Charlotte looked confused.

"That was shortly after they met," Helen explained, surprised her friend had apparently forgotten the episode, since Charlotte had answered Ruth's knock at the door. "They'd been corresponding for a while. Paul was in the marines. Well, he still is, but that's not the point."

Charlotte chose a cookie. "It's coming back to me now," she said. "They had a lovely romance, didn't they?"

"Oh, yes."

She took a bite. "Mmm. Delicious. Now, remind me again how they met."

Helen settled back in her chair and picked up her own cup of tea. This was such a wonderful story. Her own love story was part of it, too. All those years ago during the Second World War. There were fewer and fewer people who knew what that war had *really* been like.

For more than fifty years she'd refused to talk about that time, refused to even think about her adventures and ordeals. She'd lost so much—and yet, she'd gained, too. At the urging of the few friends she'd confided in, including Charlotte, she'd finally told Ruth what had happened. Ruth and her Paul. Afterward, her granddaughter had said that her experiences were more than family history; they were *history*.

"Helen," Charlotte murmured, shaking her out of

her reverie. "You were going to tell me about Ruth and Paul."

"Oh, yes. The story of how they fell in love…" She settled back, listening to the comforting click of Charlotte's needles, and began.

One

Ruth Shelton hurried out of her classroom-management lecture at the University of Washington, where she was completing her master's of education degree. Clutching her books, she dashed across campus, in a rush to get home. By now the mail would have been delivered to her small rental house three blocks from the school.

"Ruth," Tina Dupont called, stopping her in midflight. "There's another antiwar rally this afternoon at—"

"Sorry, I've got to run," Ruth said, jogging past her friend and feeling more than a little guilty. Other students cleared a path for her; wherever she was headed must have seemed urgent—and it was, but only to her. Since Christmas, four months ago, she'd been corresponding with Sergeant Paul Gordon, USMC, who was stationed in Afghanistan. There'd been recent reports of fighting, and she hadn't received a letter or an email from Paul in three days. Three interminable days. Not since they'd initially begun their correspondence had there been such a lapse. Paul usually wrote every day and she did, too. They emailed as often as possible. Ruth had strong feelings about the war in Iraq, although her opinions didn't match those of her parents.

Earlier in the school year, Ruth had been part of a protest rally on campus. But no matter what her political views on the subject, she felt it was important to support American troops wherever they might be serving. In an effort to do that, Ruth had voluntarily mailed a Christmas card and letter to a nameless soldier.

Paul Gordon was the young man who'd received that Christmas card, and to Ruth's surprise he'd written her back and enclosed his photograph. Paul was from Seattle and he'd chosen her card because of the Seattle postmark. He'd asked her lots of questions—about her history, her family, her interests—and closed with a postscript that said he hoped to hear from her again.

When she first got his letter, Ruth had hesitated. She felt she'd done her duty, supported the armed services in a way she was comfortable doing. This man she'd never met was asking her to continue corresponding with him. She wasn't sure she wanted to become that involved. Feeling uncertain, she'd waited a few days before deciding.

During that time, Ruth had read and reread his letter and studied the head shot of the clean-cut handsome marine sergeant in dress uniform. His dark brown eyes had seemed to stare straight through her—and directly into her heart. After two days, she answered his letter with a short one of her own and added her email address at the bottom of the page. Ruth had a few concerns she wanted him to address before she could commit herself to beginning this correspondence. Being as straightforward and honest as possible, she explained her objections to the war in Iraq. She felt there was a more legitimate reason for troops to be in Afghanistan and wanted to know his stand. A few days later he emailed her. Paul didn't mince words. He told her he believed the United States had done the right thing in entering Iraq and gave his reasons. He left it up to her to decide if she wanted to continue their correspondence. Ruth emailed him back and once again listed her objections to the American presence in the Middle East. His response came a day later, suggesting they "agree to disagree." He ended the email with the same question he'd asked her earlier. Would she write him?

At first, Ruth wasn't going to. They were diametrically opposed in their political views. But in the end, even recognizing the conflict between their opinions, she did write. Their correspondence started slowly. She enjoyed his wry wit and his unflinching determination to make a difference in the world. His father had fought in Vietnam, he said, and in some ways the war in Afghanistan seemed similar—the hostile terrain, the unpredictability of the enemy, the difficult conditions. For her part, she mentioned that at twenty-five she'd returned to school to obtain her master's of education degree. Then, gradually, without being fully aware of how it had happened, Ruth found herself spending part of every day writing or emailing Paul. Despite the instant nature of email, and its convenience, they both enjoyed interspersing their online messages with more formal letters. There was something so…permanent about a real letter. As well, depending on his duty assignment, Paul didn't always have computer access.

After they'd been corresponding regularly for a couple of months, Paul asked for her picture. Eventually she'd mailed him her photograph, but only after she'd had her hair and makeup done at one of those "glamour" studios. Although she wasn't fashion-model beautiful, she considered herself fairly attractive and wanted to look her absolute best for Paul, although she didn't entirely understand why it mattered so much. For years, she'd been resigned to the fact that she wasn't much good at relationships. In high school she'd been shy, and while she was an under-graduate, she'd dated a little but tended to be reserved and studious. Her quiet manner didn't seem to appeal to the guys she met. It was only when she stepped in front of a classroom that she truly became herself. She loved teaching, every single aspect of it. In the process, Ruth lost her hesitation and her restraint, and to her astonish-ment discovered that this enthusiasm had begun to spill over into the rest of her life. Suddenly men started to no-tice her. She enjoyed the attention—who wouldn't?—and had dated more in the past few months than in the prece-ding four years.

For the picture, her short brown hair had been styled in loose curls. Her blue eyes were smiling and friendly, which was exactly the impression she hoped to convey. She was a little shocked by the importance of Paul's re-action—by her need that he find her attractive.

She waited impatiently for his response. A week later she received an email. Paul seemed to like what he saw in her photograph and soon they were writing and email-ing back and forth at a feverish pace. A day without some form of communication from Paul felt empty now.

Ruth had never had a long-distance relationship be-fore, and the growing intensity of her feelings for this man she'd never met took her by surprise. She wasn't a teenager with a schoolgirl crush. Ruth was a mature, re-sponsible adult. Or at least she had been until she slipped a simple Christmas card into the mailbox—and got a reply from a handsome marine sergeant named Paul Gordon.

Ruth walked quickly to the rental house she shared with Lynn Blumenthal, then ran up the front steps to the porch. Lynn was eighteen and away from home and family for the first time. The arrangement suited both of them, and despite the disparity in their ages and interests, they'd gotten along fairly well. With her heart pounding hard, Ruth forced herself to draw in a deep breath as she started toward the mailbox.

The screen door flew open and Lynn came out. "What are you doing home?" she asked, then shook her head. "Never mind, I already know. You're looking for a letter from soldier boy."

Ruth wasn't going to deny the obvious. "I haven't heard from him in three days."

Lynn rolled her eyes. "I don't understand you."

"I know." Ruth didn't want to get into another discussion with her roommate. Lynn had made her feelings about this relationship known from the outset, although as Ruth had gently tried to tell her, it was none of her business. That didn't prevent the younger woman from expressing her views. Lynn said that Ruth was only setting herself up for heartache. A part of Ruth actually agreed, but by the time she realized what was happening, she was emotionally involved with Paul.

"You hardly ever see Clay anymore," Lynn chastised, hands on her hips. "He called and asked about you the other night."

Ruth stared at the small black mailbox. "Clay and I are just friends."

"Not according to him."

It was true that they'd been seeing each other quite a bit following a Halloween party last October. Like her, Clay Matthews was obtaining his master's of education, and they seemed to have a lot in common. But her interest in him had started to wane even before she'd mailed that Christmas card to Paul. The problem was, Clay hadn't noticed.

"I'm sorry he's disappointed."

"Clay is decent and hardworking, and the way you've

treated him the last few months is…is terrible." Lynn, who at five foot ten stood a good seven inches taller than Ruth, could be intimidating, especially with her mouth twisted in that grimace of disapproval.

Ruth had tried to let Clay down easily, but it hadn't worked. They'd gone to the library together last Thursday. Unfortunately, that had been a mistake. She'd known it almost right away when Clay pressured her to have coffee with him afterward. It would've been better just to end the relationship and forget about staying friends. He was younger, for one thing, and while that hadn't seemed important earlier, it did now. Perhaps it was wrong to compare him to Paul, but Ruth couldn't help it. Measured against Paul, Clay seemed immature, demanding and insecure.

"You said he phoned?" Frowning, she glanced at Lynn.

Lynn nodded. "He wants to know what's going on."

Oh, brother! Ruth couldn't have made it plainer had she handed him divorce papers. Unwilling to be cruel, she'd tried to bolster his ego by referring to all the positive aspects of his personality—but apparently, that had only led him to think the opposite of what she was trying to tell him. He'd refused to take her very obvious hints, and in her frustration, she'd bluntly announced that she wasn't interested in seeing him anymore. That seemed pretty explicit to her; how he could be confused about it left Ruth shaking her head.

The fact that he'd phoned and cried on her roommate's shoulder was a good example of what she found adolescent about his behavior. She was absolutely certain Paul would never do that. If he had a problem, he'd take it directly to the source.

"I think you're being foolish," Lynn said, and added, "Not that you asked my opinion."

"No, I didn't," Ruth reminded her, eyeing the mailbox again. There was an ornamental latticework design along the bottom, and looking through it, she could tell that the day's mail had been delivered. The envelope inside was white, and her spirits sank. There *had* to be something from Paul. If not a real letter, then an email.

"He wanted me to talk to you," Lynn was saying.

"Who did?" Ruth asked distractedly. She was dying to open the mailbox, but she wanted to do it in privacy.

"Clay," Lynn cried, sounding completely exasperated. "Who else are we talking about?"

Suddenly Ruth understood. She looked away from the mailbox and focused her attention on Lynn. "You're attracted to him, aren't you?"

Lynn gasped indignantly. "Don't be ridiculous."

"Sit down," Ruth said, gesturing toward the front steps where they'd often sat before. It was a lovely spring afternoon, the first week of April, and she needed to clear the air with her roommate before this got further out of hand.

"What?" Lynn said with a defensive edge. "You've got the wrong idea here. I was just trying to help a friend."

"Sit," Ruth ordered.

"I have class in twenty minutes and I—" Lynn paused, scowling at her watch.

"Sit down."

The eighteen-year-old capitulated with ill grace. "All right, but I know what you're going to say." She folded her arms and stared straight ahead.

"I'm fine with it," Ruth said softly. "Go out with him if you want. Like I said earlier, I'm not interested in Clay."

"You would be if it wasn't for soldier boy."

Ruth considered that and in all honesty felt she could say, "Not so."

"I don't understand you," Lynn lamented a second time. "You marched in the rally against the war in Iraq. Afghanistan isn't all that different, and now you're involved with Paul what's-his-face and it's like I don't even know you anymore."

"Paul doesn't have anything to do with this."

"Yes, he does," Lynn insisted.

"I'm not going to have this conversation with you. We agree on some points and disagree on others. That's fine. We live in a free society and we don't have to have the same opinion on these issues or anything else."

Lynn sighed and said nothing.

"I have the feeling none of this is really about Paul," Ruth said with deliberate patience. She hadn't known Lynn very long; they lived separate lives and so far they'd never had a problem. As roommates went, Ruth felt she was fortunate to have found someone as amicable as Lynn. She didn't want this difference of opinion about Clay—and Paul—to ruin that.

The other girl once again looked pointedly at her watch, as if to suggest Ruth say what she intended to say and be done with it.

"I don't want to see Clay," she said emphatically.

"You might have told him that."

"I tried."

Lynn glared at her. "You should've tried harder."

Ruth laughed, but not because she was amused. For whatever reason, Clay had set his sights on her and wasn't about to be dissuaded. Complicating matters, Lynn was obviously interested in him and feeling guilty and unsure of how to deal with her attraction.

"Listen," Ruth said. "I didn't mean to hurt Clay. He's a great guy and—"

"You shouldn't have lied to him."

Ruth raised her eyebrows. "When did I lie to him?"

"Last week you said you were going to visit your grandmother in Cedar Cove and that was why you couldn't go out with him this weekend. I overheard you," she murmured.

Oh, that. "It was a white lie," Ruth confessed. She definitely planned to visit her grandmother, though. Helen Shelton lived across Puget Sound in a small community on the Kitsap Peninsula. Ruth had spent Thanksgiving with her grandmother and visited for a weekend before Christmas and then again close to Valentine's Day. Her last visit had been early in March. She always enjoyed her time with Helen, but somehow the weeks had slipped away and here it was April already.

"A lie is a lie," Lynn said adamantly.

"Okay, you're right," Ruth agreed. "I should've been honest with Clay." Delaying had been a mistake, as she was now learning.

That seemed to satisfy her roommate, who started to get to her feet. Ruth placed her hand on Lynn's forearm, stopping her. "I want to know why you're so upset about this situation with Clay."

"I told you.… I just don't think this is how people should treat each other."

"I don't like the way Clay's put you in the middle. This is between him and me. He had no right to drag you into it."

"Yes, but—"

"You're defending him?"

Lynn shrugged. "I guess."

"Don't. Clay's a big boy. If he has something to say,

then he can come to me all on his own. When and if he does, I'm going to tell him *again* that I'm no longer interested in dating him. I'm—"

"Stuck on some gun-wielding—"

A look from Ruth cut her off.

"Okay, whatever," Lynn muttered.

"What I want you to do is comfort him," Ruth said, patting Lynn's arm.

"I could, I suppose."

"Good," Ruth said, hoping to encourage her. "He might need someone to talk to, and since you're sensitive to his feelings, you'd be the perfect choice."

"You think so?"

Ruth nodded. Lynn stood up and went inside to get her books; she left with a cheerful goodbye as if they'd never had an argument. With her roommate gone, Ruth leaped off the step and across the porch to the mailbox. Lifting the top, she reached inside, holding her breath as she pulled out the electric bill in its white envelope, a sales flyer—and a hand-addressed air mail letter from Sergeant Paul Gordon.

Two

April 2

My Dear Ruth,

We've been out on a recon mission for the last four days and there wasn't any way I could let you know. They seemed like the longest four days of this tour, and not for the reasons you might think. Those days meant I couldn't write you or receive your letters. I've been in the marines for eight years now and I've never felt like this about mail before. Never felt this strongly about a woman I've yet to meet, either. Once we were back in camp, I sat down with your letters and read through each one. As I explained before, there are times we can't get online and this happened to be one of those times. I realize you've probably been wondering why I wasn't in touch. I hope you weren't too concerned. I would've written if I could.

I have good news. I'm coming home on leave....

Ruth read Paul's letter twice. Yes, he'd definitely said he was headed home, to Seattle, for two weeks before flying to Camp Pendleton in California for additional training. He hoped to spend most of his leave with her. His one request was that Ruth make as much time for him as her studies would allow and, if possible, keep her weekends free.

If Ruth thought her heart had been beating hard a few minutes earlier, it didn't compare to the way it pounded now. She could barely breathe. Never had she looked forward to meeting anyone more.

Sitting on the edge of her bed, Ruth picked up the small framed photograph she kept on her nightstand. Paul's image was the first thing she saw when she woke and the last before she turned off her light. In four months, he'd become an important part of her life. Now, with his return to Seattle, their feelings for each other would stand the real test. Writing letters and email messages was very different from carrying on a face-to-face conversation....

At the end of his letter, Paul suggested they meet at 6:00 p.m. on Saturday, April 16, at Ivar's restaurant on the Seattle waterfront. She didn't care what else was on her schedule; any conflicting arrangement would immediately be canceled.

Rather than begin her homework, Ruth sat down and wrote Paul back, her fingers flying over the computer keys as she composed her response. Yes, she would see him there. Nothing could keep her away. While she was nervous at the prospect of meeting Paul, she was excited, too.

Her letter was coming out of the printer when the phone rang. Absently Ruth grabbed the receiver, holding it against her shoulder as she opened the desk drawer and searched for an envelope.

"Hello?"

"Ruth, it's your grandmother."

"Grandma," Ruth said, genuinely pleased to hear from Helen. "I've been meaning to call you and I haven't. I'm sorry."

Her grandmother chuckled. "I didn't call to make you feel guilty. I'm inviting you to lunch."

"When?"

"In a couple of weeks—on Sunday the seventeenth if that works for you. I figured I'd give you plenty of time to fit me into your schedule. I thought we'd sit out on the patio, weather permitting, and enjoy the view of the cove."

Her grandmother's duplex was on a hill overlooking the water with the lighthouse in the distance. Her grandparents had lived in Cedar Cove for as long as Ruth could remember, and Helen had stayed there after her husband's death. Because Ruth had been born and raised in Oregon, she'd visited the small Washington town often through the years. "I've wanted to get over to see you."

"I know, I know, but unless we both plan ahead, it won't happen. In no time you'll have your master's degree and then you'll move on and we'll both regret the missed opportunities. I don't want that."

"I don't, either." Her Grandma Shelton was Ruth's favorite relative. She was highly educated, which wasn't particularly common for a woman her age, and spoke French and German fluently. She'd worked as a translator from the 1950s through the '80s, specializing in French novels, which she translated into English. Her father hadn't said much about his mother's life prior to her marriage, and one of the reasons Ruth had chosen to attend the University of Washington was so she could get to know her grandmother better.

"I can put you down for lunch, then?"

"Yes, that would be lovely." Her gaze fell on Paul's

letter and Ruth realized that the date her grandmother had suggested was the first weekend Paul would be in town. He'd specifically asked her to keep as much of that two-week period free as she could. She wanted to spend time with him and yet she couldn't refuse her grandmother. "Grandma, I'm looking at my calendar and—"

"Is there a conflict?"

"Not…exactly. I've sort of got a date," she said, assuming she and Paul would be seeing each other. It would be ideal if he could join her. "It isn't anything official, so I—"

"Then you do have another commitment."

"No…" This was getting complicated. "Well, not exactly," she said again.

"I wasn't aware that you were dating anyone special. Who is he?"

The question hung there for a moment before Ruth answered. "His name is Paul Gordon and we aren't really dating." She would've continued, except that her grandmother broke in.

"Your parents didn't say anything about this." The words were spoken as if there must be something untoward about Paul that Ruth didn't want to divulge.

"No, Mom and Dad wouldn't," Ruth said, not adding that she hadn't actually mentioned Paul to her parents. She'd decided it wasn't necessary to enlighten them about this correspondence yet. Explaining her feelings about Paul to her family would be difficult when everyone knew her political views. More importantly, she wasn't sure how she felt about him and wouldn't be until they'd met.

So far, they were only pen pals, but this was the man she dreamed about every night, the man who dominated her thoughts each and every day.

"Grandma, I haven't said anything to Mom and Dad because I haven't officially met Paul yet."

"Is this..." Her grandmother hesitated. "Is this one of those...those *internet* relationships?" She spit out the word as though meeting a man via the internet was either illegal or unseemly—most likely both.

"No, Grandma, it's nothing like that."

"Then why don't your parents know about him?"

"Well, because...because he's a soldier in Afghanistan." There—it was out.

Her announcement was greeted by silence. "There's something wrong with that?" she eventually asked.

"No..."

"You say it like you're ashamed."

"I'm *not* ashamed," Ruth insisted. "I like Paul a great deal and I'm proud of his service to our country." She downplayed her political beliefs as she expanded on her feelings. "I enjoy his letters and like him more than I probably should, but I don't like the fact that he's a soldier."

"You sound confused."

Ruth sighed. That was certainly an accurate description of how she felt.

"So this Paul will be in Seattle on leave?"

"Yes. For two weeks."

"He's coming here to meet you?"

"His family also lives in the area."

"Invite him along for lunch," her grandmother said. "I want to meet him, too."

"You do?" Ruth's enthusiasm swelled. "That's great. I thought of it, but I wasn't sure how you'd feel about having him join us."

"I meant what I said. I want to meet him."

"We've only been writing for a few months. I don't know him well, and..." She let the rest fade.

"It'll be fine, Ruth," her grandmother assured her. Helen always seemed to understand what Ruth was feeling. She'd found ways to encourage the special bond between them.

"Grandpa was a soldier when you first met him, wasn't he?" Ruth remembered her father telling her this years ago, although he'd also said his mother didn't like to talk about those years. Ruth assumed that was because of Grandpa Sam's bad memories of the war, the awful things he'd seen and experienced in Europe. She knew her grandparents had met during the Second World War, fallen in love and married soon afterward. Ruth's father had been born in the baby boom years that followed, and her uncle Jake had arrived two years later. Ruth was Helen's only granddaughter, but she had three grandsons.

"Oh, yes." She sighed wistfully. "My Sam was so handsome, especially in his uniform." Her voice softened perceptibly.

"How long did you know him before you were married?"

Her grandmother laughed. "Less than a year. In wartime everything's very intense. People married quickly because you never knew if you'd still be alive tomorrow. It was as if those of us who were young had to cram as much life into as short a time as possible."

"The war was terrible, wasn't it?"

Helen sighed before whispering, "All war is terrible."

"I agree," Ruth said promptly.

"So you and this soldier you've never met are discussing marriage?" her grandmother asked after a moment.

"No!" Ruth nearly choked getting out her denial. "Paul and me? No, of course not. I promise you the subject has never even come up." They hadn't written about kissing or touching or exchanged the conventional romantic endearments. That didn't mean she hadn't *dreamed* about what it would be like to be held by Paul Gordon. To kiss him and be caressed by him. She'd let her imagination roam free....

"So you say," her grandmother said with amusement in her voice. "By all means, bring your friend. I'll look forward to meeting him."

That was no doubt true, Ruth thought, but no one looked forward to meeting Paul Gordon more than she did.

Three

"How do I look?" Ruth asked her roommate. She hated to sound so insecure, but this was perhaps the most important meeting of her life and Ruth was determined to make a perfect impression.

"Fabulous," Lynn said, her face hidden behind the latest issue of *People* magazine.

"I might believe you if you actually looked at me." Ruth held on to her patience with limited success. The relationship with her roommate had gone steadily downhill since the confrontation on the porch steps two weeks earlier. Apparently Clay wasn't interested in dating Lynn. What Ruth did know was that Clay hadn't contacted either of them since, and her roommate had been increasingly cold and standoffish. Ruth had tried to talk to her but that hadn't done any good. She suspected that Lynn *wanted* to be upset, so Ruth had decided to go about her own business and ignore her roommate's disgruntled mood. This might not be the best strategy, but it was the only way she could deal with Lynn's attitude.

Her roommate heaved a sigh; apparently lifting her head a couple of inches required immense effort. Her eyes were devoid of emotion as she gave Ruth a token appraisal. "You look all right, I guess."

These days, that was high praise coming from Lynn. Ruth had spent an hour doing her hair, with the help of a curling iron and two brushes. And now it was raining like crazy. This wasn't the drizzle traditionally associated with the Pacific Northwest, either. This was *rain*. Real rain. Which spelled disaster for her hair, since her umbrella wouldn't afford much protection.

If her hair had taken a long time, choosing what to wear had demanded equal consideration. She had a pretty teal-and-white summer dress from last year that made her eyes look soft and dreamy, but the rain had altered *that* plan. Now she was wearing black pants and a white cashmere sweater with a beige overcoat.

"You're meeting at Ivar's, right?"

"Right." Ruth didn't remember telling her roommate. They were barely on speaking terms.

"Too bad."

"Too bad what?"

Lynn sighed once more and set aside the magazine. "If you must know, soldier boy phoned and said you should meet him outside the restaurant." She grinned nastily. "And in case you haven't noticed, it's pouring out."

"I'm supposed to meet him outside?"

"That's what he said."

Ruth made an effort not to snap at her. "You didn't think to mention this before?"

Lynn shrugged. "It slipped my mind."

Ruth just bet it did. Rather than start an argument, she collected her raincoat, umbrella and purse. Surely she would receive a heavenly reward for controlling her temper. Lynn would love an argument but Ruth wasn't going to give her one; she wasn't going to play childish games with her roommate. The difference in their ages had never seemed more pronounced than it had in the past two weeks.

Because of the rain, Ruth couldn't find convenient street parking and was forced to pay an outrageous amount at a lot near the restaurant. She rushed toward Ivar's, making sure she arrived in plenty of time. Lynn's sour disposition might have upset Ruth if not for the fact that she was finally going to meet the soldier who'd come to mean so much to her.

Focusing on her hair, dress and makeup meant she'd paid almost no attention to something that was far more important—what she'd actually say when she saw Paul for the first time. Ideas skittered through her mind as she crossed the street.

Ruth hoped to sound witty, articulate and well informed. She so badly wanted to impress Paul and was afraid she'd stumble over her words or find herself speechless. Her other fear was that she'd take one look at him and burst into tears. It could happen; she felt very emotional about meeting this man she'd known only through letters and emails.

Thankfully, by the time she reached Ivar's, the rain had slowed to a drizzle. But it was still wet out and miserably gray. Her curls, which had been perfectly styled, had turned into tight wads of frizz in the humid air. She was sure she resembled a cartoon character more than the fashion model she'd strived for earlier that afternoon.

After the longest ten-minute wait of her life, Ruth checked her watch and saw that it was now one minute past six. Paul was late. She pulled her cell phone from her bag; unfortunately Paul didn't answer *his* cell, so she punched out her home number. Perhaps he'd been delayed in traffic and had called the house, hoping to connect with her.

No answer. Either Lynn had left or purposely chosen not to pick up the receiver. Great, just great.

To her dismay, as she went to toss her cell phone back inside her purse, she realized the battery was low. Why hadn't she charged it? Oh, no, that would've been *much* too smart.

All at once Ruth figured it out. Paul wasn't late at all. Somehow she'd missed him, which wouldn't be that difficult with all the tourist traffic on the waterfront. Even in the rain, people milled around the area as if they were on the sunny beaches of Hawaii. Someone needed to explain to these tourists that the water dripping down from the sky was cold rain. Just because they'd dressed for sunshine didn't mean the weather would cooperate.

Despite her umbrella, her hair now hung in tight ringlets all around her head. Either of two things had happened, she speculated. Perhaps her appearance was so drastically changed from the glamour photo she'd sent him that Paul hadn't recognized her and assumed she'd stood him up. The other possibility was even less appealing. Paul had gotten a glimpse of her and decided to escape without saying a word.

For a moment Ruth felt like crying. Rather than waste the last of her cell phone battery phoning her roommate again, she stepped inside the restaurant to see if Paul had left a message for her.

She opened the door and lowered her umbrella. As she did, she saw a tall, lean and very handsome Paul Gordon get up from a chair in the restaurant foyer.

"Ruth?"

"Paul?" Without a thought, she dropped the umbrella and moved directly into his embrace.

Then they were in each other's arms, hugging fiercely.

When it became obvious that everyone in the crowded foyer was staring at them, Paul finally released her.

"I was outside—didn't you tell Lynn that's where we were meeting?"

"No." He brushed the wet curls from her forehead and smiled down at her. "I said inside because I heard on the weather forecast that it was going to rain. And—" he rolled his eyes "—I forgot my cell phone. I'm not used to carrying one around."

"Of *course* you said inside." Ruth wanted to kick herself for being so dense. She should've guessed what Lynn was up to; instead, she'd fallen right into her roommate's petty hands. "I'm so sorry to keep you waiting."

A number of people were still watching them but Ruth didn't care. She couldn't stop looking at Paul. He seemed unable to break eye contact with her, too.

The hostess came forward. "Since your party's arrived," she said with a smile, "I can seat you now."

"Yes, please." Paul helped Ruth off with her coat and set the umbrella beside several others so it could dry. Then, as if they'd known and loved each other all their lives, he reached for her hand and linked her fingers with his as they walked through the restaurant.

The hostess seated them by the window, which overlooked the dark, murky waters of Puget Sound. Rain ran in rivulets down the tempered glass, but as far as Ruth was concerned it could have been the brightest, sunniest day in Seattle's history.

Paul continued to hold her hand on top of the table.

"I was worried about what I'd say once we met," she said. "Then when we did, I just felt so glad, the words didn't seem important."

"I'd almost convinced myself you'd stood me up." He yawned, covering his mouth with the other hand, and she realized he was probably functioning on next to no sleep.

"Stood you up? I would've found a way to get here no matter what." She let the truth of that show in her eyes. She had the strongest feeling of *certainty,* and an involuntary sense that he was everything she'd dreamed.

He briefly looked away. "I would've found a way to get to you, too." His fingers tightened around hers.

"When did you last sleep?" she asked.

His mouth curved upward in a half smile. "I forget. A long time ago. Maybe I should've suggested we meet tomorrow instead, but I didn't want to wait a minute longer than I had to."

"Me, neither," she confessed.

He smiled again, that wonderful, intoxicating smile.

"When did you land?" she asked, because if she didn't stop staring at him she was going to embarrass herself.

"Late this morning," he told her. "My family—well, you know what families are like. Mom's been cooking for days and there was a big family get-together this afternoon. I wanted to invite you but—"

"No, I understand. You couldn't because—well, how could you?" That didn't come out right, but Paul seemed to know what she was trying to say.

"You're exactly like I pictured you," he said, leaning forward to touch her cheek.

"You imagined me drenched?"

He chuckled. "I imagined you beautiful, and you are."

His words made her blush. "I'm having a hard time believing you're actually here," she said.

"I am, too."

The waitress came for their drink order. Ruth hadn't even looked at her menu or thought about what she'd like to drink. Because she was wet and chilled, she ordered hot tea and Paul asked for a bottle of champagne.

"We have reason to celebrate," he announced. Then, as if it had suddenly occurred to him, he said, "You do drink alcohol, don't you?"

She nodded quickly. "Normally I would've asked for wine, but I wanted the tea so I could warm up. I haven't decided what to order yet." She picked up the menu and scanned the entrées.

The waitress brought the champagne and standing ice bucket to the table. "Is there something special you're celebrating?" she asked in a friendly voice.

Paul nodded and his eyes met Ruth's. "We're celebrating the fact that we found each other," he said.

"Excellent." She removed the foil top and wire around the cork and opened the bottle with a slight popping sound. After filling the two champagne flutes, she left.

Ruth took her glass. "Once again, I'm so sorry about what happened. Let me pay for the champagne, please. You wouldn't have had a problem finding me if I'd—"

"I wasn't talking about this evening," he broke in. "I was talking about your Christmas card."

"Oh."

Paul raised his glass; she raised hers, too, and they clicked the rims gently together. "Do you believe in fate?" he asked.

Ruth smiled. "I didn't, but I've had a change of heart since Christmas."

His smile widened. "Me, too."

Dinner was marvelous. Ruth didn't remember what she'd ordered or anything else about the actual meal. For all she knew, she could've been dining on raw seaweed. It hardly mattered.

They talked and talked, and she felt as if she'd known Paul her entire life. He asked detailed questions about her family, her studies, her plans after graduation, and seemed genuinely interested in everything she said. He talked about the marines and Afghanistan with a sense of pride at the positive differences he'd seen in the country. After dinner and dessert, they lingered over coffee and at nine-thirty Paul paid the tab and suggested they walk along the waterfront. She eagerly agreed. Her umbrella was now merely an encumbrance because the rain had stopped, so they brought it back to her car before they set off.

The clouds had drifted away and the moon was glowing, its light splashing against the pier as they strolled hand in hand. Although she knew Paul had to be exhausted from his long flight and the family gathering, she couldn't deny herself these last few minutes.

"You asked me to keep the weekends free," Ruth murmured, resting her head against his shoulder.

"Did you?"

She sighed. "Not tomorrow."

"Do you have a date with some other guy?"

She leaned back in order to study his face, trying to discern whether he was serious. "You're joking, right?" she said hesitantly.

He shrugged. "Yes and no. You have no obligation to me and vice versa."

"Are *you* seeing someone else?"

"No." His response was immediate.

"I'm not, either," she told him. She wanted to ask how he could even *think* that she would be. "I promised my grandmother I'd visit tomorrow."

"Your grandmother?" he repeated.

"She invited you, too."

He arched his brows.

"In fact, she insisted I bring you."

"So you've mentioned me to your family."

She'd told him in her letters that she hadn't. "Just her. We've become really close. I'm sure you'll enjoy meeting her."

"I'm sure I will, too."

"You'll come, won't you?"

Paul turned Ruth into his arms and gazed down at her. "I don't think I could stay away."

And then he kissed her. Ruth had fantasized about this moment for months. She'd wondered what it would be like when Paul kissed her, but nothing she'd conjured up equaled this reality. Never in all her twenty-five years had she experienced anything like the sensation she felt when Paul's mouth descended on hers. Stars fell from the sky. She saw it happen even with her eyes tightly closed. She heard triumphant music nearby; it seemed to surround her. But once she opened her eyes, all the stars seemed to be exactly where they'd been before. And the music came from somebody's car radio.

Paul wore a stunned look.

"That was...very nice," Ruth managed.

Paul nodded in agreement, then cleared his throat. "Very."

"Should I admit I was afraid of what would happen when we met?" she asked.

"Afraid why? Of what?"

"I didn't know what to expect."

"I didn't either." He slid his hand down her spine and moved a step away. "I'd built this up in my mind."

"I did, too," she whispered.

"I was so afraid you could never live up to my image of you," Paul told her. "I figured we'd meet and I'd get you out of my system. I'd buy you dinner, thank you for your letters and emails—and that would be the end of it. No woman could possibly be everything I'd envisioned you to be. But you are, Ruth, you are."

Although the wind was chilly, his words were enough to warm her from head to foot.

"I didn't think you could be what I'd imagined, either, and I was right," Ruth said.

"You were?" He seemed crestfallen.

She nodded. "Paul, you're even more wonderful than I'd realized." At his relieved expression, she said, "I underestimated how strong my feelings for you are. Look at me, I'm shaking." She held out her hand as evidence of how badly she was trembling after his kiss.

He shook his head. "I feel the same way—nervous and jittery inside."

"That's lack of sleep."

"No," he said, and took her by the shoulders. "That's what your kiss did to me." His eyes glittered as he stared down at her.

"What should we do?" she asked uncertainly.

"You're the one with reservations about falling for a guy in the service."

Her early letters had often referred to her feelings about exactly that. Ruth lowered her gaze. "The fundamental problem hasn't changed," she said. "But you'll eventually get out, won't you?"

He hesitated, and his dark eyes—which had been so warm seconds before—seemed to be closing her out. "Eventually I'll leave the marines, but you should know it won't be anytime in the near future. I'm in for the long haul, and if you want to continue this relationship, the sooner you accept that, the better."

Ruth didn't want their evening to end on a negative note. When she'd answered his letter that first time, she'd known he was a military man and it hadn't stopped her. She'd gone into this with her eyes wide open. "I don't have to decide right away, do I?"

"No," he admitted. "But—"

"Good," she said, cutting him off. She couldn't allow their differences to come between them so quickly. She sensed that Paul, too, wanted to push all that aside. When she slipped her arms around his waist and hugged him, he hugged her back. "You're exhausted. Let's meet in the morning. I'll take you over to visit my grandmother and we can talk some more then."

Ruth rested her head against his shoulder again and Paul kissed her hair. "You're making this difficult," he said.

"I know. I'm sorry."

"Me, too," he whispered.

Ruth knew they'd need to confront the issue soon. She could also see that settling it wasn't going to be as easy as she'd hoped.

Four

Paul met Ruth at the Seattle terminal at ten the next morning and they walked up the ramp to board the Bremerton ferry. The hard rain of the night before had yielded to glorious sunshine.

Unlike the previous evening, when Paul and Ruth had talked nonstop through a three-hour dinner, it seemed that now they had little to say. The one big obstacle in their relationship hung between them. They sat side by side on the wooden bench and sipped hot coffee as the ferry eased away from the Seattle dock.

"You're still thinking about last night, aren't you?" Ruth said, carefully broaching the subject after a lengthy silence. "About you being in the military, I mean, and my objections to the war in Iraq?"

He nodded. "Yeah, there's the political aspect and also the fact that you don't seem comfortable with the concept of military life," he said.

"I'm not, really, but we'll work it out," she told him, and reached for his free hand, entwining their fingers. "We'll find a way."

Paul didn't look as if he believed her. But after a couple of minutes, he seemed to come to some sort of decision.

He brought her hand to his lips. "Let's enjoy the time we have today, all right?"

Ruth smiled in agreement.

"Tell me about your grandmother."

Ruth was more than willing to change the subject. "This is my paternal grandmother, and she's lived in Cedar Cove for the past thirty years. She and my grandfather moved there from Seattle after he retired because they wanted a slower pace of life. I barely remember my grandfather Sam. He died when I was two, before I had any real memories of him."

"He died young," Paul commented sympathetically.

"Yes… My grandmother's been alone for a long time."

"She probably has good friends in a town like Cedar Cove."

"Yes," Ruth said. "And she's still got friends she's had since the war. It's something I admire about my grandmother," she continued. "She's my inspiration, and not only because she speaks three languages fluently and is one of the most intelligent women I know. Ever since I can remember, she's been helping others. Although she's in her eighties, Grandma's involved with all kinds of charities and social groups. When I enrolled at the University of Washington, I intended for the two of us to get together often, but I swear her schedule's even busier than mine."

Paul grinned at her. "I know what you mean. It's the same in my family."

By the time they stepped off the Bremerton ferry and took the foot ferry across to Cedar Cove, it was after eleven. They stopped at a deli, where Paul bought a loaf of fresh bread and a bottle of Washington State gewürztraminer to take with them. At quarter to twelve, they trudged up the hill toward her grandmother's duplex on Poppy Lane.

When they arrived, Helen greeted them at the front door and ushered Paul and Ruth into the house. Ruth hugged her grandmother, whose white hair was cut stylishly short. Helen was thinner than the last time Ruth had visited and seemed more fragile somehow. Her grandmother paused to give Paul an embarrassingly frank look. Ruth felt her face heat as Helen spoke.

"So, you're the young man who's captured my granddaughter's heart."

"Grandma, this is Paul Gordon," Ruth said hurriedly, gesturing toward Paul.

"This is the soldier you've been writing to, who's fighting in Afghanistan?"

"I am." Paul's response sounded a bit defensive, Ruth thought. He obviously preferred not to discuss it.

In an effort to ward off any misunderstanding, Ruth added, "My grandfather was a soldier when Grandma met him."

Helen nodded, and a faraway look stole over her. It took her a moment to refocus. "Come, both of you," she said, stepping between them. She tucked her arm around Ruth's waist. "I set the table outside. It's such a beautiful afternoon, I thought we'd eat on the patio."

"We brought some bread and a bottle of wine," Ruth said. "Paul got them."

"Lovely. Thank you, Paul."

While Ruth sliced the fresh-baked bread, he opened the wine, then helped her grandmother carry the salad plates outside. An apple pie cooled on the kitchen counter and the scent of cinnamon permeated the sunlit kitchen.

They chatted throughout the meal; the conversation was light and friendly as they lingered over their wine.

Every now and then Ruth caught her grandmother staring at Paul with the strangest expression on her face. Ruth didn't know what to make of this. It almost seemed as if her grandmother was trying to place him, to recall where she'd seen him before.

Helen had apparently read Ruth's mind. "Am I embarrassing your beau, sweetheart?" she asked with a half smile.

Ruth resisted informing her grandmother that Paul wasn't her anything, especially not her beau. They'd had one lovely dinner together, but now their political differences seemed to have overtaken them.

"I apologize, Paul." Helen briefly touched his hand, which rested on the table. "When I first saw you—" She stopped abruptly. "You resemble someone I knew many years ago."

"Where, Grandma?" Ruth asked.

"In France, during the war."

"You were in France during World War II?" Ruth couldn't quite hide her shock.

Helen turned to her. "I haven't spoken much about those days, but now, toward the end of my life, I think about them more and more." She pushed back her chair and stood.

Ruth stood, too, thinking her grandmother was about to carry in their empty plates and serve the pie.

Helen motioned her to sit. "Stay here. There's something I want you to see. I think perhaps it's time."

When her grandmother had left them, Ruth looked at Paul and shrugged. "I have no idea what's going on."

Paul had been wonderful with her grandmother, thoughtful and attentive. He'd asked a number of questions during the meal—about Cedar Cove, about her life with Sam—and listened intently when she responded.

Ruth knew his interest was genuine. Together they cleared the table and returned the dishes to the kitchen, then waited for Helen at the patio table.

It was at least five minutes before she came back. She held a rolled-up paper that appeared to be some kind of poster, old enough to have yellowed with age. Carefully she opened it and laid it flat on the cleared table. Ruth saw that the writing was French. In the center of the poster, which measured about eighteen inches by twenty-four, was a pencil sketch of two faces: a man and a woman, whose names she didn't recognize. Jean and Marie Brulotte.

"Who's that?" Ruth asked, pointing to the female.

Her grandmother smiled calmly. "I am that woman."

Ruth frowned. Helen had obviously used a false name, and although she'd seen photographs of her grandmother as a young woman, this sketch barely resembled the woman she knew. The man in the drawing, however, seemed familiar. Gazing at the sketch for a minute, she realized the face was vaguely like Paul's. Not so much in any similarity of features as in a quality of…character, she supposed.

"And the man?"

"That was Jean-Claude," Helen whispered, her voice full of pain.

Paul turned to Ruth, but she was at a complete loss and didn't know what to tell him. Her grandfather's name was Sam and she'd never heard of this Jean or Jean-Claude. Certainly her father had never mentioned another man in his mother's life.

"This is a wanted poster," Paul remarked. "I speak some French—studied it in school."

"Yes. The Germans offered a reward of one million francs to anyone who turned us in."

"You were in France during the war and you were *wanted?*" This was more than Ruth could assimilate. She sat back down; so did her grandmother. Paul remained standing for a moment longer as he studied the poster.

"But…it said Marie. Marie Brulotte."

"I went by my middle name in those days. Marie. You may not be aware that it was part of my name because I haven't used it since."

"But…"

"You and Jean-Claude were part of the French Resistance?" Paul asked. It was more statement than question.

"We were." Her grandmother seemed to have difficulty speaking. "Jean-Claude was my husband. We married during the war, and I took his name with pride. He was my everything, strong and handsome and brave. His laughter filled a room. Sometimes, still, I think I can hear him." Her eyes grew teary and she dabbed at them with her linen handkerchief. "That was many years ago now and, as I said, I think perhaps it's time I spoke of it."

Ruth was grateful. She couldn't let her grandmother leave the story untold. She suspected her father hadn't heard any of this, and she wanted to learn whatever she could about this unknown episode in their family history before it was forever lost.

"What were you doing in France?" Ruth asked. She couldn't comprehend that the woman she'd always known as a warm and loving grandmother, who baked cookies and knit socks for Christmas, had been a freedom fighter in a foreign country.

"I was attending the Sorbonne when the Germans invaded. You may recall that my mother was born in France, but her own parents were long dead. I was studying French literature. My parents were frantic for me

to book my passage home, but like so many others in
France, I didn't believe the country would fall. I assured
my mother I'd leave when I felt it was no longer safe.
Being young and foolish, I thought she was overreact-
ing. Besides, I was in love. Jean-Claude had asked me to
marry him, and what woman in love wishes to leave her
lover over rumors of war?" She laughed lightly, shaking
her head. "France seemed invincible. We were convinced
the Germans wouldn't invade, convinced they'd suffer a
humiliating defeat if they tried."

"So when it happened you were trapped," Paul said.

Her grandmother drew in a deep breath. "There was
the Blitzkrieg.… People were demoralized and defeated
when France surrendered after only a few days of fighting. We were aghast that such a thing could happen.
Jean-Claude and a few of his friends decided to resist
the occupation. I decided I would, too, so we were married right away. My parents knew nothing of this."

"How did you join the Resistance?" Paul asked as Ruth
looked at her grandmother with fresh eyes.

"Join," she repeated scornfully. "There was no place
to *join,* no place to sign up and be handed a weapon
and an instruction manual. A group of us students, naive
and foolish, offered resistance to the German occupation. Later we learned there were other groups, eventually united under the leadership of General de Gaulle.
We soon found one another. Jean-Claude and I—we were
young and too stupid to understand the price we'd pay,
but by then we'd already lost some of our dearest friends.
Jean-Claude and I refused to let them die in vain."

"What did you do?" Ruth breathed. She leaned closer
to her grandmother.

"Whatever we could, which in the beginning was pit-
ifully little. The Germans suffered more casualties in

traffic accidents. At first our resistance was mostly symbolic." A slow smile spread across her weathered face. "But we learned, oh yes, we learned."

Ruth was still having difficulty taking it all in. She pressed her hand to her forehead. She found it hard enough to believe that the sketch of the female in this worn poster was her own grandmother. Then to discover that the fragile, petite woman at her side had been part of the French Resistance…

"Does my dad know any of this?" Ruth asked.

Helen sighed heavily. "I'm not sure, but I doubt it. Sam might have mentioned it to him. I've only told a few of my friends. No one else." She shook her head. "I didn't feel I could talk to my sons about it. There was too much that's disturbing. Too many painful memories."

"Did you…did you ever have to kill anyone?" Ruth had trouble even getting the question out.

"Many times," Helen answered bluntly. "Does that surprise you?"

It shocked Ruth to the point that she couldn't ask anything else.

"The first time was the hardest," her grandmother said. "I was held by a French policeman." She added something derogatory in French, and although Ruth couldn't understand the language, some things didn't need translation. "Under Vichy, some of the police worked hard to prove to the Germans what good little boys they were," she muttered, this time in English. "I'd been stopped and questioned, detained by this pig of a man. He said he was taking me to the police station. I had a small gun with me that I'd hidden, a seven millimeter."

Ruth's heart raced as she listened to Helen recount this adventure.

"The pig didn't drive me to the police station. Instead

he headed for open country and I knew that once he was outside town and away from the eyes of any witnesses, he would rape and murder me."

Ruth pressed her hand to her mouth, holding back a gasp of horror.

"You'd trained in self-defense?" Paul asked.

Her grandmother laughed. "No. How could we? There was no time for such lessons. But I realized that I didn't need technique. What I needed was nerve. This beast of a man pulled his gun on me but I was quicker. I shot him in the head." She paused at the memory of that terrifying moment. "I buried him myself in a field and, as far as I know, he was never found." She wore a small satisfied look. "His mistake," she murmured, "was that he tightened his jaw when he reached for his gun—and I saw. I'd been watching him closely. He was thinking of what might happen, of what could go wrong. He was a professional, and I was only nineteen, and yet I knew that if I didn't act then, it would've been too late."

"Didn't *you* worry about what could happen?" Ruth asked, unable to grasp how her grandmother could ever shoot another human being.

"No," Helen answered flatly. "I *knew* what would happen. We all did. We didn't have a chance of surviving, none of us. My parents would never have discovered my fate—I would simply have disappeared. They didn't even know I'd married Jean-Claude or changed my name." She stared out at the water. "I don't understand why I lived. It makes no sense that God would spare me when all my friends, all those I loved, were killed."

"Jean-Claude, too?"

Her eyes filled and she slowly nodded.

"Where was he when you were taken by the policeman?" Paul asked.

Her grandmother's mouth trembled. "By then, Jean-Claude had been captured."

"The French police?"

"No," she said in the thinnest of whispers. "Jean-Claude was being held by the Gestapo. That was the first time they got him—but not the last."

Ruth had heard about the notorious German soldiers and their cruelty.

Helen straightened, and her back went rigid. "I could only imagine how those monsters were torturing my husband." Contempt hardened her voice.

"What did you do?" Ruth glanced at Paul, whose gaze remained riveted on her grandmother.

At first Helen didn't answer. "What else could I do? I had to rescue him."

"You?" Paul asked this with the same shock Ruth felt.

"Yes, me and…" Helen's smile was fleeting. "I was very clever about it, too." The sadness returned with such intensity that it brought tears to Ruth's eyes.

"They eventually killed him, didn't they?" she asked, hardly able to listen to her grandmother's response.

"No," Helen said as she turned to face Ruth. "I did."

Five

"You killed Jean-Claude?" Ruth repeated incredulously.

Tears rolling down her cheeks, Helen nodded. "God forgive me, but I had no choice. I couldn't allow him to be tortured any longer. He begged me to do it, begged me to end his suffering. That was the second time he was captured, and they were more determined than ever to break him. He knew far too much."

"You'd better start at the beginning. You went into Gestapo headquarters?" Paul moved closer as if he didn't want to risk missing even one word. "Was that the first time or the second?"

"Both. The first time, in April 1943, I rescued him. I pretended I was pregnant and brought a priest to the house the Gestapo had taken over. I insisted with great bravado that they force Jean-Claude to marry me and give my baby a name. I didn't care if they killed him, I said, but before he died I wanted him to give my baby his name." She paused. "I was very convincing."

"So you weren't really pregnant?" Ruth asked.

"No, of course not," her grandmother replied. "It was a ploy to get into the house."

"Was the priest a real priest?"

"Yes. He didn't know I was using him, but I had no alternative. I was desperate to get Jean-Claude out alive."

"The priest knew nothing," Ruth said, meeting Paul's eyes, astounded by her grandmother's nerve and cunning.

"The Father knew nothing," the older woman concurred, smiling grimly. "But I needed him, so I used him. Thankfully the Gestapo believed me, and because they wanted to keep relations with the Church as smooth as possible, they brought Jean-Claude into the room."

Ruth could picture the scene, but she didn't know if she'd ever possess that kind of bravery.

"Jean-Claude was in terrible pain, but he nearly laughed out loud when the priest asked him if he was the father of my child. Fortunately he didn't have to answer because our friends had arranged a distraction outside the house. A firebomb was tossed into a parked vehicle, which exploded. All but two Gestapo left the room. I shot them both right in front of the priest, and then Jean-Claude and I escaped through a back window."

"Where did you find the courage?" Ruth asked breathlessly.

"Courage?" her grandmother echoed. "That wasn't courage. That was fear. I would do anything to save my husband's life—and I did. Then, only a few weeks later, I was the one who killed him. What took courage was finding the will to live after Jean-Claude died. *That* was courage, and I would never have managed if it hadn't been for the American soldier who saved my life. If it hadn't been for Sam."

"He was my grandfather," Ruth explained to Paul.

"I want to know more about Jean-Claude," Paul said, placing his arm around Ruth's shoulders. It felt good to be held by him and she leaned into his strength, his solid warmth.

Her grandmother's eyes grew weary and she shook her head. "Perhaps another day. I'm tired now, too tired to speak anymore."

"We should go," Paul whispered.

"I'll do the dishes," Ruth insisted.

"Nonsense. You should leave now," Helen said. "You have better things to do than talk to an old lady."

"But we *want* to talk to you," Ruth told her.

"You will." Helen looked even more drawn. "Soon, but not right now."

"You'll finish the story?"

"Yes," the old woman said hoarsely. "I promise I'll tell you everything."

While her grandmother went to her room to rest, Ruth and Paul cleaned up the kitchen. At first they worked in silence, as if they weren't quite sure what to say to each other. Ruth put the food away while Paul rinsed the dishes and set them inside the dishwasher.

"You didn't know any of this before today?" he asked, propping himself against the counter.

"Not a single detail."

"Your father never mentioned it?"

"Never." Ruth wondered again how much her father actually knew about his mother's wartime adventures. "I'm sure you were the one who prompted her."

"Me?" Paul asked. "How?"

"More than anything, I think you reminded her of Jean-Claude." Ruth tilted her head to one side. "It's as if this woman I've known all my life has suddenly become a stranger." Ruth finished wiping down the counters. She knew they'd need to leave soon if they were going to catch the ferry.

"Maybe you'd better check on her before we go," Paul said.

She agreed and hurried out of the kitchen. Her grandmother's eyes opened briefly when Ruth entered the cool, silent room. Reaching for an afghan at the foot of the bed, Ruth covered her with it and kissed the papery skin of her cheek. She'd always loved Helen, but she had an entirely new respect for her now.

"I'll be back soon," Ruth promised.

"Bring your young man."

"I will."

Helen's response was low, and at first Ruth didn't understand her and strained to hear. Gradually her voice drifted off. Ruth waited until Helen was asleep before she slipped out of the room.

"She's sleeping?" Paul asked, setting aside the magazine he was reading when Ruth returned to the kitchen.

Ruth nodded. "She started talking to me in French. I so badly wish I knew what she said."

They left a few minutes later. Absorbed in her own thoughts, Ruth walked down the hill beside Paul, neither of them speaking as they approached the foot ferry that would take them from Cedar Cove to Bremerton.

Once they were aboard, Paul went to get them coffee from the concession stand. While he was gone, Ruth decided she had to find out how much her family knew about her grandmother's war exploits. She opened her purse and rummaged for her cell phone.

Paul brought the coffee and set her plastic cup on the table.

Ruth glanced up long enough to thank him with a smile. "I'm calling my parents."

Paul nodded, tentatively sipping hot coffee. Then, in

an obvious effort to give her some privacy, he moved to stand by the rail, gazing out at the water.

Her father answered on the third ring. "Dad, it's Ruth," she said in a rush.

"Ruthie! It's nice to hear from you."

Her father had never enjoyed telephone conversations and generally handed the phone off to Ruth's mother.

"Wait—I need to talk to you," Ruth said.

"What's up?"

That was her dad, too. He didn't like chitchat and wanted to get to the point as quickly as possible.

"I went over to see Grandma this afternoon."

"How is she? We've been meaning to get up there and see her *and* you. I don't know where the time goes. Thanksgiving was our last visit."

How is she? Ruth wasn't sure what to say. Her grandmother seemed fragile and old, and Ruth had never thought of her as either. "I don't know, Dad. She's the same, except—well, except she might have lost a few pounds." Ruth looked over at Paul and bit her lip. "I… brought a friend along with me."

"Your roommate? What's her name again?"

"Lynn Blumenthal. No, this is a male friend."

That caught her father's attention. "Someone from school?"

"No, we met sort of…by accident. His name is Paul Gordon and he's a sergeant in the marines. We've been corresponding for the past four months. But Paul isn't the reason I'm phoning."

"All right, then. What is?"

Ruth dragged in a deep breath. "Like I said before, I was visiting Grandma."

"With this marine you're seeing," he reiterated.

"Yes." Ruth didn't dare look at Paul a second time.

Nervously, she tucked a strand of hair behind her ear and leaned forward, lowering her voice. "Grandma was in France during World War II. Did you know that?"

Her father paused. "Yes, I did."

"Were you aware that she was a member of the French Resistance?"

Again he paused. "My father said something shortly before he died, but I never got any more information."

"Didn't you ask your mother?"

"I tried, but she refused to talk about it. She said some things were better left buried and deflected all my questions. Do you mean to say she told you about this?"

"Yes, and, Dad, the stories were incredible! Did you know Grandma was married before she met Grandpa Sam?"

"What?"

"Her husband's name was Jean-Claude."

"A Frenchman?"

"Yes." She tried to recall his surname from the poster. "Jean-Claude…Brulotte. That's it. He was part of the movement, too, and Grandma, your *mother,* went into a Gestapo headquarters and managed to get him out."

"My mother?" The question was loud enough for Paul to hear from several feet away, because his eyebrows shot up as their eyes met.

"Yes, Dad, *your* mother. I was desperate to learn more, but she got tired all of a sudden, and neither Paul nor I wanted to overtax her. She's taking a nap now, and Paul and I are on the ferry back to Seattle."

Ruth heard her father take a long, ragged breath.

"All these years and she's never said a word to me. My dad did, as I told you, but he didn't give me any details, and I never believed Mom's involvement amounted to much—more along the lines of moral support, I always figured. My dad was over there and we knew that's where he met Mom."

"Did they ever go back to France?" Ruth asked.

"No. They did some traveling, but mostly in North America—Florida, Mexico, Quebec…"

"I guess she really was keeping the past buried," Ruth said.

"She must realize she's getting near the end of her life," her father went on, apparently thinking out loud. "And she wants us to know. I'm grateful she was willing to share this with you. Still, it's pretty hard to take in. My mother…part of the French Resistance. She told me she was in school over there."

"She was." Ruth didn't want her father to think Helen had lied to him.

"Then how in heaven's name did she get involved in that?"

"It's a long story."

"What made her start talking about it now?" her father asked.

"I think it's because she knows she's getting old, as you suggested," Ruth said. "And because of Paul."

"Ah, yes, this young man you're with."

"Yeah."

Her father hesitated. "I know you can't discuss this with Paul there, so give us a call later, will you? Your mother's going to want to hear about this young man."

"Yes, Daddy," she said, thinking with some amusement that she sounded like an obedient child.

"I'll call Mom this evening," her father said. "We need to set up a visit ourselves, possibly for the Memorial Day weekend."

After a quick farewell, she clicked off the phone and put it back in her purse.

Paul, still sipping his coffee, approached her again. She picked up her own cup as he sat down beside her.

"I haven't enjoyed an afternoon more in years," Paul said. "Not in years," he added emphatically.

Ruth grinned, then drank some of her cooling coffee. "I'd like to believe it was my company that was so engaging, but I know you're enthralled with my grandmother."

"And her granddaughter," Paul murmured, but he said it as if he felt wary of the fact that he found her appealing.

Ruth took his hand. "We haven't settled anything," he reminded her, tightening his hold on her fingers.

"Do we have to right this minute?"

He didn't answer.

"I want to see you again," she told him, moving closer.

"That's the problem. I want to see you again, too."

"I'm glad." Ruth didn't hide her relief.

Paul's responding smile was brief. "Fine. We'll do this your way—one day at a time. But remember, I only have two weeks' leave."

She could sense already that these would be the shortest two weeks of her life.

"By the time I ship out, we should know how we feel. Agreed?"

"Agreed."

He nodded solemnly. "Do you own a pair of in-line skates?" he asked unexpectedly.

"Sure, but I don't have them in Seattle. I can easily rent a pair, though."

"Want to go skating?"

"When?"

"Now?"

Ruth laughed. "I'd love to, with one stipulation."

"What's that?"

Ruth hated to admit how clumsy she was on skates. "If I fall down, promise you'll help me up."

"I can do that."

"If I get hurt…"

"If you get hurt," Paul said, "I promise to kiss you and make it better."

Ruth had the distinct feeling that she wasn't going to mind falling, not one little bit.

Six

Helen Shelton
5-B Poppy Lane
Cedar Cove, Washington
April 23

Dearest Charlotte,
Forgive me for writing rather than calling. It must
seem odd, since we're neighbors as well as friends.
It's just that sometimes writing things out makes it
easier to think them through....

I have some news, by the way. You haven't met
my granddaughter, Ruth, but you've heard me speak
of her. Well, she was over last week with a soldier
she's been writing to, who's on leave from Afghanistan. He's a delightful young man and it was easy
to see that her feelings for him are quite intense. His
name is Paul Gordon. When Ruth first introduced
us, I'm afraid I embarrassed us both by staring at
him. Paul could've been Jean-Claude's grandson,
the resemblance is that striking.

For the past few weeks, I've been remembering
and dreaming about my war experiences. You've

encouraged me for years to write them down. I've tried, but couldn't make myself do it. However... I don't know if this was wise but I told Ruth and her young man some of what happened to me in France. I know I shocked them both.

My son phoned later the same day, and John was quite upset with me, especially since I'd told Ruth and not him. I tried to explain that these were memories I've spent most of my life trying to forget. I do hope he understands. But Pandora's box is open now, and my family wants to learn everything they can. I've agreed to allow Ruth to tape our conversations, which satisfies everyone. I'm afraid you're right, my dear friend—I should've told my children long ago.

Do take care of yourself and Ben. I hope to see you soon.

Bless you, dear Charlotte,

Your friend always,

Helen

"I want you to meet my family," Paul said a little more than a week after their first date. They'd spent every available moment together; they'd been to the Seattle Center and the Space Needle, rowing on Lake Washington, out to dinner and had seen a couple of movies. Sitting on the campus lawn, he'd been waiting for Ruth after her last class of the day. He stood when she reached him, and Ruth saw that he wasn't smiling as he issued the invitation.

"When?"

"Mom and Dad are at the house."

"You mean you want me to meet them *now?*" Ruth asked as they strolled across the lush green grass toward the visitors' parking lot. If she'd known she was meeting

Paul's parents she would've been better prepared. She would've done something about her hair and worn a different outfit and…

"Yeah," Paul muttered.

Ruth stopped and he walked forward two or three steps before he noticed. Frowning, he glanced back.

"What's going on here?" she asked, clutching her books to her chest.

Paul looked everywhere but at her. "My parents feel they should meet you, since I'm spending most of my time in your company. The way they figure it, you must be someone important in my life."

Ruth's heart did a happy little jig. "Am I?" she asked flirtatiously.

A rigid expression came over him, betraying none of his feelings. "I don't know the answer to that yet."

"Really?" she teased.

"Listen, Ruth, I'm not handing you my heart so you can break it. You don't want to be involved with a soldier. Well, I'm a soldier, and either you accept that or at the end of these two weeks, it's over."

He sounded so…so military. As if he thought a relationship could be that simple, that straightforward. Life didn't divide evenly into black and white. There were plenty of gray areas, too. All right, so Paul had a point. In the back of her mind, Ruth hoped that, given time, Paul would decide to get out of the war business. She wasn't the kind of woman who'd be content to sit at home while the man she loved was off in some faraway country risking his life. Experiencing dreadful things. Suffering. Maybe dying.

"You'd rather I didn't meet your family?" she asked.

"Right."

That hurt. "I see."

Some of her pain must have been evident in her voice, because Paul came toward her and tucked his finger beneath her chin. Their eyes met for the longest moment. "If my family meets you, they'll know how much I care about you," he said quietly.

Ruth managed to smile. "I'm glad you care, because I care about you, too," she admitted. "A *lot*."

"That doesn't solve anything."

"No, it doesn't," she said, leaning forward so their lips could meet. She half expected Paul to pull away, but he didn't.

Instead, he groaned and forcefully brought his mouth to hers. Their kiss was passionate, deep—honest. She felt the sharp edges of her textbooks digging painfully into her breasts, and still Ruth melted in his arms.

"You're making things impossible," he mumbled when he lifted his head from hers.

"I've been known to do that."

Paul reached for her hand and led her into the parking lot. "I mentioned your grandmother to my parents," he said casually as he unlocked the car doors.

"Ah," Ruth said, slipping into the passenger seat. "That explains it."

"Explains what?"

"Why your family wants to meet me. I've brought you to *my* family. They feel cheated."

Paul shook his head solemnly. "I really don't think that's it. But…speaking of your grandmother, when can we see her again?"

"Tomorrow afternoon, if you like. I talked to her this morning before my classes and she asked when we could make a return visit."

"You're curious about what happened, aren't you?" Paul asked as he inserted the key into the ignition.

"Very much," Ruth said. Since their visit to Cedar Cove, she'd thought about her grandmother's adventures again and again. She'd done some research, too, using the internet and a number of library books on the war. In fact, Ruth was so fascinated by the history of the Resistance movement, she'd found it difficult to concentrate on the psychology essay she was trying to write.

She'd had several days to become accustomed to the idea of Helen's exploits during the Second World War. And yet she still had trouble imagining the woman she knew as a fighter for the French Resistance.

"She loved Jean-Claude," Paul commented.

Ruth nodded. Her grandmother had loved her husband enough to kill him—a shocking reality that would not have made sense at any other time in Helen's life. And then, at some point after that, Helen had met her Sam. How? Ruth wondered. Helen said he'd rescued her, but what were the circumstances? When did they fall in love? Family history told her that Sam Shelton had fought in the European campaign during the Second World War. He'd been in France toward the end of the war, she recalled. How much had he known about Helen's past?

Ruth could only hope her grandmother would provide some answers tomorrow.

The meeting with Paul's family was going well. Ruth was charmed by his parents, who immediately welcomed her. Barbara, his mother, had an easy laugh and a big heart. She brought Ruth into the kitchen and settled her on a stool at the counter while she fussed with the dinner salad.

Paul and his father, Greg, were on the patio, firing up the grill and chatting. Every now and then, Ruth caught Paul stealing a glance in her direction.

"I want to help," Ruth told his mother.

"Nonsense," Barbara Gordon said as she tore lettuce leaves into a large wooden bowl. "I'm just so pleased to finally meet you. It was as if Paul had some secret he was keeping from us."

Ruth smiled and sipped her glass of iced tea.

"My father was career military—in the marines," Barbara said, chopping tomatoes for the salad. "I don't know if that was what induced Paul to join the military or not, but I suspect it had an influence."

"How do you feel about him being stationed so far from home?" Ruth asked, curious to hear his mother's perspective. She couldn't imagine any mother wanting to see her son or daughter at that kind of risk.

Barbara sighed. "I don't like it, if that's what you're asking. Every sane person hates war. My father didn't want to fight in World War II, and I cried my eyes out the day Greg left for Vietnam. Now here's my oldest son in Afghanistan."

"It seems most generations are called upon to serve their country, doesn't it?" Ruth said.

Barbara agreed with a short nod. "Freedom isn't free— for us or for the countries we support. Granted, in hindsight some of the conflicts we've been involved in seem misguided, but unfortunately war appears to be part of the human condition."

"Why?" Ruth asked, although she didn't really expect a response.

"I think every generation has asked that same question," Barbara said thoughtfully, putting the salad aside. She began to prepare a dressing, pouring olive oil and balsamic vinegar into a small bowl. "Paul told me you have a problem with his unwillingness to leave the marines at the end of his commitment. Is that right?"

A little embarrassed by the question, Ruth nodded. "I do."

"The truth is, as his mother, I want Paul out of the marines, too, but that isn't a decision you or I can make for him. My son has always been his own person. That's how his father and I raised him."

Ruth's gaze followed Paul as he stood with his father by the barbecue. He looked up and saw her, frowning as if he knew exactly what she and his mother were talking about. Ruth gave him a reassuring wave.

"You're in love with him, aren't you?" his mother asked, watching her closely.

The question took Ruth by surprise. "I'm afraid I am." Ruth didn't *want* to be—something she hadn't acknowledged openly until this moment. He'd described his reluctance to hand her his heart to break. She felt the same way and feared he'd end up breaking hers.

There seemed to be a tacit agreement not to broach these difficult subjects during dinner.

The four of them sat on the patio around a big table, shaded by a large umbrella. His mother had made corn bread as well as the salad, and the steaks were grilled to perfection. After dinner, Ruth helped with the cleanup and then Paul made their excuses.

"We're going to a movie?" she whispered on their way out the door, figuring he'd used that as a convenient pretext for leaving.

"I had to get you out of there before my mother started showing you my baby pictures."

"I'll bet you were a real cutie."

"You should see my brother and sister, especially the nude photos."

Ruth giggled.

Instead of the theater, they headed for Lake Washington and walked through the park, licking ice-cream cones, talking and laughing. Ruth couldn't remember laughing with anyone as much as she did with Paul.

He dropped her off after ten, walked her up to the front porch and kissed her good-night.

"I'll pick you up at noon," he said. "After your morning class."

"Noon," she repeated, her arms linked around his neck. That seemed too long. Despite her fears, despite the looming doubts, she *was* in love with him.

"You're sure your grandmother's up to having company so soon?" he asked.

"Yes." Ruth pressed her forehead against his shoulder. "I think the real question's whether we're ready for the next installment. I don't know if I can bear to hear exactly what happened to Jean-Claude."

"Perhaps not, but she needs to tell us."

"Yes," Ruth said. "She couldn't talk about it before."

"I know." Paul kissed her again.

Ruth felt at peace in his arms. Only when she stopped to think about the future, *their* future, did she become uncertain and confused.

Seven

Ruth and Paul sat with Helen at the kitchen table in her Cedar Cove house as rain dripped rhythmically against the windowpane. The day was overcast and dreary, as it frequently was during spring in the Pacific Northwest.

Helen reached for the teapot in the middle of the table and filled each of their cups, then offered them freshly baked peanut-butter cookies arranged on a small dessert plate. Ruth recognized the plate from her childhood. She and her grandmother had often had tea together when she was a youngster. Her visits to Cedar Cove were special; her grandmother had listened while Ruth chattered endlessly, sharing girlish confidences. It was during those private little tea parties that they'd bonded, grandmother and granddaughter.

Today the slow ritual of pouring tea and passing around cookies demanded patience. Ruth badly wanted to throw questions at Helen, but she could see that her grandmother would resume her story only when she was ready. Helen seemed to be bracing herself for this next installment.

"I've been thinking about the things I mentioned on your last visit," Helen finally said, sipping her tea. Steam rose from the delicate bone-china cup. "It was a lot for you to absorb at one time."

"I didn't know *anything* about your adventures, Grandma." And they truly were adventures, of a kind few people experienced these days. *Real* adventures, with real and usually involuntary risks.

Helen grimaced. "My children didn't, either. But as I said before, it's time." Helen set the fragile cup back in its saucer. "Your father phoned and asked me about all of this." She paused, a look of distress on her face. "I hope he'll forgive me for keeping it from him all these years."

"I'm sure he will," Ruth told her.

Helen obviously wanted to believe that. "He asked me to tell him more, but I couldn't," she said sadly.

"I'm sure Dad understood."

"I couldn't relive those memories again so soon."

Ruth laid a comforting hand on her grandmother's arm. This information of Helen's was an important part of her family history. Today, with Helen's agreement, she'd come prepared with a small tape recorder. Now nothing would be lost.

"Jean-Claude had a wonderful gift," her grandmother said, breaking into the story without preamble. "He was a big man who made friends easily—a natural leader. Our small group trusted him with our lives."

Paul smiled encouragingly.

"Within a few minutes of meeting someone, he could figure out if he should trust that person," Helen continued. "More and more people wanted to join us. We started with a few students like ourselves, who were determined to resist the Nazis. Soon, others found us and we connected with groups across France. We all worked together as we lit fires of hope."

"Tell me about the wanted poster with your picture and Jean-Claude's," Ruth said.

Her grandmother smiled ruefully, as if that small piece of notoriety embarrassed her. "I'm afraid Jean-Claude and I acquired a somewhat exaggerated reputation. Soon almost everything that happened in Paris as part of the Resistance movement was attributed to us, whether we were involved or not."

"Such as?"

"There was a fire in a supply depot. Jean-Claude and I wished we'd been responsible, but we weren't. Yet that was what prompted the Germans to post our pictures." A smile brightened her eyes. "It was a rather unflattering sketch of Jean-Claude, he told me, although I disagreed."

"Can you tell me some of the anti-Nazi activities you were able to undertake?" Ruth asked, knowing her father would want to hear as much of this as his mother could recall.

Helen considered the question. "Perhaps the most daring adventure was one of Jean-Claude's. There was an SS officer, a horrible man, a pig." This word was spit out, as if even the memory of him disgusted her. "Jean-Claude discovered that this officer had obtained information through torturing a fellow Resistance member, information that put us all at risk. Jean-Claude decided the man had to die and that he would be the one to do it."

Paul glanced at Ruth, and he seemed to tell her that killing an SS officer would be no easy task.

Helen sipped her tea once more. "I feared for Jean-Claude."

"Is this when he…died?" Ruth asked.

"No." For emphasis, her grandmother shook her head. "That came later."

"Go on," Paul urged.

"One night Jean-Claude left me and another woman in a garden in the suburbs, at the home of a sympathetic schoolteacher who'd made contact with our group. He and his wife went out for the evening. Jean-Claude instructed us to dig a grave and fill it with quicklime. We were to wait there for his return. He left with two other men and I was convinced I'd never see him again."

"But you did," Ruth said.

The old woman nodded. "According to Jean-Claude, it was either kill the SS officer or he would take us all down. He simply knew too much."

"What did Jean-Claude do?"

"That is a story unto itself." Helen sat even straighter in her chair. "This happened close to the final time he was captured. He knew, I believe, that he would die soon, and it made him fearless. He took more and more risks. And he valued his own life less and less." Her eyes shone with tears as she gazed out the rain-blurred window, lost in a world long since past.

"The SS officer had taken a room in a luxury hotel on the outskirts of Paris," Helen went on a minute later. "He was in the habit of sipping a cognac before retiring for the evening. When he called for his drink, it was Jean-Claude who brought it to him wearing a waiter's jacket. I don't know how he killed the SS man, but he did it without alerting anyone. He made sure there was no blood. The problem was getting the body out of the hotel without anyone seeing."

"Why? Couldn't he just leave it there?"

"Why?" Helen repeated, shaking her head. "If the man's body had been discovered, the entire staff would have been tortured as punishment. Eventually someone would have broken. In any event, Jean-Claude smuggled the body out."

"How did he do it?"

"Jean-Claude was clever. His friends hauled him and the body of the SS officer up the chimney. First the dead man and then the live one. That was necessary, you see, because there was a guard at the end of the hallway."

"But once they got to the rooftop, how did he manage?"

"It was an effort," Helen said. "Jean-Claude told me they tossed the body from that rooftop to the roof of another building and then another—an office building. They lowered him down in the elevator. When the men arrived with the body, we all worked together and buried him quickly."

"The SS officer's disappearance must have caused trouble for the Resistance," Paul said.

Helen nodded ardently. "Oh, yes."

"When was Jean-Claude captured the second time?" Ruth asked. She was intensely curious and yet she dreaded hearing about the death of this brave man her grandmother had loved.

Helen's eyes glistened and she lifted her teacup with an unsteady hand. "It isn't what you think," she prefaced, and the cup made a slight clinking sound as it rattled against the saucer. Helen placed both hands in her lap and took a moment to compose herself. "We were headed for the Metro—the subway. By then I'd bleached my hair and we'd both changed our appearances as much as possible. I don't think my own mother would have recognized me. Jean-Claude's, either," she added softly, her voice a mere whisper.

Paul reached for Ruth's hand, as if sensing that she needed his support.

When her grandmother began to speak again, it was in French. She switched languages naturally, apparently without realizing she'd done so. All at once, she covered her face and broke into sobs.

Although Ruth hadn't understood a word, she started crying, too, and gently wrapped her arms around her grandmother's thin shoulders. Hugging her was the only thing she could do to ease this remembered pain.

"It's all right, it's all right," Ruth cooed over and over. "You don't need to tell us any more."

Paul agreed. "This is too hard on her—and you," he said.

They stayed for another hour, but it was clear that reliving the past had exhausted her grandmother. She seemed so frail now, even more than during the previous visit.

While her grandmother rested in her room, Ruth cleared the table. As she took care of the few dishes, her eyes brimmed with tears again. It was agonizing to think about the horrors her grandmother had endured.

"When she was speaking French, she must've been reliving the day Jean-Claude died," Ruth said, turning so her back was pressed against the kitchen counter.

Paul nodded. "She was," he answered somberly.

Ruth studied him as she returned to the kitchen table, where he sat. "You said you speak French. Could you understand what she was saying?"

He nodded again. "At the Metro that day, Jean-Claude was picked up in a routine identity check by the French police. Through pure luck, Helen was able to get on the train without being stopped. She had to stand helplessly inside the subway car and watch as the police hauled him to Gestapo headquarters." Paul paused long enough to give her an odd smile. "The next part was a tirade against the police, whom she hated. Remember last week when she explained that some of the French police were trying to prove their worth to the Germans? Well, apparently Jean-Claude was one of their most wanted criminals."

"They tortured him, didn't they?" she asked, although she already knew the answer.

"Yes." Paul met her eyes. "Unmercifully."

Ruth swallowed hard.

"Helen tried to save him. Disregarding her own safety, she went in after him, only this time she went alone. No sympathetic priest." Paul's face hardened. "They dragged her into the basement, where Jean-Claude was being tortured. They had him strung up by his arms. He was bloody and his face was unrecognizable."

"No!" Ruth hid her eyes with both hands.

"They taunted him. Said they had his accomplice and now he would see her die."

Ruth could barely talk. "They…were going to…kill Helen—in front of Jean-Claude?"

"From what she said, it wouldn't have been an easy death. The point was for Jean-Claude to watch her suffer—to watch her die a slow, agonizing death."

"Dear God in heaven."

"She didn't actually say it," Paul continued. "She didn't have to spell it out, but Jean-Claude obviously hadn't been broken. Seeing her suffer would have done it, though, and your grandmother knew that. She also knew that if he talked, it would mean the torture and death of others in the Resistance." Paul looked away for a moment. "Apparently he and his friends had helped a number of British pilots escape German detection. At risk was the entire underground effort. Jean-Claude knew more than anyone suspected."

"Helen couldn't let that happen," Ruth said.

"No, and Jean-Claude understood that, too."

"Remember when she said she was the one who killed him? She didn't mean that literally, did she?"

"She did."

This was beginning not to make sense. "But… how?"

Paul braced his elbows on the table. "Her voice started to break at that point and I didn't catch everything. She talked about a cyanide tablet. I'm not sure how she got hold of it. But I know she kissed him…. A final kiss goodbye. By this stage she was too emotional to understand clearly."

The pieces started to fall together for Ruth. "She gave him the pill—you mean instead of taking it herself?"

"That's what it sounded like to me," he said hoarsely.

"Was this when he asked her to kill him? And then she kissed him and transferred the pill?"

"I think so." Paul cleared his throat, but his voice was still rough. "She said Jean-Claude had begged her to kill him. He spoke to her in English, which the Germans couldn't understand."

Ruth pictured the terrible scene. Helen and Jean-Claude arguing. If Helen swallowed the pill, she'd be dead and the Gestapo would lose their bargaining chip. Even knowing that, Jean-Claude couldn't bear to see his wife die. It truly would have broken him.

"Speaking in another language added enough confusion that she had the opportunity to do what he asked," Ruth speculated.

"Last time she told us about being driven by fear instead of courage," Paul reminded her. "I'm sure she didn't stop to think about what she was doing—she couldn't. Nor could she refuse Jean-Claude."

Ruth wanted to bury her face in her hands and weep.

"Jean-Claude thanked her," Paul said.

"She would have refused." Ruth could see it all in her mind, the argument between them.

"I'm convinced she did refuse at first. She loved Jean-Claude—he was her husband."

Ruth couldn't imagine a worse scenario.

Paul's voice dropped slightly. "She said Jean-Claude had never begged for mercy, never pleaded for anything, but he told her he couldn't bear any more pain. Above all, he couldn't bear it if they killed her. He begged her to let him die."

"He loved her that much," Ruth said in a hushed whisper.

"And she loved him that much, enough to spare him any more torture, even at the risk of her own death."

"They didn't kill her, though," Ruth said, stating the obvious. "Even though they must have figured out that she was responsible for his death?"

Paul's eyes widened as if he couldn't explain that any more than she could. "She didn't say what happened next."

Ruth stood, anxious now to see her grandmother before they left. "I'm going to check on her."

Ruth went to her grandmother's room to find her resting fitfully. Helen's eyes fluttered open when Ruth stepped quietly past the threshold.

"Have I shocked you?" Helen asked, holding out her hand to Ruth.

"No," Ruth told her grandmother, who had to be the bravest woman she'd ever know. She sat on the edge of the bed and whispered, "Thank you, Grandma—for everything you did. And for doing Paul and me the honor of sharing it with us."

Helen smiled and touched her cheek. "You've been crying."

Taking her grandmother's hand between her own, she kissed the old woman's knuckles. A lump filled her throat and she couldn't find the words to express her love.

"When did you meet Grandpa?" she finally asked.

Helen smiled again and her eyes drifted shut. "Two years later. He was one of the American soldiers who came with Patton's army to free us from the concentration camp."

This was a completely different aspect of the story.

"When it was learned that I was an American citizen, I was immediately questioned and when my citizenship was verified, I was put on a ship and sent home."

"Two years," Ruth said in a choked voice. "You were in a camp for *two years?*" Just when she thought there was nothing more to horrify her, Helen revealed something else.

"Buchenwald… I don't want to talk about it," Helen muttered.

No wonder her grandmother had never spoken of those years. The memories were far worse than the worst Ruth had been able to imagine.

Her grandmother brushed the hair from Ruth's forehead. "I want you to know I like your young man."

"He reminded you of Jean-Claude, didn't he?"

Her smile was weak, which told Ruth how drained this afternoon's conversation had left Helen. "Not at first, but then he smiled and I saw Jean-Claude in Paul's eyes." She swallowed a couple of times and added, "I wanted to die after Jean-Claude did. I would've done anything if only the Germans had put me out of my living hell. They knew that and decided it was better to let me live and remember, each and every day, that I'd killed my own husband." A tear slid down her face. "I can't speak of it anymore."

Ruth understood. "I'll leave you to rest. Try to sleep."

Her grandmother's answering sigh told Ruth how badly she needed that just then.

"Come back and see me soon," she called as Ruth stood.

"I will, I promise." She bent down to kiss the soft cheek.

Paul was waiting for her in the living room, flipping through the *Cedar Cove Chronicle,* but he got up when she returned. "Is she all right?"

Ruth shrugged. "She's tired." Her eyes were watering again, despite her best efforts not to cry. She couldn't stop thinking about the pain her grandmother had endured and kept hidden all these years.

Paul held open his arms and she walked into his embrace as naturally as she slipped on a favorite coat. Once there, she began to cry—harsh, broken sobs she thought would never end.

Eight

As before, Ruth and Paul spoke little on the ferry ride back to Seattle.

Ruth's entire perspective on her grandmother had changed. Until now, she'd always viewed the petite, gentle woman as…well, her grandmother. All of a sudden Ruth was forced to realize that Helen had been young once, and deeply involved in events that had changed or destroyed many lives. She'd been an ordinary young woman from a fairly privileged background. She'd been a student, fallen in love, enjoyed a carefree existence. Then this ordinary young woman had been caught up in extraordinary circumstances—and risen to their demands.

Ruth was curious about the connection between her grandmother's life during the war and her life afterward. Clearly the link was her grandfather, whom she'd never had a chance to know.

Paul stood with Ruth at the railing as the ferry glided through the relatively smooth waters of Puget Sound. The rain had stopped, and although the sky remained cloudy and gray, the air was fresh with only the slightest hint of brine.

"Every story I hear leaves me amazed that this incredible woman is my grandmother," Ruth said fervently, grateful that Paul was beside her.

"I know. I'm overwhelmed, and I just met her."

They exchanged tentative smiles, and then they both sighed—in appreciation, Ruth thought, of everything Helen Shelton had been and done.

"I wish I'd known my grandfather," she said. "He seems to have been the one who gave my grandmother a reason to live. He loved her and she loved him." Ruth knew that from every word her grandmother and her dad had said about Sam Shelton.

"How old were you when he died?" Paul asked.

"Two or so." She turned so she could look directly at Paul. "When I saw my grandmother in her bedroom, she said he was with a group of soldiers who freed the prisoners in the concentration camp."

"She was in a concentration camp?"

Ruth nodded. "She was there at least a couple of years."

Paul frowned, obviously upset.

"I can't *bear* to think what her life was like in one of those obscene places," Ruth said.

"It would've been grim. You're right—they were obscene. Places of death."

Ruth didn't welcome the reminder. "I'm so glad you've been with me on these visits," she told him. Paul's presence helped her assimilate the details her grandmother had shared. He'd given her a feeling of comfort and companionship as they'd listened to these painful wartime experiences. Ruth believed there was something about Paul that had led Helen to divulge her secrets.

After the ferry docked, they walked along the Seattle waterfront, where they ate clam chowder, followed by fish and chips, for dinner. Their mood was somber, and yet, strangely, Ruth felt a sense of peace.

The next day, after her classes, she hurried back to her rental house and ran into Lynn. As much as possible, Ruth had avoided her roommate. Her relationship with Lynn had been awkward ever since the argument over Clay. Lynn's lie, which she'd told in an effort to keep Ruth from meeting Paul, hadn't helped.

Lynn was coming out just as Ruth leaped up the porch steps. Her roommate hesitated.

Ruth did, too. She'd never said anything to Lynn about her intentional mix-up that first night she was meeting Paul. Her classes would be over in June, and she was more than ready to move out.

"Hi," Lynn offered uncertainly.

Ruth's pace slowed as she waited, half expecting Lynn to make some derogatory remark about Paul. Because Ruth had been with him so often lately, she'd had very little contact with her roommate.

"Are you seeing Paul again?" The question lacked the scornful tone she'd used when referring to him previously. She seemed more prompted by curiosity than anything else.

"We're meeting some friends of his later. Why?" Ruth couldn't help being suspicious. If he'd phoned with a change of plan, she needed to know about it. She knew from experience that Lynn couldn't be trusted to relay the message.

Lynn shrugged. "No reason."

"Is there something you aren't telling me?" Ruth's voice was calm.

Her roommate had the grace to blush. "He didn't call, if that's what you're asking."

"Like I could believe you."

"You can—okay, maybe what I did that night was stupid."

"Maybe?" Ruth echoed.

"All right, it was. I was upset because of Clay." She didn't meet Ruth's eyes. "I thought Clay was really hot and you dumped him for soldier boy, and I thought that was just wrong."

"I don't need you to decide who I'm allowed to date." Ruth couldn't keep the anger out of her voice. What Lynn had tried to do still rankled. If her cell phone battery hadn't been low, she and Paul might have missed each other completely. That sent chills down her spine.

Lynn released a long sigh. "I'll admit it—you were right about Clay."

"How so?"

"He's…he's stuck on himself."

Ruth suspected that meant he wasn't interested in Lynn.

"I…I like Paul," her roommate confessed.

Ruth wasn't even aware that Lynn had met him and said so.

"He stopped by one afternoon when he thought you were back from class, only you weren't, and I was here. We talked for a bit. Then he left to look for you at the library."

Funny that neither had mentioned the incident earlier. "I had the impression you were dead set against him."

"Not him," Lynn said. "I'm against the war in Iraq.… I thought you were, too."

"I don't like war of any kind. This war or any war, including Afghanistan. Still, the United States is involved in the Middle East, and no matter what, it's our young men and women who are fighting there. Politics aside, I want to support our troops."

"I know." Lynn suddenly seemed to find something absolutely mesmerizing about her shoes.

Ruth moved past her on the porch. "I'd better go in and change."

"Ruth," Lynn said sharply. Ruth turned to face her. "I'm sorry about the other night. That really was an awful thing to do. I was upset and I took it out on you."

Ruth had pretty much figured that out on her own. "Paul and I connected, so no harm done."

"I know, and I'm glad you did because I think Paul is great. I know he's a soldier and all, but he's a nice guy. I only met him once, but I could see he's ten times the man Clay will ever be. He's the kind of guy I hope to meet."

Paul had obviously impressed her during their brief exchange. She wondered what they'd talked about.

"All's well that ends well," Ruth said.

"Shakespeare, right?" Lynn asked. "In other words, all is forgiven?"

Ruth laughed and nodded, then started into the house.

Paul picked her up at five-thirty and they drove to a Mexican restaurant in downtown Kent. Paul had arranged for her to meet his best friend.

Brian Hart and his wife, Carley, were high school sweethearts and Brian had known Paul for most of his life.

"We go way back," Brian said when they were introduced. He slid out of the booth and they exchanged handshakes, with Paul standing just behind Ruth, his hand on her shoulder.

"I'm pleased to meet you both." They were a handsome couple. Carley was a delicate blonde with soulful blue eyes, and her husband was tall and muscular, as if he routinely worked out.

"We're pleased to meet you, too," Carley said when Ruth slipped into the booth across from her.

Paul got in beside Ruth.

"I insisted Paul introduce us," Carley said as she reached for a chip and dipped it in the salsa. "Every time we tried to get together during his leave, he already had plans with you."

Ruth hadn't thought of it that way, but realized she'd monopolized his time. "I guess I should apologize for that."

"We only have the two weeks," Paul explained.

"You'll be back in Seattle after the training, won't you?" Brian asked.

"Maybe, but…" Paul hesitated and glanced at Ruth.

"We only just met and…" Ruth let the rest fade. He would be back and they'd see each other again, but only if she could accept his career in the military.

This fourteen-day period was a testing time for them both, and at the end they had a decision to make.

"I'm giving Ruth two weeks to fall head over heels in love with me." Paul said it as if it were a joke.

"If she doesn't, there's definitely something wrong with her," Carley joked back.

Ruth smiled, but she felt her heart sinking. She hadn't made her decision yet; the truth was, she'd been putting it off until the last possible minute.

Time was dwindling and soon, in a matter of days, Paul would be leaving. She wasn't ready—wasn't ready to decide and wasn't ready for him to go.

Brian and Carley had to be home before eight because of their babysitter, so they left the restaurant first.

Ruth had enjoyed the spicy enchiladas, the margarita and especially the teasing between Paul and Brian. Carley had told story after story of the two boys and their high school exploits, and they'd all laughed and joked together.

Paul and Ruth lingered in the booth over cups of dark coffee, gazing into each other's eyes. He'd switched places so he could sit across from her. If she'd met him under any other circumstance, there'd be no question about her feelings. None! It was so easy to fall in love with this man. In fact, it was already too late; even Paul's mother had seen that. Ruth *knew* him. After all the letters and emails, all the conversations, she felt as if he'd become part of her life.

"I know what you're thinking," Paul said unexpectedly.

"What am I thinking?" she asked with amusement.

"You're wondering why I find life in the military so attractive."

She shrugged. "Close."

"Do you want to know my answer?"

Ruth was aware of his reasons, but wanted to hear him out, anyway. "Sure, go ahead."

"I like the structure, the discipline, the knowledge that I'm doing something positive to bring about freedom and democracy in the world."

This was where it got troubling for Ruth.

Before she could state her own feelings, Paul stopped her. "I know you don't agree with me, and I accept that, but I am who I am."

"I didn't challenge that—I wouldn't."

He stiffened, then reached for his coffee and held it at arm's length, cupping his hands around the mug. "True enough, but the minute I started talking, you looked like you wanted to challenge my answer."

She hadn't known her feelings were that transparent.

"I guess now is as good a time as any to ask where I stand with you."

"What do you mean?" An uneasy feeling began to creep up her spine. They had only a couple of days before he was scheduled to leave, and she was going to need every minute of that time to concentrate on this relationship.

"You know what I'm asking, Ruth."

She did. She met his eyes. "I'm in love with you, Paul."

"I'm in love with you, too." He stretched his hand across the table and intertwined their fingers.

Her heart nearly sprang out of her chest with happiness and yet tears filled her eyes.

To her astonishment, Paul laughed. "This is supposed to be a happy moment," he told her.

"I *am* happy, but I'm afraid, too."

"Of what?"

"Of you leaving again. Of your involvement in the military. Of you fighting in a war, any war."

"It's what I do."

"I know." Still, she had difficulty reconciling her emotions and beliefs with the way Paul chose to make his living.

"But you don't like it," he said, his voice hard.

"No."

He sighed harshly. "Then tell me where we go from here."

Ruth wished she knew. "I can't answer that."

His eyes pleaded with her. "I can't answer it for you, Ruth. You're going to have to make up your mind about us."

She'd known it would come down to this. "I'm not sure I can. Not yet."

He considered her words. "When do you think you'll be able to decide?"

"Let's wait until you've finished your training and we see each other again.... We'll both have a better idea then, don't you think?"

"No. I might not be coming back to Seattle. I have to know soon. Now. Tonight." He paused. "I realize I sound unfair and pushy, and I apologize."

"Apologize for what?" she asked. Her hand tightened around his fingers. She could feel him pulling away from her, if not physically, then emotionally.

"I've been trained to be decisive. Putting things off only leads to confusion. We've been writing for months."

"Yes, I know, but—"

"We've spent every possible minute of my leave together."

"Yes…"

"I love you, Ruth, but I won't lie to you. I'm not leaving the marines. I've chosen the military as my career and that means I could be involved in conflicts all over the world. I have to know if you can accept that."

"I…"

"If you can't, we need to walk away from each other right now. I don't want to drag this out. You decide."

Ruth didn't want a part-time husband. "I want a man who'll be a husband to me and a father to my children. A man of peace, not war." She didn't mean to sound so adamant.

Paul didn't respond for a long moment. "I think we have our answer." He slid out of the booth and waited for her. They'd paid earlier, so there was nothing to do but go out to the parking lot.

Ruth wasn't finished with the conversation, even if Paul was. "I need time," she told him.

"The decision's made."

"You're pressuring me," she protested. "I've still got two days, remember?"

"It doesn't work that way," he said.

"But this isn't fair!"

"I already admitted it wasn't." He opened the passenger door, and a moment later, he joined her in the car. "I wish now I'd waited and we still had those two days," he said bleakly. "But we don't."

He started the car and Ruth noticed that his fingers had tensed on the steering wheel.

Ruth bit her lip. "Sure we do. Let's just pretend we didn't have this conversation and enjoy the time we have left. You can do that, can't you?" Her voice took on a pleading quality.

"I wish I could, but...I can't." He inhaled deeply. "The decision is made," he said again.

They didn't have much to say during the rest of the ride to the university district. When Paul pulled up in front of the rental house, Ruth noticed the lights were on, which meant Lynn was home.

They sat side by side in the car without speaking until Paul roused himself to open his door. He walked around to escort her from the passenger side, then accompanied her to the porch.

Ruth half expected him to kiss her. He didn't.

"Will I see you again?" she asked as he began to leave.

He turned back and stood there, stiff and formal. "Probably not."

"You mean this is it? This is goodbye...as if I meant nothing...as if we were strangers?" She felt outraged that he could abandon her like this, without a word. It was unkind and unfair...and life wasn't that simple.

"Is there anything left to say?" he asked.

"Of course there is," she cried. She didn't know what, but surely there was *something*. Hurting and angry, Ruth gestured wildly with her arms. "You can't be serious! Are you really going to walk away? Just like that?"

"Yes." The word was devoid of emotion.

"You aren't going to write me again?"

"No."

This was unbelievable.

"Call me?"

"No."

She glared at him. "In other words, you're going to act as if you'd never even met me, as if I'd never mailed that Christmas card."

A hint of a smile flickered over his tightly controlled features. "I'm certainly going to give it my best shot."

"Fine, then," she muttered. If he thought so little of her, then he could do as he wished. She didn't want to be with a man who didn't care about her feelings, just his own.

Nine

True to his word, Paul didn't get in touch with her after their Tuesday-night dinner. The first day, her anger carried her. Then she convinced herself that he'd contact her before he left for Camp Pendleton. Not so. Paul Gordon—correction, *Sergeant* Paul Gordon, USMC—was out of her life and that was perfectly fine with her. Only it wasn't.

A week later, as she sat in her "Theories of Learning" class, taking notes, her determination faltered. She wanted to push all thoughts of Paul out of her mind forever; instead, he was constantly there.

What upset her most was the cold-blooded way he'd dismissed her from his life. It seemed so easy for him, so…simple. She was gone for him, as if she meant nothing. That hurt, and it didn't stop hurting.

Ruth blinked, forcing herself to listen to the lecture. If she flunked this course, Paul Gordon would be to blame.

After class she walked across campus, her steps slow and deliberate. She felt no urge to hurry. But when her cell phone rang, she nearly dropped her purse in her eagerness. Could it be Paul? Had he changed his mind?

Had he found it impossible to forget her, the same way she couldn't forget him? A dozen more questions flew through her mind before she managed to answer.

"Hello?" She sounded excited and breathless at the same time.

"Ruth." The familiar voice of a longtime friend, Tina Dupont, greeted her. They talked for a few minutes, and arranged to meet at the library at the end of the week. Four minutes after she'd answered her cell, it was back in her purse.

She was too restless to sit at home and study, which was how she'd spent every night since her last date with Paul, so she decided to go out. That was what she needed, she told herself with forced enthusiasm. Find people, friends, a party. Something to do, somewhere to be.

Although it was midafternoon, she took the bus down to the waterfront, where she'd met Paul the first night. That wasn't a smart idea. She wasn't up to dealing with memories. Before she could talk herself out of it, Ruth hopped on the Bremerton ferry. A visit with her grandmother would lift her spirits in a way nothing else could. Besides, if Helen felt strong enough, she wanted to hear the rest of the story, especially the role her grandfather had played.

As she stepped off the foot ferry from Bremerton to Cedar Cove, it occurred to Ruth that she should've phoned first. But it was unlikely her grandmother would be out. And if she was, Ruth figured she could wander around Cedar Cove for a while. That would help fill the void threatening to swallow her whole.

The trudge up the hill to her grandmother's house seemed twice as steep and three times as long. Funny, when she'd been with Paul, the climb hadn't even winded her. That was because she'd been laughing and joking with him, she remembered—and wished she hadn't. Alone, hands shoved in her pockets, she felt drained of energy.

Reaching 5-B Poppy Lane, she saw that the front door to her grandmother's duplex stood open, although the old-fashioned wooden screen was shut. The last remaining tulips bloomed in primary colors as vivid as the rainbow. Walking up the steps, Ruth rang the doorbell. "Grandma! Are you home?"

No one answered. "Grandma?"

Alarm jolted through her. Had something happened to her grandmother? She pounded on the door and was even more alarmed when a white-haired woman close to her grandmother's age came toward her.

"Hello," the older lady said pleasantly. "Can I help you?"

"I'm looking for my grandmother."

The woman unlatched the screen door and swung it open. "You must be Ruth. I don't think Helen was expecting you. I'm Charlotte Rhodes."

"Charlotte," Ruth repeated. "Helen's spoken of you so often. It's wonderful to meet you."

"You, too," Charlotte said, taking Ruth's hand. "I'm happy to make your acquaintance."

Ruth nodded, but she couldn't stop herself from blurting out, "Is anything wrong with my grandmother?"

"Oh, no, not at all. We're sitting on the patio, talking and knitting. Helen's counting stitches and asked me to get the door. She assumed it was a salesman and my job was to get rid of him...or her." Charlotte laughed. "Not that *I'm* much good at that. Just the other day, a Girl Scout came to my door selling cookies. When I bought four boxes, she announced that every kid comes to my house first, because I'll buy anything. Especially for charity."

Ruth grinned. "I think my grandmother must be like that, too."

"Why do you suppose she sent *me* to the door?" Charlotte joked. "Your grandmother's knitting a Fair Isle sweater. It's her first one and she asked me over to get her started."

"Perhaps I should come back at a more convenient time?" Ruth didn't want to interrupt the two women.

"Nonsense! She'd never forgive me if you left. Besides, I was just gathering my things to head on home. My husband will be wondering what's kept me so long." Charlotte led the way through the house.

As soon as Ruth stepped onto the brick patio, her grandmother's eyes lit up with pleasure. "Ruth! What a welcome surprise."

Ruth bent forward and kissed Helen's cheek.

Charlotte Rhodes collected her knitting, saying she'd talk to Helen at the Senior Center on Monday, and left.

"Sit down, sit down," Helen urged, motioning at the chair next to her. "Help yourself to iced tea if you'd like." Strands of yarn were wrapped around both index fingers as she held the needles. One was red, the other white. "You can find a glass, can't you?"

"Yes, of course, but I'm fine," Ruth assured her, enjoying the sunshine and the sights and sounds of Cedar Cove. The earth in her grandmother's garden smelled warm and clean—the way it only smelled in spring. Inhaling deeply, Ruth sat down, staring at the cove with its sparkling blue water.

"Where's Paul?" her grandmother asked, as if noticing for the first time that he wasn't with her.

Ruth's serenity was instantly destroyed and she struggled to disguise her misery. "He went to the marines' camp in California."

"Oh." Her grandmother seemed disappointed. "I imagine you miss him."

Ruth decided to let the comment slide.

"I liked him a great deal," her grandmother said, rubbing salt into Ruth's already wounded heart. Helen's focus was on her knitting, but when Ruth didn't immediately respond, she looked up.

Ruth met her eyes and exhaled forcefully. "Would you mind if we didn't discuss Paul?"

Her request was met with a puzzled glance. "Why?"

Ruth decided she might as well tell her. "We won't be seeing each other again."

"Really?" Her grandmother's expression was downcast. "I thought highly of that young man. Any particular reason?"

"Actually," Ruth said, "there are several. He's in the military, which you already know."

Her grandmother carefully set her knitting aside and reached for her glass of iced tea, giving Ruth her full attention. "You knew that when you first met, I believe."

"Yes, I did, but I assumed that in time he'd be released from his commitment and return to civilian life. He told me that won't be the case, that the military's his career." *In for the long haul,* as he'd put it. Granted, she'd known about his dedication to the marines from the beginning, but he'd known about her feelings, too. Did her preferences matter less than his?

"I see." Her grandmother studied her.

Ruth wondered if she truly did. "What really upsets me is the heartless way he left. I told him I wasn't sure I could live with the fact that he'd chosen the military." The memory angered her, and she raised her voice. "Then Paul had the audacity to say I wouldn't be hearing from him again and he…he just walked away." Ruth hadn't planned to spill out the whole story minutes after she arrived, but she couldn't hold it inside a second longer.

Her grandmother's response shocked her into silence. Helen *smiled*.

"Forgive me," her grandmother said gently, leaning forward to give Ruth's hand a small squeeze. "Sam did something similar, you see."

The irritation died instantly. "I wanted to ask you about my grandfather."

A peaceful look came over Helen. "He was a wonderful man. And he saved me."

"From the Germans, you mean?"

Helen shook her head. "Technically, it was General Patton and the Third Army who saved us. Patton knew what Buchenwald was. He knew that a three-hour wait meant twenty-thousand lives because the Germans had been given orders to kill all prisoners before surrendering. Against every rule of caution, Patton mounted an attack, cutting off the SS troops from the camp. Because of his decisive move, the Germans were forced to flee or surrender. By that time, the German soldiers knew they were defeated. They threw down their guns and surrendered. Sam was with Patton on the march, so, yes, he contributed to my rescue and that of countless others. But when I say your grandfather saved me, I mean he saved me from myself."

"I want to hear about him, if you're willing to tell me." Ruth straightened, perching on the edge of her seat.

Her grandmother closed her eyes. "I cannot speak about the years in Buchenwald, not even to you."

Ruth reached for Helen's hand, stroking the soft skin over the gnarled and prominent knuckles. "That's fine, Grandma."

"I wanted to die, wished it with all my heart. Without

Jean-Claude, it was harder to live than to die. Living was the cruelest form of punishment." Tears pooled in her eyes and she blinked them away.

"When the Americans came," Helen continued, "the gates were opened and we were free. It was a delicious feeling—freedom always is—but one never appreciates it until it's taken away. The soldiers spoke English, and I went to them and explained that I was an American. I had no identification or anything to prove my claim, so I kept repeating the address where my parents lived in New York. I was desperate to get word to them that I was alive. They hadn't heard from me in almost five years.

"One of the soldiers brought me to their headquarters. I was completely emaciated, and I'm sure my stench was enough to nauseate anyone standing within twenty feet. The young man then took me to his lieutenant, whose name was Sam Shelton. From that moment forward, Sam took care of me. He saw that I had food and water, clothes and access to showers and anything else I needed."

Ruth shuddered at the thought of her grandmother's physical and mental condition following her release.

Her grandmother paused to take a deep breath, and when she spoke again, it was in another language, what Ruth assumed was German. Pressing her hand on Helen's, she stopped her. "Grandma, English, please."

Her grandmother frowned. "Sorry."

"Was that German?"

She shrugged, eyes wild and confused. "I don't know."

After all those years inside a German camp, it made sense that she'd revert to the language. In her mind she'd gone back to that time, was reliving each incident.

"Go on. Please," Ruth urged.

Helen sighed. "I don't remember much about those first days of freedom."

Ruth could easily understand that.

"Still, every memory I have is of the lieutenant at my side, watching over me. I was hospitalized, and I think I slept almost around the clock for three days straight, waking only long enough to eat and drink. Yet every time I opened my eyes, Sam was there. I'm sure that's not possible, but that's how I remember it."

She picked up her tea with a trembling hand and sipped the cool liquid. "After a week—maybe more, I don't know, time meant nothing to me—I was transported out of Germany and placed on a ship going to America. Sam wrote out his name and home address in Washington State and gave it to me. I didn't know why he'd do that."

"Did you keep it?" Ruth asked.

"I did," Helen confessed, "although I didn't think I'd ever need it. By the time I got back to New York, I was still skin and bones. My own parents didn't even recognize me. My mother looked at me and burst into tears. I was twenty-four years old, and I felt sixty."

Ruth was in her twenties and couldn't imagine living through any of what her grandmother had described.

"Five months after I got home, Sam Shelton knocked on the door of my parents' brownstone. I'd gained weight and my hair had grown back, and when I saw him I barely remembered who he was. He visited for two days and we talked. He'd come to see how I was adjusting to life in America."

Ruth had wondered about that, too. It couldn't have been easy.

"I hadn't done very well. My parents owned a small bakery and I worked at the counter, but I had no life in me, no joy. Now that I was free, I felt I had nothing to live for. My husband was dead, and I was the one who'd killed him. I told this American soldier, whom I hardly knew, all of this. I told him I preferred to die. I told him everything—not one thing did I hold back. He listened and didn't interrupt me with questions, and when I was finished he took my hand and kissed it." The tears came again, spilling down her cheeks. "He said I was the bravest woman he'd ever known."

"I think you are, too," Ruth said, her voice shaky.

"Sam told me he was part of D-day," Helen said. "His company was one of the first to land on Omaha Beach. He spoke of the fighting there and the bravery of his men. He'd seen death the same way I had. Later, in the midst of the fighting, he'd stumbled across the body of his own brother. He had no time to mourn him. He didn't understand why God had seen fit to spare him and not his brother.

"This lieutenant asked the very questions I'd been asking myself. I didn't know why I should live when I'd rather have died with Jean-Claude—or instead of him." She paused again, as if to regain her composure.

"After that, Sam said he'd needed to do a lot of thinking, and praying, and it came to him that his brother, his men, had sacrificed their lives so that others could live in freedom. God had spared him, and me, too, and it wasn't up to either of us to question why. As for Jean-Claude and Tim, Sam's brother, they had died in this terrible but necessary *war*. For either of us to throw away our lives now would be to dishonor them—my husband and Sam's brother."

"He was right, you know."

Her grandmother nodded. "Sam left after that one visit. He wished me well and said he hoped I'd keep in touch. I waited a week before I wrote the first letter. Sam hadn't given me many details of his war experiences, but deep down I knew they'd been as horrific as my own. In that, we had a bond."

"So you and Grandpa Sam wrote letters to each other."

Helen nodded again. "For six months we wrote, and every day I found more questions for him to answer. His letters were messages of encouragement and hope for us both. Oh, Ruth, how I wish you'd had the opportunity to know your grandfather. He was wise and kind and loving. He gave me a reason to live, a reason to go on. He taught me I could love again—and then he asked me to marry him." Helen drew in a deep breath. "Sam wrote and asked me to be his wife, and I said no."

"You refused?" Ruth asked, incredulous.

"I couldn't leave my parents a second time.... Oh, I had a dozen excuses, all of them valid."

"How did he convince you?"

Her smile was back. "He didn't. In those days, one didn't hop on a plane or even use the phone unless it was a dire emergency. For two weeks he was silent. No letters and no contact. Nothing. When I didn't hear from him, I knew I never would again."

This was the reason her grandmother had smiled when Ruth told her she hadn't heard from Paul.

"I couldn't stand it," Helen admitted. "This soldier had become vitally important to me. For the first time since Jean-Claude died, I could *feel*. I could laugh and cry. I knew Sam was the one who'd taken this heavy burden of pain from my shoulders. Not only that, he loved me. Loved me," she repeated, "and I'd turned him down when he asked me to share his life."

"What did you do next?"

Helen smiled at the memory. "I sent a telegram that

said three words. *Yes. Yes. Yes.* Then I boarded a train and five days later, I arrived in Washington State. When I stepped off the platform, my suitcase in hand, Sam was there with his entire family. We were married two weeks later. I knew no one, so he introduced me to his best friends and the women they loved. Those four became my dearest friends. They were the people who helped me adjust to normal life. They helped me find my new identity." She shook her head slowly. "Not once in all the years your grandfather and I were together did I have a single regret."

Ruth's eyes were teary. "That's a beautiful love story."

"Now you're living one of your own."

Ruth didn't see it like that. "I don't want to be a military wife," she said. "I can't do it."

"You love Paul."

Ruth noted that her grandmother hadn't made it a question. Helen knew that Ruth's heart was linked with Paul's. He was an honorable man, and he loved her. They didn't need to have the same political beliefs as long as they respected each other's views.

"Yes, Grandma, I love him."

"And you miss him the same way I missed Sam."

"I do." It was freeing to Ruth to admit it. The depression that had hung over her for the past week lifted.

All at once Ruth knew exactly what she was going to do. Her decision was made.

Ten

Barbara Gordon answered the doorbell, and the moment she saw Ruth, her eyes lit with delight. "Ruth, I'm so glad to see you!"

Ruth was instantly ushered into the house. She hadn't been sure what kind of reception she'd get. After all, she'd disappointed and possibly hurt the Gordons' son.

"I was so hoping you'd stop by," Barbara continued as she led her into the kitchen.

Obediently Ruth followed. "I came because I don't have a current address for Paul."

"You plan on writing him?" Barbara seemed about to leap up and down and clap her hands.

"Actually, no."

The happiness drained from the other woman's eyes.

"I know it's a bit old-fashioned, but I thought I'd send him a telegram."

The delight was back in place. "Greg," she shouted over her shoulder. "Ruth is here."

Almost immediately Paul's father joined them in the kitchen. His grin was as wide as his wife's had been. "Good to see you, good to see you," he said expansively.

"What did I tell you?" Barbara insisted.

The two of them stood there staring at her.

"About Paul's address?" Ruth prodded.

"Oh, yes." As if she'd woken from a trance, Barbara Gordon hurried into the other room, leaving Ruth alone with Paul's father.

It was awkward at first, and Ruth felt the least she could do was explain the reason for her visit. "I miss Paul so much," she told him. "I need his address."

Greg Gordon nodded. "He's missing you, too. Big-time."

Ruth's heart filled with hope. "He said that?"

"Not in those exact words," Greg stated matter-of-factly. "But rest assured, my son is pretty miserable."

"That's *wonderful*." Now it was Ruth who wanted to leap up and down and clap her hands.

"My son is miserable and you're happy?" Greg asked, but a teasing light glinted in his eyes.

"Yes…no… Yes," she quickly amended. "I just hope he's been as miserable as I have."

Greg's smile faded. "No question there."

The phone rang once; Barbara must have answered it right away. Within a few minutes she returned to the kitchen, carrying a portable phone. "It's for you."

Greg started toward her.

"Not you, honey," she said, gesturing at Ruth. "The call is for Ruth."

"Me?" She was startled. No one knew she'd come here. Anyone wanting to reach her would automatically call her cell. Her frown disappeared as she realized who it must be.

"Is it Paul?" she asked, her voice low and hopeful.

"It is. He thinks Greg's about to get on the line." She clasped her husband's elbow. "Come on, honey, let's give

Ruth and Paul some privacy." She was halfway out of the room when she turned back, caught Ruth's eye and winked.

That was just the encouragement Ruth needed. Still, she felt decidedly nervous as she picked up the phone resting on the kitchen counter. After the way they'd parted, she didn't know what to expect or how to react.

"Hello, Paul," she said, hoping to sound calm and confident, neither of which she was.

Her greeting was followed by a slight hesitation. "Ruth?"

"Yes, it's me." Her voice was downright cheerful—and more than a little forced.

"What are you doing at my parents' place?" he asked gruffly.

"Visiting."

Again he paused, as if he wasn't sure what to make of this. "I'd like to speak to my father."

"I'm sorry, he and your mother left the room so you and I could talk."

"About what?" He hadn't warmed to her yet.

"Your calling ruins everything," she told him. "I was going to send you a telegram. My grandmother sent one to my grandfather sixty years ago."

"A telegram?"

"I know it's outdated. It's also rather romantic, I thought."

"What did you intend to say in this telegram?"

"I hadn't decided. My first idea was to say the same thing Helen said to my grandfather. It was a short message—just three little words."

"I love you?" He was warming up now.

"No."

"No?" He seemed skeptical. "What else could it be? Helen loved him, didn't she?"

"Oh, yes, but that was understood. Oh, Paul, I heard the rest of the story and it's so beautiful, so compelling, you'll see why she loved him as much as she did. Sam helped her look to the future and step out of the past."

"You're avoiding the question," he said.

That confused her for a moment. "What's the question?"

"Do you love me enough to accept me as a marine?"

"I wasn't sending *that* answer by way of Western Union." The answer that was going to change her life....

"You can tell me now," he said casually.

"Before I do, you have to promise, on your word of honor as a United States marine, that you'll never walk away from me like that again."

"You think it was easy?" he demanded.

"I don't care if it was easy or not, you can't ever do it again." His abandonment had hurt too much.

"All right," he muttered. "I promise I'll never walk away from you again."

"Word of honor?"

"Word of honor."

He'd earned it now. "I'm crazy about you, Paul Gordon. *Crazy*. Crazy in love with you. If having the marines as your career means that much to you, then I'll adjust. I'll find a way to make it work. But you need to compromise, too, when it comes to my career. I can't just leave a teaching job in order to follow you somewhere."

The last thing Ruth expected after her admission was a long stretch of silence.

Then, "Are you serious? You'll accept my being in the military?"

"Yes. Do you think I'd do this otherwise?"

"No," he told her. "But what you don't know is that I've been thinking about giving up the marines."

"Because of me?"

"Yes."

"You were?" Never once had it occurred to Ruth that he'd consider such a thing.

"My dad and I have had a couple of long talks about it," he went on to say.

"Tell me more."

"You already know this part—I'm crazy about you, too. I wasn't convinced I could find a way to live the rest of my life without you. One option I've looked into is training. I've talked to my commander about it, and he thinks it's a good possibility. I'd be able to stay in the marines, but I'd be stationed in one place for a while."

Ruth slumped onto a kitchen stool, feeling deliciously weak, too weak to stay upright. "Oh, Paul, that's wonderful!"

"I felt like a fool," he said. "I made my big stand, and I honestly felt I was right, but I didn't have to force you to decide that very minute. My pride wouldn't allow me to back off, though."

"Pride carried me the first week," she said. "Then I went to see my grandmother, and she told me how she met my grandfather at the end of the war. Their romance was as much of an adventure as everything else she told us."

"She's a very special woman," Paul said. "Just like her granddaughter."

"I'll tell you everything later."

"I can't wait to hear it. I'm just wondering if history might repeat itself."

"How?"

"I'm wondering if you'll be my wife."

"That's the perfect question," Ruth said, and it *was* perfect for what she had in mind.

She closed her eyes and sighed deeply. "I do believe I'll send you that telegram after all."

Yes. Yes. Yes.

Epilogue

Paul reached for Ruth's hand beneath the dining-room table. Ruth smiled and gave his hand a squeeze.

"Dinner was fabulous, Grandma," Ruth said. She'd never expected her grandmother to go to all this effort. "I wish you hadn't worked so hard, though. Paul and I would've taken you out to eat."

"Nonsense. It's Christmas Eve. Besides, I rarely get the opportunity to cook for anyone these days. I enjoyed it. And it's such a treat to have the two of you all to myself."

"Thank you so much for everything—especially the stockings. You know we'll treasure them."

"And thank *you,* my darling, for the beautiful memoir you've created."

Ruth had made a new version of Helen's story, including a number of photographs she'd found through her research. She'd scanned the poster declaring Helen and her first husband, Jean-Claude, criminals. She'd also inserted some details Helen had remembered more recently. Finally, she'd had it professionally bound and it was, even if she said so herself, a beautiful piece of work. The memoir was for her grandmother, true, but it was also for everyone in the Shelton family, now and in the future.

Ruth stood and carried the empty dinner plates to the sink. "Paul and I will do the dishes."

"No need."

"We insist," Paul said.

"I don't want to waste a minute of our time together with dishes," Helen told him. "I hardly ever see you as it is."

"Well, that should be changing soon," Ruth said with a smile.

"I've requested Seattle as my next duty station," Paul explained. "My parents are here, too, and we both love the Pacific Northwest."

"California is fine, but this is where we want to make our home," Ruth added.

"Let me get coffee—and the pie," Helen said, walking into the kitchen behind them.

"You mean, there's pie, as well as those yummy cookies?" Paul's eyes lit up.

"Green tomato mincemeat. The tomatoes are from Charlotte Rhodes's garden. It's the best you'll ever taste."

"I love mincemeat," Ruth said, resisting the urge to poke her husband, who was making a face.

Helen smiled. "Give it a try and if you don't like it, I also have fruitcake."

"I believe I'll pass on both."

Ruth's grandmother ignored his comment and quietly dished up three small slices of pie with vanilla ice cream. Ruth helped her bring the plates into the dining room. Paul followed, carrying two cups and saucers, steaming with freshly brewed coffee. Ruth had declined, saying the pie was enough for her.

"One taste," she said, waving her fork at him.

Paul grinned. "I doubt anyone could refuse you, Ruth. Especially me."

"You keep thinking that, okay?"

Ruth watched as her husband sliced off a sliver of the pie. She laughed when she saw his expression change.

"Hey, this is *good*."

Helen looked equally pleased. "I'll tell Charlotte she made a convert out of you." She paused to sip her coffee. "What are your plans for Christmas Day?"

Paul reached for Ruth's hand once more. "First, we're making you breakfast tomorrow morning. It's the least we can do." Helen had invited them to stay the night, and they'd accepted. "Then we're driving to Seattle to spend the day with my parents."

"And we're going to visit Mom and Dad for New Year's," Ruth said.

"Our Christmas vacation worked out perfectly, since I was able to get a week's leave at the same time Ruth finished teaching for the semester."

"There's nothing like being with family over the holidays." Helen nodded.

"I couldn't agree more." Ruth turned to her husband, who sent her a smile. "Besides, we have news to share... the kind of news we wanted to tell you in person."

Helen stared at them expectantly.

"We're going to make you a great-grandma," Ruth announced, and awaited her grandmother's reaction. To her surprise, Helen said nothing.

"Grandma Shelton, did you hear?" Paul prodded.

Helen's face broke into a huge smile. "Congratulations. When are you due?"

"Not until June."

"June? What a perfect month for a birthday."

"Oh, Grandma, you'd say that about any month."

"Probably," Helen agreed. "I apologize for not responding right away. I was trying to calculate if I had enough time to knit you a special baby blanket and an extra Christmas stocking before then. I suspect I do."

"Oh, Grandma," Ruth said, struggling not to laugh.

"This is a blessed Christmas," Helen said simply, happiness radiating from her face. "There was a time I didn't believe I'd ever know joy again and yet I feel it every single day."

"Merry Christmas, Grandma."

"Merry Christmas to both of you. No—" she raised her coffee cup in a toast "—to all *three* of you."

* * * * *

A CEDAR COVE CHRISTMAS

To our dear friend
Rhett Palmer
"The Mayor of the Airwaves"

Prologue

"I can't believe Grace is willing to do this on Christmas Eve," Mary Jo said, slipping the frilly red dress over Noelle's head. The one-year-old fussed, objecting to the fact that her face was momentarily covered.

"It's Noelle's birthday," Mack reminded her.

Not that Mary Jo needed reminding...

"A year ago today you stepped off the foot ferry to Cedar Cove..."

"And met you," she finished for him.

"At the library..."

"Because Grace thought I needed medical attention."

"Which you did," Mac continued, smiling at their exchange, "because you were about to give birth."

"Only I didn't know that at the time."

"No one did."

Noelle squealed.

"Except Noelle," Mary Jo said. "Right, sweetie?" She nuzzled her daughter's face. "Happy birthday, baby girl."

"Ma Ma."

"That's right, sweetie. That's me."

"Ma Ma," Noelle repeated and gleefully clapped her hands.

"Are my two girls ready to party?" Mack asked. He had his coat on and a big collection of birthday and Christmas gifts tied up in a large bag that made Mary Jo think of something Santa would haul around. "We don't want to keep everyone waiting."

Grace had invited half of Cedar Cove—or so it seemed to Mary Jo—to her Christmas Eve bash, which was also Noelle's birthday party. All three of Mary Jo's brothers planned to attend, which was only fitting since they'd lost out on the chance to welcome their niece into the world a year ago. Mary Jo still had to grin whenever she thought about her brothers racing around the county like Keystone Kops frantically searching for their missing sister.

Grace's two daughters and their families would be at the ranch as well, along with Grace's dear friend Olivia and Olivia's husband, Jack. And Charlotte and Ben Rhodes were on the invitation list, too, as well they should be.

Then, of course, there were Mack's parents, Roy and Corrie McAfee. His oldest sister, Gloria, had sent her regrets. She was a sheriff's deputy and unfortunately she'd pulled the Christmas Eve shift. His other sister, Linnette, who lived in North Dakota, was a new mom herself and had mailed a gift Noelle had cheerfully ripped open that morning. It was a pull toy that made popping sounds with every step. Mack had laughed and promised revenge. Mary Jo could see a toy drum set in little Wade Mason's future.

Oh, yes, this was going to be quite the party and one Mary Jo had never expected. But then, she hadn't expected *any* of this. That day exactly a year ago—when she'd come from Seattle with the desperate, and misguided, idea of finding Noelle's birth father—had changed her life.

What she'd found was love, friends, a home, a whole new family. Not that there was anything wrong with her old one, but the people of Cedar Cove had expanded her family above and beyond anything she could ever have dreamed of.

"I'll get the car warmed up and then come back and help you and Noelle," Mack said.

"Okay, darling."

"Darling?" Mack's eyebrows rose ever so slightly, giving him a sexy, enticing look. "I have to say I prefer that to the nickname the guys at the firehouse have for me."

"And what's that?"

"You think I'm going to tell you? Not on your life."

"Loverboy?"

He laughed, shook his head and disappeared out the front door. Mack returned a couple of minutes later to carry Noelle to the car. "You ready?"

"Ready."

Noelle, bundled up in her winter coat with the faux-fur hem and edging around the hood, raised her tiny arms up to Mack. Her daughter had reached out to Mack a year ago, too. And Mack had responded—to both of them.

Love, family, friends—a place to belong. Her first Christmas in Cedar Cove had given her all that. And this, her second one, was a celebration of the first.

Christmas Eve. It was a night for remembering and rejoicing in *two* birthdays, wasn't it?

One

A year ago

Even though she was listening to Christmas carols on her iPod, Mary Jo Wyse could hear her brothers arguing. How could she not? Individually, the three of them had voices that were usually described as booming; together they sounded like an entire football stadium full of fans. All three worked as mechanics in the family-owned car repair business and stood well over six feet. Their size alone was intimidating. Add to that their voices, and they'd put the fear of God into the most hardened criminal.

"It's nearly Christmas," Linc was saying. He was the oldest and, if possible, loudest of the bunch.

"Mary Jo said he'd call her before now," Mel said.

Ned, her youngest brother, remained suspiciously quiet. He was the sensitive one. Translated, that meant he'd apologize after he broke David Rhodes's fingers for getting his little sister pregnant and then abandoning her.

"We've got to do *something*," Linc insisted.

The determination in his voice gave her pause. Mary Jo's situation was complicated enough without the involvement of her loving but meddlesome older brothers.

However, it wasn't *their* fault that she was about to have a baby and the father was nowhere in sight.

"I say we find David Rhodes and string him up until he agrees to marry our sister."

Mary Jo gasped. She couldn't help it. Knowing Linc, he'd have no qualms about doing exactly that.

"I think we should, too—if only we knew where he was," she heard Mel say.

Unable to sit still any longer, Mary Jo tore off her earphones and burst out of her bedroom. She marched into the living room, where her brothers stood around the Christmas tree, beers in hand, as its lights blinked cheerfully. Ever since their parents had been killed in a car accident six years earlier, her older brothers had considered themselves her guardians. Which was ridiculous, since she was over twenty-one. Twenty-three, to be precise. She hadn't been legally of age at the time of their deaths, but her brothers seemed to forget she was now an adult.

All four of them still lived in the family home. Mel and Ned were currently seeing women, but neither relationship seemed all that serious. Linc had recently broken up with someone. Mary Jo was the only one eager to leave, chafing as she did at her brothers' attempts to decree how she should live her life.

Admittedly she'd made a mess of things; she couldn't deny it. But she was trying to deal with the consequences, to act like the adult she was. Yes, she'd made a massive error in judgment, falling for an attractive older man and doing what came all too naturally. And no, she didn't need her brothers' assistance.

"Would you guys mind your own business," she demanded, hands on her hips. At five-three she stared up at her brothers, who towered above her.

She probably looked a sight, although at the moment

her appearance was the least of her problems. She was dressed in her old flannel nightgown, the one with the Christmas angels on it, her belly stretched out so far it looked like she'd swallowed a giant snow globe. Her long dark hair fell in tangles, and her feet were bare.

Linc frowned back at her. "You're our sister and that makes you our business."

"We're worried about you," Ned said, speaking for the first time. "You're gonna have that baby any day."

"I don't know nothin' about birthing no babies," Mel added in a falsetto voice.

If he was trying to add humor to the situation, Mary Jo wasn't amused. She glared at him angrily. "You don't have to worry about delivering my baby. This child is my concern and mine alone."

"No, he isn't."

From the very minute she'd tearfully announced her pregnancy four months ago, her brothers had decided the baby was a boy. For some reason, the alternative never seemed to occur to them, no matter how often she suggested it.

"You're depriving this baby of his father," Linc said stubbornly. It was a lament he'd voiced a hundred times over the past months. "A baby *needs* a father."

"I agree," Mary Jo told him. "However, I haven't seen David in weeks."

Mel stepped forward, his disapproval obvious. "What about Christmas? Didn't he tell you he'd be in touch before Christmas?"

"He did." But then David Rhodes had made a lot of promises, none of which he'd kept. "He said he'd be visiting his family in the area."

"Where?" Ned asked.

"Cedar Cove," she supplied and wondered if she should've told her three hotheaded brothers that much.

"Let's go there and find him," Linc said.

Mary Jo held up both hands. "Don't be crazy!"

"Crazy," Linc echoed with a snort of indignation. "I refuse to let you have this baby alone."

"I'm not alone," Mary Jo said. She gestured toward them. "I have the three of you, don't I?"

Her brothers went pale before her eyes. "You...you want us in the delivery room?" Mel asked in weak tones. He swallowed visibly. "You're joking, right?"

Mary Jo had delayed registering for birthing classes because David had promised to attend them with her. Only he hadn't managed to show up for the first session or the one after that or the following one, either. Giving up on him, Mary Jo had begun a session that week—a lot later in the pregnancy than she should have. She'd gone by herself and left the class in tears. Although she'd considered asking Ned if he'd be her birthing partner, she hadn't found the courage to do it yet. And she wasn't sure he'd be the best choice, anyway. Her other options were her girlfriends Casey and Chloe; however, Casey was terrified by the idea and Chloe, married last year, was expecting her own baby.

"Right." She struggled to maintain her composure. "That was a joke."

They released a collective sigh.

"You're distracting us from what's important here." Obviously, Linc wasn't going to be put off. "I want to talk to David Rhodes, just him and me, man to man." He clenched his hands at his sides.

"And when Linc's finished, I want a turn," Mel said, plowing his fist into his open palm.

Mary Jo rolled her eyes. She'd defended David to her

brothers countless times. She'd defended him to Casey and Chloe—the only other people who knew David was her baby's father. Casey worked with her at the insurance company in Seattle, so she'd met David, since he'd come to their office for meetings every few weeks, representing corporate headquarters in California. David had charmed just about everybody—with the possible exception of Casey.

He'd always had such good excuses for missing the birthing classes, and she'd believed him. It was easy to do because she so badly wanted to trust him. He claimed to love her and while the pregnancy certainly hadn't been planned, he'd seemed genuinely pleased when she'd told him. There were a few legal and financial matters that needed to be cleared up, he'd explained, but as soon as they were dealt with, he'd marry her.

For a number of months Mary Jo had convinced her brothers that David's intentions were honorable. Now, though, she had to resign herself to the fact that David wasn't willing or able to marry her. She realized she didn't know as much about him as she should. Granted, he was older by at least twenty years, but her infatuation had led her to dismiss the significance of that. Now Mary Jo had to doubt his sincerity. She hadn't heard from him in more than two weeks and he wasn't answering his cell phone, and even during their last conversation, he'd been preoccupied and abrupt. He'd mentioned that he'd be in Cedar Cove for Christmas with his father and stepmother and would call her then.

"Do you *want* to marry David?" Ned asked. He was the only brother to take her feelings into consideration.

"Of course she wants to marry him," Linc answered, scowling at him. "She's about to have his baby, isn't she?"

"I believe I can answer for myself." Mary Jo calmly turned toward her oldest brother. "Actually—"

"You're getting married," Linc broke in.

"I won't have you holding a gun on David!"

Linc shook his head, expression puzzled. "I don't own a gun."

She sighed; her brothers could be so literal sometimes. "I was speaking figuratively," she said loftily.

"Oh." Linc frowned. "Well, I'm not talking figures, I'm talking facts." He raised one finger. "You're having a baby." He raised a second. "The father of that baby needs to accept his responsibilities."

"He will," Mary Jo murmured, although any hope that David would take care of her and the baby had long since been dashed.

"Yes, he will," Mel said firmly, "because we're going to make sure he does."

"And that includes putting a wedding band on your finger," Linc informed her, giving her a look that said he wouldn't tolerate any argument.

The baby kicked as though in protest and Mary Jo echoed the child's feelings. She no longer knew what she wanted. In the beginning she'd been head-over-heels in love with David. He was the most exciting man she'd ever met, and without even trying, he'd swept her off her feet. Mary Jo had been thrilled when he paid attention to her, a lowly accounting clerk. Compared to the boyfriends she'd had—as naive and inexperienced as she'd been herself—David was a romantic hero. An older man, confident, witty, indulgent.

"Mary Josephine," Mel said loudly. "Are you listening?"

Blinking to clear her thoughts, Mary Jo focused on her middle brother. "I guess not, sorry."

"Sorry?" Mel stormed. "We're talking about your future here and the future of your son."

Despite the seriousness of the situation, Mary Jo yawned. She couldn't help it. She covered her mouth with one hand and placed the other on her protruding belly. "I'm going to bed," she declared.

"Mary Jo!" Linc shouted after her as if she were a marine recruit and he was her drill instructor. "We need to decide what to do *here* and *now*."

"Can't we talk about it in the morning?" She was too exhausted to continue this argument with her brothers at—she glanced toward the antique clock—almost midnight.

"No."

"Linc, be reasonable."

"We have to get this settled." Mel joined forces with his older brother.

Again Ned didn't speak. He cast her a look of quiet sympathy but he wasn't taking sides. Mary Jo could see that he felt Linc and Mel were right—not about becoming Mrs. Rhodes but about the need to make some kind of decision.

"Okay, okay, but we've already said everything there is to say." She sagged onto the sofa and tried to keep her eyes open.

Linc glanced at the clock, too. "As of about one minute ago, it's officially Christmas Eve. Rhodes promised to be in touch *before* Christmas."

Exhaling a deep sigh, Mary Jo shrugged. "He might've said *on* Christmas. I've forgotten."

"Well, I haven't." Mel's feet were braced wide apart, his arms folded across his chest.

"I haven't forgotten, either." Linc, too, crossed his arms. They looked like bouncers at a tough bar, but Mary

Jo feared the person they'd toss out on his ear would be David Rhodes.

And he'd deserve it; she knew that. He'd deceived her not once, not twice, but a dozen times or more. Still, some of the responsibility was hers. Even though she was aware that he'd abused her trust, she'd foolishly believed him, giving him chance after chance. Now her brothers were trying to save her from him—and from herself.

"David said he'd contact you *before* Christmas," Linc reminded her. "That gives him less than twenty-four hours."

"Yes, it does." Her agreeing with him was sure to confuse her well-meaning brothers.

Apparently shocked by her unaccustomed meekness, Linc narrowed his eyes, then checked the clock again. "Yup, less than twenty-four hours. It's time you realized he has no intention of doing the proper thing."

Mary Jo couldn't argue with that. She was just tired of discussing it. "You never know," she said, forcing a note of optimism into her voice.

"Then you're living in a dream world, little sister," Mel said through gritted teeth.

Ned sat down next to Mary Jo and reached for her hand. "Linc and Mel are right," he told her gently.

"About what?" She was so exhausted, her vision had started to blur.

"Someone needs to get in touch with David. If we can't find him, then one of his family members. He has to be held accountable."

Linc snorted again. "David Rhodes has to make an honest woman of you."

If Mary Jo heard that one more time she was going to scream. "I *am* an honest woman! I don't need David or any man to validate what each of you should already know."

"Yeah, yeah," Linc muttered. "Don't get your knickers in a knot. It's only an expression."

"What we all want," Mel began, as if to clarify their thoughts, "is for you to be happy—*with* the father of your baby."

Mary Jo doubted that was even possible. She'd lost faith in David and as much as she wanted to believe he loved her and cared about their child, the evidence stated otherwise.

"He's not giving us any choice," Linc said, his dark eyes menacing. "We're going to find him and—"

"Linc, please. Hold off for a few days. Please." She hated to plead but it was Christmas and she didn't want to see the holiday ruined for any of them. She was protecting David—again—and the irony didn't escape her. Despite all these months of intermittent contact and broken promises, Mary Jo still felt the urge to shield him from her brothers.

But her real concern was for Linc, Mel and Ned. She didn't want *them* ending up in jail because of David.

"We're not waiting another minute!" Mel boomed. "If David's in Cedar Cove, we're going to track him down."

"No. Please," she said shakily.

"You don't have a say in this anymore."

"Linc, it's my life! Listen to me. I—"

"We've listened to you enough," her oldest brother said matter-of-factly. "Now the three of us have decided to take matters into our own hands."

Mary Jo couldn't let her brothers get involved. She shuddered as she imagined them charging into Cedar

Cove on Christmas Eve, bent on forcing David to marry her.

No, she couldn't allow that to happen. Resolute, she stood up and started for her bedroom. "We'll finish discussing this in the morning," she said in as dignified a voice as she could manage.

Linc seemed about to argue, but her fatigue must have shown because he hesitated, then nodded reluctantly. "There'll be no avoiding it, understand?"

"Perfectly."

"Night, sweetie." He threw his arms around her in a quick hug, as did Mel and then Ned.

Mary Jo slept soundly for six hours and woke in a cold sweat. She knew she'd never be able to stop her interfering brothers from invading Cedar Cove, embarrassing her and possibly doing bodily harm to David. The only solution she could think of was to get there first and warn David and/or his family.

With that in mind, Mary Jo left her brothers a note and slipped quietly out of the house.

Two

Cedar Cove was a festive little town, Mary Jo thought when she stepped off the ferry. It was a place that took Christmas seriously. Even the terminal was decorated, with bells hanging from the ceiling and large snowflakes in the windows. She'd never been here before and was pleasantly surprised by its charm. After taking the Washington State ferry from downtown Seattle to Bremerton, she'd caught the foot ferry across Sinclair Inlet to the small town David had mentioned.

He'd only talked about it that one time. She'd had the impression he didn't like it much, but she hadn't understood why.

She looked around.

A lighthouse stood off in the distance, picturesque against the backdrop of fir trees and the green waters of the cove. Waves rhythmically splashed the large rocks that marked the beach. Adjusting her purse strap on her shoulder and getting a tighter grip on her bag, Mary Jo walked down the pier into town.

Large evergreen boughs stretched across the main street of Cedar Cove—Harbor Street, according to the sign—and from the center of each hung a huge ornament.

There were alternating wreaths, angels and candles. The lightposts were festooned with holly. The effect of all these decorations was delightful and it raised her spirits—until she remembered why she was in Cedar Cove.

It was ten in the morning on Christmas Eve, and everyone seemed to have places to go. So did Mary Jo, except that she was in no hurry to get there, and who could blame her? This was likely to be a painful confrontation.

Not sure where to start searching for David's family and desperate to collect her thoughts, Mary Jo stopped at a coffee house called Mocha Mama's about a block from the waterfront. This, too, was decorated and redolent of Christmas scents—fir, cinnamon, peppermint. And the rich, strong aroma of fresh coffee. The place was nearly empty. The only other person there was a young man who stood behind the counter; he was writing or drawing something in a sketchbook and appeared to be immersed in his task, whatever it was.

"Merry Christmas," Mary Jo said cheerfully, wondering if her words sounded as forced as they felt. She pulled off her wool hat and gloves, cramming them in her pockets.

Her presence startled the young man, who wore a name tag that identified him as Shaw. He glanced up, blinked in apparent confusion, then suddenly smiled. "Sorry. Didn't see you come in. What can I get you?"

"I'd like one of your decaf candy cane mochas, Shaw."

"What size?"

"Oh, grande—is that what you call it here? Medium. One of those." She pointed at a stack of cups.

His eyes went to her stomach, which protruded from the opening of her wool coat. She could no longer fasten more than the top three buttons.

"You're gonna have a baby," Shaw said, as if this information should be a surprise to her.

"Yes, I am." She rested a protective hand on her belly.

Shaw began to prepare her mocha, chatting as he did. "It's been pretty quiet this morning. Maybe 'cause it's Christmas Eve," he commented.

Mary Jo nodded, then took a chair by the window and watched people walk briskly past. The town seemed to be busy and prosperous, with people popping in and out of stores along the street. The bakery had quite a few customers and so did a nearby framing shop.

"I haven't seen you around here before," Shaw said. He added whipped topping and a candy cane to her cup and handed it to her.

"I'm visiting," Mary Jo explained as she got up to pay for her drink. Shaw seemed to be full of information; he might be just the person to ask about David. She poked a folded dollar bill into the tip jar. "Would you know any people named Rhodes in this area?" she asked speculatively, holding her drink with both hands.

"Rhodes, Rhodes," Shaw repeated carefully. He mulled it over for a moment, then shook his head. "The name's familiar but I can't put a face to it."

"Oh." She couldn't quite hide her disappointment. Carrying her mocha, she returned to the table by the window and gazed out at the street again. Her biggest fear was that her three brothers would come rolling into town in their huge pickup, looking like vigilantes out of some old western. Or worse, a bunch of hillbillies. Mary Jo decided she *had* to get to David and his family first.

"Just a minute," Shaw said. "There *is* a Rhodes family in Cedar Cove." He reached behind the counter and pulled out a telephone directory.

Mary Jo wanted to slap her forehead. Of course! How stupid. She should've checked the phone book immediately. That was certainly what her brothers would do.

"Here," Shaw said, flipping the directory around so she could read the listings. As it happened, there was a B. Rhodes, a Kevin Rhodes and three others—and Mary Jo had no way of knowing which of these people were related to David. The only thing to do was to call every one of them and find out.

"Would you mind if I borrowed this for a few minutes?" she asked.

"Sure, go ahead. Tell me if there's anything I can do to help."

"Thanks."

"Consider it a random act of kindness."

"Not so random." Mary Jo smiled as she brought the phone book back to her table. She rummaged for her cell phone; she hadn't remembered to charge it before she left and was relieved to see that she had nearly a full battery. She dialed the number for B. Rhodes and waited through several rings before a greeting came on, telling her that Ben and Charlotte weren't available and inviting her to leave a message. She didn't. She actually spoke to the next Rhodes, who sounded young and didn't know anyone named David. Of the last three, the first had a disconnected phone line and the other two didn't answer.

Mary Jo had assumed it would be easy to find David in a town as small as Cedar Cove. Walking down Harbor Street, she'd seen a sign for Roy McAfee, a private investigator. She hadn't expected to need one, and even if she could afford to pay someone else to search for David Rhodes, it wasn't likely that Mr. McAfee would accept a case this close to Christmas.

"Any luck?" Shaw asked.

"None." Without knowing the name of David's father, she couldn't figure out what her next step should be. There were three, possibly four, potential candidates, since she'd managed to rule out just one. Her only consolation was the fact that if *she* was having trouble, so would her brothers.

"I can think of one person who might be able to help you," Shaw said thoughtfully.

"Who?"

"Grace Harding. She's the head librarian and she knows practically everyone in town. I'm not sure if she's working this morning but it wouldn't do any harm to go there and see."

"The library is where?" Being on foot and pregnant definitely imposed some limitations, especially now that it had started to snow.

"How'd you get here?" Shaw asked.

"Foot ferry."

He grinned. "Then you walked right past it when you got off. It's the building with the large mural on the front. You won't have any trouble finding it."

Mary Jo had noticed two such murals. She supposed it wouldn't be difficult to distinguish which one was the library. Eager to talk to Grace Harding, she left the remainder of her drink behind. She put the wool hat back on her head and pulled on her gloves. It was cold and the few snowflakes that had begun to drift down seemed persistent, like a harbinger of more to come. The Seattle area rarely experienced a white Christmas, and under other circumstances Mary Jo would've been thrilled at the prospect of snow.

As Shaw had predicted, she didn't have a problem locating the library. The mural of a frontier family was striking, and the library doors were decorated with

Christmas wreaths. When she stepped inside, she saw dozens of cut-out snowflakes suspended from the ceiling in the children's area, as well as a display of seasonal picture books, some of which—like *A Snowy Day*—she remembered from her own childhood. A large Christmas tree with book-size wrapped gifts underneath stood just inside the small lobby. One look told Mary Jo that this was a much-used and much-loved place.

She welcomed the warmth, both emotional and physical. There was a woman at the counter, which held a sign stating that the library would close at noon. Glancing at the clock on the wall, Mary Jo was surprised to see that it was already ten-forty-five.

She approached the front counter. "Excuse me. Are you Grace Harding?" she asked in a pleasant voice.

"Afraid not. Should I get her for you?"

"Yes, please."

The woman disappeared into a nearby office. A few minutes later, she reappeared with another middle-aged woman, who greeted Mary Jo with a friendly smile. She wore a bright red turtleneck sweater under a festive holly-green jumper. Her right arm seemed to be thickly bandaged beneath her long sleeve.

"I'm Grace Harding," she announced. "How can I help you?"

Mary Jo gave the woman a strained smile. "Hello, my name is Mary Jo Wyse and—" The baby kicked—hard—and Mary Jo's eyes widened with shock. She placed her hands against her stomach and slowly exhaled.

"Are you okay?" Grace asked, looking concerned.

"I…think so."

"Perhaps you should sit down."

Numbly Mary Jo nodded. This was all so…unseemly. She hated making a fuss, but she suspected the librarian was right and she did need to sit. Thankfully, Ms. Harding came around the counter and led her to a chair. She left for a moment and returned with a glass of water.

"Here, drink this."

"Thank you." Mary Jo felt embarrassed, since almost everyone in the library was staring at her. No doubt she made quite a spectacle and people probably thought she'd give birth any second. Actually, her due date wasn't for another two weeks; she didn't think there was any danger the baby would arrive early, but this was her first pregnancy and she couldn't really tell. She could only hope....

Grace took the chair beside hers. "How can I help you?" she asked again.

Mary Jo gulped down all the water, then put the glass down beside her.

Taking a deep breath, she clasped her hands together. "I'm looking for a man by the name of David Rhodes."

Right away Mary Jo saw that the other woman stiffened.

"You know him?" she asked excitedly, ignoring any misgivings over Grace's reaction. "Is he here? He said he'd be visiting his father and stepmother in Cedar Cove. It's important that I talk to him as soon as possible."

Grace sagged in her chair. "Oh, dear."

"Oh, dear," Mary Jo repeated. "What does that mean?"

"Well..."

"Is David in town?"

Grace shook her head, but her expression was sympathetic. "I'm afraid not."

Mary Jo's heart sank. She should've known not to trust David. This was obviously another lie.

"What about his father and stepmother? Are they available?" If she didn't tell David's family about the baby, then her brothers surely would. The information would be better coming from her. The image of her brothers barging into these people's home lent a sense of urgency to her question.

"Unfortunately," Grace went on, "Ben and Charlotte have taken a Christmas cruise."

"They're gone, then," Mary Jo said in a flat voice. She recalled the message on their phone; ironically, Ben had been the first Rhodes she'd called. Maybe she should be relieved they were out of town, but she wasn't. Instead, a deep sadness settled over her. The uncertainty would continue. Whatever happened, she accepted the likelihood of being a single mother, but her brothers would do their best to prevent it.

"According to a friend of mine, they're coming back sometime tomorrow," Grace told her.

"On Christmas Day?"

"Yes, that's what I understand, at any rate. I can find out for sure if you'd like."

"Yes, please."

Grace looked tentative. "Before I phone Olivia—she's the friend I mentioned—I should tell you that her mother is married to Ben Rhodes."

"I see."

"Would you mind if I asked you a question?"

"Of course not." Although she already knew what that question would be…

"Is your baby…is David Rhodes—"

Rather than respond, Mary Jo closed her eyes and hung her head.

Grace touched her arm gently. "Don't be upset, dear," she murmured. "None of that matters now."

The answer to Grace's question was obvious. Why

else would someone in an advanced state of pregnancy come looking for David and his family—especially on Christmas Eve?

As she opened her eyes, Grace squeezed her hand reassuringly.

"I haven't seen or heard from David in weeks," Mary Jo admitted. "He occasionally calls and the last time he did, he said he was coming here to spend Christmas with his family. My brothers want to make him marry me, but… but that isn't what *I* want."

"Of course you don't."

At least Grace shared her point of view. "I've got to talk to Mr. and Mrs. Rhodes as soon as I can and explain that even if David offered to marry me, I don't think it's the right thing for me or my baby."

"I don't either," Grace said. "David isn't to be trusted."

Mary Jo grinned weakly. "I'm afraid I have to agree with you. But this is their grandchild. Or…or Ben's, anyway. Maybe they'll be interested in knowing the baby. Maybe David'll want some kind of relationship." She turned to Grace and said earnestly, "Shouldn't I give them that choice?"

"Yes, that's exactly what you should do." Grace squeezed her hand again. "I'll go call Olivia and get right back to you. She'll know Charlotte and Ben's travel schedule. However, it does seem to me that they're due home on the twenty-fifth."

"Thank you," Mary Jo murmured. She was feeling light-headed and a bit queasy, so she intended to stay where she was until Grace came back. It didn't take long.

Grace sat down next to her again. "I spoke with Olivia

and she confirmed that Charlotte and Ben will indeed be home tomorrow afternoon."

"Oh…good." Still, Mary Jo wasn't sure what she should do next. If she went home, her brothers would be impossible. They'd be furious that she'd left with no warning other than a brief note. In any case, they were probably on their way to Cedar Cove now. And with some effort, they'd uncover the same information Mary Jo had.

"What would you like to do?" Grace asked.

"I think I'd better spend the night here," Mary Jo said. She hadn't packed a bag, but her requirements were simple. All she needed was a decent hotel. "Can you recommend a place to stay?"

"Oh, yes, there are several, including a lovely B-and-B. I'm just wondering if there'll be a problem getting a room for tonight."

"A problem?" This wasn't something Mary Jo had considered.

"Let's see if there's anything at the Comfort Inn. It's close by and clean."

"That would be great. Thank you so much," Mary Jo said.

Here it was, Christmas Eve, and she felt as if she'd found an angel to help her. An angel fittingly named Grace…

Three

Grace Harding studied the young pregnant woman beside her. So David Rhodes was the father of her baby. Not a surprise, she supposed, but it made her think even less of him. Certainly Olivia had told her plenty—about his deceit, his loans that were more like theft, since he never seemed to have any intention of repaying his father, the rumors of women he'd cheated on.… That Ben Rhodes, who was one of the most decent and honorable men she'd ever met, could have a son like David defied explanation. Not only had David fathered this child, which she didn't doubt for a minute, he'd also lied to Mary Jo.

Well, Grace decided, she'd do what she could to give the poor girl a hand. And she knew Charlotte and Ben would, too.

"I'll get that list of places for you," Grace told Mary Jo, rising to her feet. The library had a sheet with phone numbers of the local bed-and-breakfasts, plus all the motels in the area. The best place in town was Thyme and Tide Bed & Breakfast, run by Bob and Peggy Beldon. However, she recalled, the couple was away for the holidays. So staying there wasn't an option. But there were several chain hotels out by the freeway.

"I'll need to be within walking distance of the Rhodes home," Mary Jo said as Grace handed her the list. "I didn't drive over."

"Don't worry. If there's a vacancy a few miles out of town I'll take you there myself and I can drop you off at Charlotte's tomorrow evening."

Mary Jo glanced up at her, brown eyes wide with astonishment. "You'd do that?"

"Of course. It wouldn't be any problem. I'm going that way myself."

"Thank you."

Grace shrugged lightly. "I'm happy to do it," she said. The offer was a small thing and yet Mary Jo seemed so grateful. "If you'll excuse me, I need to make another phone call."

"Of course." Mary Jo had taken out her cell phone, clearly ready to start her search for a room. Normally, cell phone use in the library was discouraged but in this case Grace couldn't object.

Grace returned to her office. She'd promised to call Olivia back as soon as she could. Although they spoke almost every day, their conversations over the past week had been brief. With so much to do before Christmas, there hadn't been time to chat.

Sitting at her desk, Grace picked up the receiver and punched in Olivia's number. Her dearest friend was at home today, but unfortunately not because it was Christmas Eve. Judge Olivia Griffin had been diagnosed with breast cancer and had undergone surgery; she'd begin chemotherapy and radiation treatments early in the new year. She'd taken a leave of absence from the bench. The last month had been frightening, especially when Olivia developed a life-threatening infection. Grace got chills just thinking about how close they'd all come to losing her.

Olivia answered on the first ring. "It took you forever to call back," she said. "Is the girl still at the library?"

"Yes. She's staying the night and then meeting with Ben and Charlotte tomorrow afternoon."

"Oh, no…"

"Should I tell her it might be better to wait?" Grace asked. Like Olivia, she hated the thought of hitting Ben with this news the minute he and Charlotte got home.

"I don't know," Olivia said. "I mean, they're going to be tired…" Her voice faded away.

"The thing is," Grace went on to say, "I really don't think it *should* wait. Mary Jo's obviously due very soon." She hesitated, unsure how much to tell Olivia. She didn't want to burden her friend. Because of her illness, Olivia was uncharacteristically fragile these days.

"I heard that hesitation in your voice, Grace Harding," Olivia scolded. "There's more to this and you're wondering if you should tell me."

There were times Grace swore Olivia could read her mind. She took a breath. "It seems David told Mary Jo he'd be spending the holidays with Ben and Charlotte."

"I knew it! That's a lie. This cruise has been planned for months and David was well aware of it. Why would he do something like this?"

Grace didn't have an answer—although she had her own opinion on David and his motives.

"He probably used the lie as another tactic to put the poor girl off," Olivia said. "The way David manipulates people and then discards them like so much garbage infuriates me." Outrage echoed in every word.

"It appears that's exactly what he did," Grace murmured. She remembered how David had tried to swindle

Charlotte out of several thousand dollars a few years ago. The man was without conscience.

"This poor girl! All alone at Christmas. It's appalling. If I could, I'd wring David's neck myself."

"I have the feeling we'd need to stand in line for that," Grace said wryly.

"No kidding," Olivia agreed. "Okay, now that I know what this Mary Jo business is all about, tell me what happened to your arm."

Instinctively Grace's hand moved to her upper right arm. "You're gonna laugh," she said, smiling herself, though at the time it'd been no laughing matter.

"Grace, from what I heard, you were in a lot of pain."

"And who told you that?"

"Justine. She ran into Cliff at the pharmacy when he was picking up your prescription."

"Oh, right." Small towns were like this. Everything was news and nothing was private. That could be beneficial—and it could be embarrassing. Olivia's daughter, Justine, knew, so Olivia's husband—the local newspaper editor—did, too. It wouldn't surprise her if Jack wrote a humorous piece on her misadventure.

"So, what happened?" Olivia repeated.

Grace saw no reason to hide the truth. "I got bitten by the camel."

"*What?* The *camel?* What camel?"

Grace had to smile again. Olivia's reaction was the same as that of Dr. Timmons. According to the young physician, this was the first time he'd ever treated anyone for a camel bite.

"Cliff and I are housing the animals for the live Nativity scene," she said. "Remember?" The local Methodist church had brought in animals for the display. Grace wasn't sure where the camel had come from but as far as she was concerned it could go back there anytime. And it would. Yesterday had been the final day of the animals' appearances; they'd be returning to their individual homes just after Christmas. True, she'd miss the donkey, since she'd grown fond of him. But the camel? Goodbye, Sleeping Beauty! Grace almost snorted at the animal's unlikely name.

"Of course," Olivia said, "the live Nativity scene. I didn't get a chance to see it. So *that's* how you encountered the camel."

"Yes, I went out to feed the dastardly beast. Cliff warned me that camels can be cantankerous and I *thought* I was being careful."

"Apparently not careful enough." Olivia sputtered with laughter.

"Hey, it isn't that funny," Grace said, slightly miffed that her friend hadn't offered her the requisite amount of sympathy. "I'll have you know it *hurt.*"

"Did he break the skin?"

"He's a she, and yes, she did." Grace's arm ached at the memory. "Sleeping Beauty—" she said the name sarcastically "—bit me through two layers of clothing."

"Did you need stitches?" The amusement had left Olivia's voice.

"No, but Dr. Timmons gave me a prescription for antibiotics and then bandaged my arm. From the bandage, you'd think it had nearly been amputated. This morning I had trouble finding a sweater that would go over the dressing."

"Poor Grace."

"That's more like it," she said in a satisfied tone.

"Let Cliff feed the camel from now on."

"You bet I will."

"Good."

"That's not all." Grace figured she might as well go for broke on the sympathy factor.

"What—the donkey bit you, too?"

"No, but the sheep stepped on my foot."

"Poor Grace."

"Thank you."

"A sheep can't weigh *that* much."

"This one did. I've got an unsightly bruise on the top of my foot." She thrust out her leg and gazed down on it. Her panty hose didn't hide the spectacularly colored bruise at all.

"Oh, poor, poor Gracie."

"You don't sound like you mean that."

"Oh, I do, I do."

"Hmph. We haven't had much of a chance to talk in the last few days, so tell me what you're doing for Christmas," Grace said.

"We're keeping it pretty low-key," Olivia told her. "Justine, Seth and Leif are coming over tonight for dinner and gifts, then we're going to church at eight. What about you and Cliff?"

"Same. Maryellen, Kelly and all the grandkids are coming for dinner and then we're heading to the Christmas Eve service. Cliff's daughter, Lisa, and her family are here as well. Tomorrow we're all going over to Maryellen and Jon's for dinner."

"Jack and I are having Christmas dinner alone. He's let on to everyone that he's cooking but between you and me, D.D.'s on the Cove is catering." Olivia laughed, clearly amused by her husband's resourcefulness. "Justine invited us," she added, "but we declined. Next year," Olivia said, and it sounded like a promise.

Everything would be back to normal by this time next

year. Olivia would be finished with her treatments this spring. Seeing what her friend had already endured, and her quiet bravery in the face of what was still to come, had given Grace a deeper understanding of Olivia. Her strength and courage impressed Grace and humbled her. Like all women their age, they'd suffered—and survived—their share of tragedy and grief. And now Olivia was coping with cancer.

Grace stood and looked out the small window that offered a view of the interior of the library. Mary Jo sat with her shoulders hunched forward, cell phone dangling from one hand.

"I have to go."

"Problems?"

"I should get back to Mary Jo."

"You'll keep me updated, won't you?" Olivia said.

"As much as I can."

"Okay, thanks. And listen, Grace, stay away from that camel!" She laughed, and then the line was disconnected.

The next time they met at the Pancake Palace, Grace intended to make Olivia pay for her coconut cream pie.

Grace called her husband quickly, then stepped out of her office and slipped into the chair next to Mary Jo. "How's it going?" she asked.

"Not so well, I'm afraid. I tried to call David. I have his cell phone number and I thought he'd answer. It's Christmas Eve and he *has* to know I'm waiting to hear from him."

Grace took Mary Jo's hand in hers. "He didn't answer?"

"Oh, it's more than that. He...he had his number changed. Last week—" she struggled to speak "—I tried to reach him at his office in California and learned that he's quit his job. We both work—worked—for the same insurance company, which is how we met."

"Oh, dear."

"I don't dare let my brothers know."

Mary Jo had mentioned them earlier.

"How many brothers?"

"Three, all of them older." She sighed. "I'd hoped David would be here with his parents, but I knew the odds that he'd told me the truth weren't good."

Grace nodded, encouraging her to continue.

"I think I told you my brothers want to make David marry me—or at least pay for all the lies he's told. They decided they were going to come and confront him, and if not David, then his family."

Grace could only imagine how distressing it would be for Ben and Charlotte to return from the vacation of a lifetime to find Mary Jo's three angry brothers waiting for them. On Christmas Day, yet.

"That's why it's important for me to talk to Ben and Charlotte first," Mary Jo concluded.

"I think you should," Grace said.

"Except…"

"Yes?" she prompted.

"Except it looks like I'll have to go back to Seattle this afternoon."

"Why?"

"I called all the places on the sheet you gave me and there aren't any vacancies."

"Nowhere? Not in the entire town? What about the Comfort Inn?"

She shook her head. "Nothing."

"You mean everything's already reserved?"

"Yes. There's no room at the Inn."

Four

"Linc," Mel shouted from the kitchen. Three Wyse Men Automotive had closed early due to the holiday.

"In a minute," Linc shouted back. "Where's Mary Jo?" He'd searched half the house and hadn't found her. He knew she'd taken the day off. Had she gone to the store, perhaps? Or to visit her friend Chloe?

"If you come to the kitchen you'll find out!"

Linc followed his brother's voice and with Ned at his heels, entered the kitchen. As soon as Mel saw him, his brother thrust a sheet of paper into his hands. "Here. This was behind the coffeemaker. Must've fallen off."

Before he'd read two words, Linc's face started to heat up. His stubborn, strong-willed, hardheaded, obstinate little sister had gone to Cedar Cove. Without her family, because she felt she knew best. Tossing the note to the ground, Linc clenched both his fists. "Of all the stupid, idiotic things to do."

"What?" Ned asked.

"Mary Jo's decided to go to Cedar Cove on her own," Mel said.

"By herself?"

"Isn't that what I said?" Mel snapped.

"It's true," Linc informed his youngest brother. "I can't believe she'd do anything this crazy."

"We drove her to it." Ned sank into a kitchen chair and splayed his fingers through his thick dark hair.

"What do you mean?" Mel challenged.

"Explain yourself," Linc ordered.

"Don't you see?" Ned gazed up at them. "All that talk about confronting David and forcing him to do the *honorable* thing. The man hasn't got an honorable bone in his body. What were we thinking?"

"What we were thinking," Linc said irritably, "is that David Rhodes is going to pay for what he did to our little sister." He looked his brothers in the eye and made sure they understood.

When their parents were killed, Mary Jo had only been seventeen. Linc, as the oldest, had been made her legal guardian, since there was no other family in the area. At the time, the responsibility had weighed heavily on his shoulders. He'd gone to his two brothers and asked for their help in raising their sister. Or at least finishing the job their parents had begun.

Both brothers had been equally committed to taking care of Mary Jo. Everything had gone smoothly, too. Mary Jo had graduated from high school the following May, and all three brothers had attended the ceremony. They'd even thrown her a party.

That autumn he'd gone with Mary Jo to the community college and signed her up for classes. She hadn't taken kindly to his accompanying her, but Linc wasn't about to let her walk around campus on her own. Not at first, anyway. Cute little girl like her? With all those lecherous college guys who couldn't keep their hands to themselves? Oh, yeah, he knew what eighteen-year-old boys were like. And he'd insisted she choose solid, practical courses, not that fluffy fun stuff they taught now.

All the brothers were proud of how well Mary Jo had done in her studies. They'd all disapproved when she'd dropped out of school and gone to work at that insurance company. More than once Linc had to bite his tongue. He'd told her no good would come of this job.

The problem with Mary Jo was that she was too eager to move out. She no longer wanted to live in the family home. For the past year, she'd talked incessantly about getting her own place.

Linc didn't understand that either. This was their *home*. Linc saw to it that Mary Jo wasn't stuck with all the cleaning, cooking and laundry. They all did their part of the upkeep—maybe not quite to her standards but well enough. That wasn't the reason she was so determined to live somewhere else.

No, Mary Jo had an intense desire for independence. From them.

Okay, maybe they'd gone overboard when it came to dating. Frankly, Linc didn't think there was a man this side of Mars who was good enough for his little sister. Mary Jo was special.

Then she'd met David Rhodes. Linc had never found out precisely when that had happened. Not once in the six months she'd been dating him had she mentioned this guy. What Linc had noticed was how happy Mary Jo seemed all of a sudden—and then, just as suddenly, she'd been depressed. That was when her mood swings started. She'd be happy and then sad and then happy again. It made no sense until he learned there was a man involved.

Even now that Mary Jo was pregnant with this man's baby, Linc still hadn't met him. In retrospect, that was

probably for the best because Linc would take real pleasure in ripping his face off.

"What are we going to do?" Mel asked.

His younger brothers were clearly worried.

Linc's hand was already in his pants pocket, fingering
his truck keys. "What can we do other than follow her to
Cedar Cove?"

"Let's talk this through," Ned suggested, coming to
his feet.

"What's there to talk about?" Mel asked. "Mary Jo's
going to have a baby. She's alone and pregnant and we
all know Rhodes isn't in Cedar Cove. He's lied to her
from the beginning. There's no way he's telling the truth
now."

"Yes, but…"

Linc looked squarely into his youngest brother's eyes.
"What do you think Mom and Dad would have us do?"
he asked, allowing time between each word to make sure
the message sank in.

Ned sighed. "They'd want us to find her."

"Exactly my point." Linc headed for the back door.

"Wait a minute." Ned raised his hand.

"Now what?" Mel said impatiently.

"Mary Jo left because she's mad."

"Well, let her be mad. By the time we arrive, she'll
be singing a different tune. My guess is she'll be mighty
glad to see us."

"Maybe," Ned agreed. "But say she isn't. Then what?"

Linc frowned. "We'll bring her home anyway."

"She might not want to come."

"She'll come." Linc wasn't about to leave his little sister with strangers over Christmas.

"If we make demands, she'll only be more determined
to stay," Ned told them.

"Do you have any other bright ideas?" Mel asked.

Ned ignored the sarcasm. "Bring her gifts," he said.

"Why?" Linc didn't understand. They all had gifts for her and the baby that she could open Christmas morning, the way she was supposed to.

"She needs to know we love her and welcome the baby."

"Of course we welcome the baby," Linc said. "He's our flesh and blood, our *nephew*."

"Hang on a minute." Mel looked pensive. "Ned has a point."

It wasn't often that Mel agreed with Ned. "What do you mean?"

"Mary Jo's pregnant, right?"

That question didn't require a response.

"And everyone knows how unreasonable women can get when they're in, uh, a delicate condition."

Linc scratched his head. "Mary Jo was like that long before she got pregnant."

"True, but she's been even more unreasonable lately, don't you think?"

Mel wasn't wrong there.

"Maybe we should bring her a gift just so she'll know how concerned we are about her and the baby. How much we care. We want her with us for Christmas, don't we?"

"What woman doesn't like gifts?" Linc said, thinking out loud.

"Yup," Ned said, smiling at Mel. "It couldn't hurt."

Linc conceded. "Okay, then, we'll each bring her a gift."

They returned to their individual bedrooms, planning to meet in the kitchen five minutes later. Linc had gone online a few weeks ago and ordered a miniature football, basketball and soccer ball for his yet-to-be-born nephew. He couldn't speak for the others, but he suspected they too had chosen gifts that were geared toward sports. At first he figured he'd bring the football, but then he reconsidered. He'd been after Mary Jo to save money and in an effort to encourage her, he'd purchased a gold coin that he planned to present on her birthday in February. Perfect. He pocketed the coin and hurried to the kitchen.

"You ready?" he asked.

"Ready," Mel echoed.

"Me, too," Ned confirmed.

The three brothers hurried out to the four-door pickup Linc drove. Mel automatically climbed into the front passenger seat and Ned sat directly behind him.

"You got your gift?" Linc asked Mel.

"Yeah. I'm bringing her perfume."

"Good idea," Linc said approvingly. "Where'd you get it?"

"I actually bought it for Annie, but I'll get her something else...."

"Ned?" Linc asked.

"Incense," his youngest brother mumbled.

"You brought her *what?*"

"Incense. She likes that stuff. It was gonna be part of her Christmas gift anyway."

"Okay..." Linc shook his head rather than ask any further questions. Whatever his brothers chose to bring Mary Jo was up to them.

He turned his key in the ignition, then rested his arm over the back of the seat and angled his head so he could see behind him as he reversed out of the driveway. He'd reached the stop sign at the end of the block before it occurred to him to ask.

"Which way?"

"North," Mel said.

"Cedar Cove is south," Ned contradicted.

"For crying out loud." Linc pulled over to the curb. Leaning across his brother, he opened the glove box and shuffled through a pile of junk until he found the Washington State map he was looking for. Dropping it on Mel's lap, he said, "Find me Cedar Cove."

Mel immediately tossed it into the backseat. "Here, Ned. You seem to think you know where it is."

"It was just a guess," Ned protested. Nevertheless he started to unfold the map.

"Well, we don't have time for guessing. Look it up." Linc put the truck back in gear and drove toward the freeway on-ramp. He assumed Ned would find Cedar Cove before he had to decide which lane to get into—north or south.

He was nearly at the ramp before Ned cried out triumphantly. "Found it!"

"Great. Which way should I go?"

Linc watched his brother through the rearview mirror as he turned the map around.

No answer.

"Which way?" Linc asked impatiently.

"South."

"You don't sound too sure."

"South," Ned said again, this time with more conviction.

Linc entered the lane that would take him in that direction. "How far is it?" he asked.

Ned stared down at the map again. "A ways."

"That doesn't tell me a darn thing. An hour or what?"

"All right, all right, give me a minute." Ned balanced the map on his knees and studied it intently. After carefully walking his fingers along the edge of the map, Ned had the answer. "I'd say…ninety minutes."

"Ninety minutes." Linc hadn't realized it was that far.

"Maybe longer."

Linc groaned silently. Traffic was heavy, which was to be expected at noon on Christmas Eve. At the rate they were crawling, it would be hours before they got there, which made their mission that much more urgent.

"Should we confront the Rhodes family first thing?" Mel asked.

"Damn straight. They need to know what he's done."

Ned cleared his throat. "Don't you think we should find Mary Jo first?"

Linc nodded slowly. "Yeah, I suppose we should."

They rode in silence for several minutes.

"Hey." Ned leaned forward and thrust his face between the two of them.

"What now?" Linc said, frustrated by the heavy traffic, which was guaranteed to be even worse once they hit Tacoma.

"How did Mary Jo get to Cedar Cove?" Mel asked.

"Good question." Linc hadn't stopped to consider her means of transportation. Mary Jo had a driver's license but didn't need a vehicle of her own, living in the city as they did. Each of the brothers owned a car and she could borrow any one of them whenever she wanted.

Ned sat back and studied the map again and after a few minutes announced, "Cedar Cove is on the Kitsap Peninsula."

"So?" Mel muttered sarcastically. The traffic was apparently making him cranky, too.

"So she took the ferry over."

That explained it. "Which ferry?" Linc asked.

"She probably caught the one from downtown Seattle to Bremerton."

"Or she might have gotten a ride," Mel said.

"Who from?" Ned asked.

"She wouldn't bother a friend on Christmas Eve." Ned seemed confident of that.

"Why not?" Mel demanded.

"Mary Jo isn't the type to call someone at the last minute and ask that kind of favor," Ned told them. "Not even Chloe or Casey—especially on Christmas Eve."

Linc agreed with his brother.

They drove in silence for another fifteen minutes before anyone spoke.

"Do you think she's okay?" Ned asked tentatively.

"Sure she is. She's a Wyse, isn't she? We're made of stern stuff."

"I mean physically," Ned clarified. "Last night she seemed so…" He didn't finish the sentence.

"Seemed what?" Linc prompted.

Ned shrugged. "Ready."

"For what?" Mel asked.

Mel could be obtuse, which was only one of his character flaws, in Linc's opinion. He was also argumentative.

"To have the baby, of course," Linc said, casting his brother a dirty look.

"Hey, there's no reason to talk to me like that." Mel shifted his weight and stared out the side window. "I've never been around a pregnant woman before. Besides, what makes *you* such experts on pregnancy and birth?"

"I read a book," Ned told them.

"No way." Linc could hardly believe it.

"I did," Ned insisted. "I figured one of us should. For Mary Jo's sake."

"So one book makes you an expert," Mel teased.

"It makes me smarter than you, anyway."

"No, it doesn't," Mel argued.

"Quit it, you two." Linc spent half his life settling squabbles between his brothers. "You." He gestured over his shoulder. "Call her cell."

Ned did, using his own. "Went right into voice mail," he said. "Must be off."

"Leave her a message, then." Linc wondered if he had to spell *everything* out for them.

"Okay. Who knows if she'll get it, though."

After that they drove in blessed silence for maybe five minutes.

"Hey, I just thought of something." Mel groaned in frustration. "If Mary Jo took the ferry, shouldn't we have done the same thing?"

Good point—except it was too late now. They were stuck in the notorious Seattle traffic, going nowhere fast.

Five

Mary Jo hated the idea of returning to Seattle having failed in her attempt to find either David or his family. He wasn't in Cedar Cove the way he'd promised; not only that, his parents weren't here, either. Ben and Charlotte Rhodes would show up the next afternoon or evening, but in the meantime...

The thought of her brothers approaching the elderly couple, shocking them with the news and their outrageous demands, made the blood rush to her face. Her situation was uncomfortable enough without her brothers riding to the rescue like the superheroes they weren't.

The fact that Mary Jo had left on Christmas Eve was only going to rile them even more. Linc, Mel and Ned were probably home from the garage by now. Or maybe they'd skipped work when they found her note on the coffeemaker and immediately set out in search of her. Maybe they were already driving up and down the streets of Cedar Cove....

Looking around, Mary Jo could see that the library was about to close. People were putting on coats and checking out their books. She wondered how an hour had disappeared so quickly. Now what? There wasn't a single vacant room in the vicinity, which meant the only thing to do was thank Grace Harding for her help and quietly leave.

She waited until the librarian stepped out of her office. The least she could do was let Grace know how much she appreciated her kindness. As she approached, Mary Jo rose from her chair.

All of a sudden the room started to sway. She'd been dizzy before but never like this. Her head swam, and for an instant she seemed about to faint. Blindly Mary Jo reached out, hoping to catch herself before she fell.

"Mary Jo!" Grace gasped and rushed to her side.

If the other woman hadn't caught her when she did, Mary Jo was convinced she would've collapsed onto the floor.

Slowly, Grace eased her into the chair. "Laurie!" she shouted. "Call 9-1-1."

"Please…no," Mary Jo protested. "I'm fine. Really, I am."

"No, you're not."

A moment later, the assistant behind the front counter hurried over to join Grace and Mary Jo. "The fire department's on the way."

Mortified beyond words, Mary Jo leaned her head back and closed her eyes. Needless to say, she'd become the library's main attraction, of far greater interest than any of the Christmas displays. Everyone was staring at her.

"Here, drink this," Grace said.

Mary Jo opened her eyes to find someone holding out a glass of water—again. Her mouth had gone completely dry and she took it gratefully. Sirens could be heard roaring toward the library, and Mary Jo would've given anything to simply disappear.

A few minutes later, two firefighters entered the library, carrying their emergency medical equipment. One of the men moved toward her and knelt down.

"Hi, there." The firefighter's voice was calm.

"Hi," Mary Jo said weakly.

"Can you tell me what happened?"

"I just got a bit light-headed. I wish they hadn't called you. I'm perfectly okay."

He ignored her comment. "You stood up?"

She nodded. "The room began to sway and I thought I was going to faint."

"I think she did faint," Grace added, kneeling down next to the firefighter. "I somehow got her back into the chair. Otherwise I'm sure she would've crumpled to the floor."

The firefighter kept his gaze on Mary Jo. He had kind eyes and, despite everything, she noticed that he was attractive in a craggy, very masculine way. He was in his late twenties, she guessed, a few years older than she was.

"My name's Mack McAfee," he said. "And that guy—" he pointed to the other firefighter "—is Brandon Hutton."

"I'm Mary Jo Wyse."

Mack smiled, maintaining eye contact. "When's your baby due?"

"January seventh."

"In about two weeks then."

"Yes."

"Have you had any other spells like this?"

Mary Jo was reluctant to confess that she had. After a moment she nodded.

"Recently?"

"Yes…"

"That's not uncommon, you know. Your body's under

a lot of strain because of the baby. Have you been experiencing any additional stress?"

She bit her lip. "A little."

"The holidays?"

"Not really."

"I'm new to town. I guess that's why I haven't seen you around," Mack said. He opened a response kit he'd brought into the library.

"Mary Jo lives in Seattle," Grace said, now standing behind Mack as the other firefighter hovered close by.

"Do you have relatives in the area?" he asked next.

"No…" She figured she might as well admit the truth. "I was hoping to see the father of my baby…only he isn't here."

"Navy?"

"No… I understood his family was from Cedar Cove, but apparently they're out of town, too."

"Ben and Charlotte Rhodes," Grace murmured.

Mack twisted around to look up at Grace. "The judge's mother, right? And her husband. Retired Navy."

"Right."

"David Rhodes is the baby's father," Mary Jo said. "We're not…together anymore." David had told her one too many lies. She knew intuitively that he'd have no desire to be part of the baby's life.

Mack didn't speak as he removed the blood pressure cuff and wrapped it around her upper arm. "How are you feeling now?" he asked.

"You mean other than mortified?"

He grinned up at her. "Other than that."

"Better," she said.

"Good." He took her blood pressure, a look of concentration on his face.

"How high is it?" Grace asked, sounding worried.

"Not bad," Mack told them both. "It's slightly elevated." He turned back to Mary Jo. "It would probably be best if you relaxed for the rest of the day. It wouldn't hurt to stay off your feet, either. Don't do anything strenuous."

"I'll...I'll try."

"Perhaps she should see a physician?" Grace said. "I'd be happy to take her to the clinic."

"No, that isn't necessary!" Mary Jo objected. "I'm so sorry to cause all this fuss. I feel fine."

Mack met her gaze and seemed to read the distress in her eyes. "As long as you rest and stay calm, I don't think you need to see a doctor."

"Thank you," she breathed.

Although the library was closing, the doors suddenly opened and a tall, regal woman walked in. She was bundled up in a wool coat with a red knit scarf around her neck and a matching knit cap and gloves.

"Olivia," Grace said. "What are you doing here?"

"Why's the aid car out front?" the other woman asked. She immediately turned to Mary Jo, and a stricken look came over her. "Are you in labor?"

"No, no, I'm just...a little light-headed," Mary Jo assured her.

The woman smiled. "I already know who this must be. Mary Jo. Are you all right?"

"This is Olivia, Charlotte Rhodes's daughter." Grace gestured at her. "She's the woman I called to get the information about Ben and Charlotte."

"Oh." Mary Jo shrank back in her chair.

"David Rhodes is my stepbrother," Olivia explained. She smiled sympathetically at Mary Jo. "Although so far, he's been nothing but an embarrassment to the family. And I can see that trend's continuing. But don't assume," she said to Mary Jo, "that I'm blaming you. I know David *far* too well."

Mary Jo nodded mutely but couldn't prevent a surge of guilt that must have reddened her face, judging by her heated cheeks. She *was* to blame, for being naive in falling for a man like David, for being careless enough to get pregnant, for letting the situation ever reach this point.

"What are you doing here?" Grace asked her friend a second time.

"I'm meeting Will at the gallery. We're going to lunch. I saw the aid car outside the library as I drove by." Olivia turned to Mary Jo again. "I was afraid something like this had happened. Thank goodness for young Mack—" they exchanged a smile "—and his partner over there." Brandon was helping an older couple with their bags of groceries and stack of books.

Mary Jo felt no less humiliated. "I should never have come," she moaned.

"I'm glad you did," Olivia said firmly. "Ben would want to know about his grandchild."

Mary Jo hadn't expected everyone to be so…nice. So friendly and willing to accept her—and her dilemma. "It's just that my brothers are upset and determined to defend my honor. I felt I should be the one to tell David's family."

"Of course you should," Olivia said in what appeared to be complete agreement.

Mack finished packing up his equipment. He placed his hand on Mary Jo's knee to gain her attention. When she looked back at him, she was struck by the caring in his gaze.

"You'll do as I suggested and rest? Don't get overexcited."

Mary Jo nodded.

"If you have any other problems, call 9-1-1. I'm on duty all day."

"I will," she promised. "Thank you so much."

Mack stood. "My pleasure." He hesitated for a moment and looked directly into her eyes. "You're going to be a good mom."

Mary Jo blinked back tears. More than anything, that was what she wanted. To be the best mother she could. Her child was coming into the world with one disadvantage already—the baby's father had no interest in him. Or her. It was all up to Mary Jo.

"Thank you," she whispered.

"Merry Christmas," Mack said before he turned to leave.

"Merry Christmas," she called after him.

"You need to rest," Olivia said with an authority few would question. "When's the last time you ate?"

"I had a decaf latte at Mocha Mama's before I came to the library."

"You need lunch."

"I'll eat," Mary Jo said, "as soon as I get back to Seattle." There was the issue of her brothers, but she'd call Linc's cell phone and let them know she was on her way home.

"You drove?" Grace asked.

"No, I took the ferry across."

Grace and Olivia glanced at each other.

"It might be a good idea if you came home with me," Olivia began. "It won't be any inconvenience and we'd enjoy having you."

Mary Jo shook her head. "I...couldn't." Although Olivia was related to David, by marriage anyway, she didn't want to intrude on their Christmas. Olivia and her family certainly didn't need unexpected company. Olivia had stated that David was an embarrassment to the family, and Mary Jo's presence only made things worse. Bad enough that she'd arrived without any warning, but it was beyond the call of duty for Olivia to take her in, and on Christmas Eve of all nights. Olivia must have plans and Mary Jo refused to ruin them.

"No," Grace said emphatically. "You're coming home with me. It's all arranged."

This invitation was just as endearing and just as unnecessary. "Thank you both." She struggled to her feet, cradling her belly with protective hands. "I can't let either of you do that. I appreciate everything, but I'm going back to Seattle."

"Nonsense," Grace said. "I've spoken to my husband and he agrees with me."

"But—"

Grace cut her off, obviously unwilling to listen. "You won't be intruding, I promise."

Mary Jo was about to argue again, but Grace talked right over her.

"We have my stepdaughter and her family visiting us, but we've got an apartment above our barn that's completely furnished. It's empty at the moment and you'd be welcome to stay there for the night."

The invitation was tempting. Still, Mary Jo hesitated.

"Didn't you hear what Mack said?" Grace reminded her. "He said it was important for you to remain calm and relaxed."

"Yes, I know, but—"

"Are you sure?" Olivia asked Grace. "Because I can easily make up the sofa bed in the den."

"Of course I'm sure."

"I don't want to interfere with your Christmas," Mary Jo said.

"You wouldn't be," Grace assured her. "You'd have your privacy and we'd have ours. The barn's close to the house, so if you needed anything it would be simple to reach me. There's a phone in the apartment, too, which I believe is still connected. If not, the line in the barn is hooked up."

The idea was gaining momentum in her mind. "Maybe I could...." Mary Jo said. As soon as she was settled, she'd call her brothers and explain that she'd decided to stay in Cedar Cove overnight. Besides, she was tired and depressed and didn't feel like celebrating. The idea of being by herself held more appeal by the minute.

Another plus was the fact that her brothers needed a break from her and her problems. For the last number of weeks, Mary Jo had been nothing but a burden to them, causing strife within the family. Thanks to her, the three of them were constantly bickering.

Ned was sympathetic to her situation and she loved him for it. But even he couldn't stand up to Linc, who took his responsibilities as head of the family much too seriously.

If her brothers were on their way to Cedar Cove, as she expected, she'd ask them firmly but politely to turn around. She'd tell them she was spending Christmas with David's family, which was, in fact, true. Sort of. By tomorrow evening, she would've met with Ben and Charlotte and maybe Olivia and the rest of David's Cedar Cove relatives. They'd resolve this situation *without* her brothers' so-called help.

"One thing," Grace said, her voice falling as she glanced over at Olivia.

"Yes?" Mary Jo asked.

"There's a slight complication."

Mary Jo should've known this was too good to be true.

"The barn's currently home to a…variety of animals," Grace went on to explain.

Mary Jo didn't understand why this should be a problem, nor did she understand Olivia's smug grin.

"There's an ox and several sheep, a donkey and—" she paused "—a camel."

"A *camel?*" Mary Jo repeated.

"A rather bad-tempered camel," Olivia put in.

Nodding, Grace pointed to her obviously bandaged arm. "You'd be well advised to keep your distance."

"That's, um, quite a menagerie you have in your barn."

"Oh, they don't belong to us," Grace said. "They're for the live Nativity scene, which ended last evening. We're housing them for the church."

"The animals won't bother me." Mary Jo smiled. "And I won't bother them."

Her smile grew wider as it occurred to her that she'd be spending Christmas Eve in a stable—something another Mary had done before her.

Six

Olivia reluctantly left the library by herself. Weak as she was these days, it made more sense for Mary Jo to go home with Grace. Nevertheless, Olivia felt a certain obligation toward this vulnerable young woman.

Olivia had never had positive feelings toward her stepbrother, and this situation definitely hadn't improved her impression of him. Ben's son could be deceptive and cruel. She knew very well that David had lied to Mary Jo Wyse. Sure, it took two to tango, as the old cliché had it—and two to get Mary Jo into her present state. But Olivia also knew that David would have misrepresented himself and, even worse, abdicated all responsibility for Mary Jo *and* his child. No wonder her family was in an uproar. Olivia didn't blame them; she would be, too.

The drive from the library to the Harbor Street Gallery took less than two minutes. Olivia hated driving such a short distance when at any other time in her life she would've walked those few blocks. The problem was that those blocks were a steep uphill climb and she didn't have the energy. The surgery and subsequent infection had sapped her of strength. Today, however, wasn't a day to dwell on the cancer that had struck her so unexpectedly, like a viper hiding in the garden. Today, Christmas Eve, was a day for gratitude and hope.

She parked outside the art gallery her brother had purchased and was renovating. Olivia had been the one to suggest he buy the gallery; he'd done so, and it seemed to be a good decision for him.

Will was waiting for her at the door. "Liv!" he said, bounding toward her in his larger-than-life way. He extended his arms for a hug. "Merry Christmas."

"Same to you," she said, smiling up at him. Her brother, although over sixty, remained a strikingly handsome man. Now divorced and retired, he'd come home to reinvent himself, leaving behind his former life in Atlanta. In the beginning Olivia had doubted his motives, but slowly he'd begun to prove himself, becoming an active member of the town—and his family—once again.

"I wanted to give you a tour of the gallery," Will told her as he led her inside.

The last time Olivia had visited the town's art gallery had been while Maryellen Bowman, Grace's daughter, was the manager. Maryellen had been forced to resign during a difficult pregnancy. The business had rapidly declined once she'd left, and eventually the gallery had gone up for sale.

Looking around, Olivia was astonished by the changes. "You did all *this* in less than a month?" The place barely resembled the old Harbor Street Gallery. Before Will had taken over, artwork had been arranged in a simple, straightforward manner—paintings and photographs on the walls, sculpture on tables.

Will had built distinctive multi-level glass cases and brought in other inventive means of displaying a variety of mediums, including a carefully designed lighting system. One entire wall was taken up with a huge quilt, unlike any she'd seen before. At first glance she had the impression of fire.

Close up, it looked abstract, with vivid clashing colors and surreal, swirling shapes. But, stepping back, Olivia identified an image that suddenly emerged—a dragon. It was fierce, angry, *red,* shooting out flames in gold, purple and orange satin against a background that incorporated trees, water and winding roads.

"That's by Shirley Bliss," Will said, following her gaze. "It took me weeks to convince her to let me put that up."

"It's magnificent." Olivia was in awe of the piece and couldn't tear her eyes from it.

"It isn't for sale, however."

"That's a shame."

Will nodded. "She calls it *Death.* She created it shortly after her husband was killed in a motorcycle accident." He slipped an arm through Olivia's. "Can't you just feel her anger and her grief?"

The quilt seemed to vibrate with emotions Olivia recognized from her own life—the time her thirteen-year-old son had drowned, more than twenty years ago. And the time, only weeks ago, that she'd been diagnosed with cancer. When she initially heard the physician say the word, she'd had a nearly irrepressible urge to argue with him. This *couldn't* be happening to her. There'd been some mistake.

That disbelief had been replaced by a hot anger at the unfairness of it. Then came numbness, then grief and finally resignation. With Jordan's death and with her own cancer, she'd experienced a tremendous loss that had brought with it fears of further loss.

Now, fighting her cancer—and that was how she thought of it, *her* cancer—she'd found a shaky serenity, even a sort of peace. That kind of acceptance was something she'd acquired with the love and assistance of her husband, Jack, her family and, as much as anyone, Grace, the woman who'd been her best friend all her life.

"My living quarters are livable now, too," Will was telling her. "I've moved in upstairs but I'm still sorting through boxes. Isn't it great how things worked out? Because of Mack," he added when Olivia looked at him quizzically.

"Getting the job here in town, you mean?"

"Yeah, since that meant he needed an apartment. At the same time, I needed out of the sublet, so it all came together perfectly."

After a quick turn around the gallery to admire the other pieces on display, Will steered her toward the door. "Where would you like to go for lunch?" he asked. "Anyplace in town. Your big brother's treating."

"Well, seeing you've got all that money burning a hole in your pocket, how about the Pancake Palace?"

Will arched his brows. "You're joking, aren't you?"

"No, I'm serious." The Pancake Palace had long been a favorite of hers and in the past month or two, she'd missed it. For years, Grace and Olivia would head over to their favorite high school hangout after aerobics class on Wednesday night. The coconut cream pie and coffee was a reward for their exertions, and the Palace was where they always caught up with each other's news.

Goldie, their favorite waitress, had served them salty French fries and iced sodas back when neither of them worried about calories. These days their once-a-week splurge reminded them of their youth, and the nostalgic appeal of the place never faded.

Some of the most defining moments of their teenage years had occurred at the Pancake Palace. It was there that eighteen-year-old Grace admitted she was pregnant, shortly before graduation.

And years later, it'd been over coffee and tears that Olivia told her Stan had asked for a divorce after Jordan's death. And later, it was where they celebrated Olivia's appointment to the bench. The Pancake Palace was a place of memories for them, good and bad.

"The Pancake Palace? You're really serious?" Will said again. "I can afford a lot better, you know."

"You asked and that's my choice."

Will nodded. "Then off to the Palace we go."

Her brother insisted on driving and Olivia couldn't fault his manners. He was the consummate gentleman, opening the passenger door for her and helping her inside. The snow that had fallen earlier dusted the buildings and trees but had melted on the sidewalks and roads, leaving them slick. The slate-gray skies promised more snow, however.

Olivia had been out with her brother plenty of times and he'd never bothered with her car door. She was his sister and manners were reserved for others.

She wondered if Will's solicitude was linked to her illness. Although he might've been reluctant to admit it, Will had been frightened. His caring comforted her, particularly since they'd been at odds during the past few years.

He assisted her out of the car and opened the door to the Pancake Palace. They'd hardly entered the restaurant when Goldie appeared.

"Well, as I live and breathe, it's Olivia!" Goldie cried. Then she shocked Olivia by throwing both sinewy arms around her. "My goodness, you're a sight for sore eyes."

"Merry Christmas, Goldie," Olivia said.

The waitress had to be close to seventy and could only

be described as "crusty." To Olivia's utter astonishment, Goldie pulled a hankie from her pink uniform pocket and dabbed at her eyes.

"I wasn't sure if I'd ever see you again," she said with a sniffle.

"Oh, Goldie…" Olivia had no idea what to say at this uncharacteristic display of affection.

"I just don't know what Grace and I would've done without you," Goldie said, sniffling even more. She wiped her nose and stuffed the hankie back in her pocket. Reaching for the coffeepot behind the counter, she motioned with her free hand. "Sit anyplace you want."

"Thank you, Goldie." Olivia was genuinely touched, since Goldie maintained strict control of who sat where.

Although Goldie had given her free rein, Olivia chose the booth where she'd sat with Grace every Wednesday night until recently. It felt good to slide across the cracked red vinyl cushion again. Olivia resisted the urge to close her eyes and breathe in the familiar scents. The coffee had always been strong and a hint of maple syrup lingered, although it was long past the breakfast hour.

Goldie automatically righted their coffee mugs and filled them. "We've got a turkey dinner with all the trimmings if you're interested," she announced.

Olivia still struggled with her appetite. "What's the soup of the day?"

Goldie frowned. "You aren't having just soup."

"But…"

"Look at you," the waitress chastised. "You're thin as a flagpole. If you don't want a big meal, then I suggest chicken pot pie."

"Sounds good to me," Will said.

Goldie ignored him. She whipped the pencil from behind her ear and yanked out the pad in her apron pocket. From sheer force of habit, or so Olivia suspected, she licked the lead. "Okay, what's it gonna be? And make up your mind, 'cause the lunch crowd's coming in a few minutes and we're gonna be real busy."

It was all Olivia could do to hide her amusement. "Okay, I'll take the chicken pot pie."

"Good choice." Goldie made a notation on her pad.

"I'm glad you approve."

"You're getting pie à la mode, too."

"Goldie!"

One hand on her hip, Goldie glared at her. "After all these years, you should know better than to argue with me." She turned to Will. "And that goes for you, too, young man."

Will raised his hands in acquiescence as Olivia sputtered. "I stand corrected," she said, grinning despite her efforts to keep a straight face.

Goldie left to place their order and Will grinned, too. "I guess *you* were told."

"I guess I was," she agreed. It was nice to know she'd been missed.

Grace would get a real kick out of hearing about this. Olivia would make a point of telling her when they met at the Christmas Eve service later that evening.

Looking out the window, Olivia studied the hand-painted snowman, surrounded by falling snow. The windowpane next to Will was adorned with a big-eyed reindeer. A small poinsettia sat on every table, and the sights and sounds of Christmas filled the room as "O, Little Town of Bethlehem" played softly in the background.

"Are you sure I can't convince you to join us for Christmas dinner?" Olivia asked her brother.

He shook his head. "I appreciate the offer, but you're not up for company yet."

"We're seeing Justine and her family tonight. It's just going to be Jack and me for Christmas Day."

"Exactly. The two of you don't need a third wheel."

"It wouldn't be like that," Olivia protested. "I hate the idea of you spending Christmas alone."

Will sat back. "What makes you think I'll be alone?"

Olivia raised her eyebrows. "You mean you won't?"

He gave a small noncommittal shrug.

"Will." She breathed his name slowly. She didn't want to bring up past history, but in her view, Will wasn't to be trusted with women. "You're seeing someone, aren't you?"

The fact that Will was being secretive didn't bode well. "Come on," she urged him. "Tell me."

He smiled. "It isn't what you think."

"She isn't married, is she?"

"No."

That, at least, was a relief.

"I'm starting over, Liv. My slate's clean now and I want to keep it that way."

Olivia certainly hoped so. "Tell me who it is," she said again.

Her brother relaxed and folded his hands on the table. "I've seen Shirley Bliss a few times."

Shirley Bliss. She was the artist who'd created the dragon, breathing fire and pain and anger.

"Shirley," she whispered. "The dragon quilt lady." Olivia hadn't even met the woman but sensed they could easily be friends.

"She's the one," Will said. "We're only getting to know

each other but I'm impressed with her. She's someone I'd definitely like to know better."

"She invited you for Christmas?"

Will shifted his weight and looked out the window. "Well, not exactly."

Olivia frowned. "Either she did or she didn't."

"Let's put it like this. She hasn't invited me *yet*."

"Good grief, Will! It's Christmas Eve. If she was going to invite you, it would've been before now."

"Perhaps." He grinned boyishly. "Actually, I thought I'd stop by her place around dinnertime tomorrow with a small gift."

"Will!"

"Hey, you can't blame a man for trying."

"Will she be by herself?"

He shook his head. "She has two kids, a teenage daughter who's a talented artist, too, and a son who's in college. I haven't met him yet."

Before Will could say anything else, Goldie arrived at their booth, carrying two chicken pot pies. She set them down and came back with two huge pieces of coconut cream pie. "Make sure you save room for this," she told them.

"I'd like to remind you I didn't order any pie," Olivia said, pretending to disapprove.

"I know," Goldie returned gruffly. "It's on the house. Think of me as your very own elf. Merry Christmas."

"Merry Christmas to you, Goldie the Elf."

Will reached for his fork and smiled over at Olivia. "I have the feeling it's going to be a merry Christmas for us all."

Olivia had the very same feeling, despite—or maybe even because of—their unexpected visitor.

Seven

Linc gritted his teeth. It was after two, and the traffic through Tacoma was bumper to bumper. "You'd think it was a holiday or something," he muttered sarcastically.

Mel's eyebrows shot up and he turned to look at Ned in the backseat.

"What?" Linc barked.

"It *is* a holiday," Ned told him.

"Don't you think I *know* that? I'm joking!"

"Okay, okay."

"You're going to exit up here," Mel said, pointing to the exit ramp for Highway 16.

Linc sighed in relief. They were getting closer, and once they found Mary Jo he intended to give her a piece of his mind. She had no business taking off like this, not when her baby was due in two weeks. It just wasn't safe.

His jaw tightened as he realized it wasn't Mary Jo who annoyed him as much as David Rhodes. If Linc could just have five minutes alone with that jerk…

"I'll bet he's married," Linc said to himself. That would explain a lot. A married man having an affair would do anything he could to hide the fact that he had a wife. He'd strung Mary Jo along, fed her a bunch of lies and then left her to deal with the consequences all on her own. Well, that wasn't going to happen. No, sir. Not while Linc was alive. David Rhodes was going to acknowledge his responsibilities and live up to them.

"Who's married?" Mel asked, staring at him curiously.

"David Rhodes," he said. "Who else?"

The exit was fast approaching and, while they still had twenty miles to go, traffic would thin out once he got off the Interstate.

"He's not," Ned said blithely from the backseat.

"Isn't what?" Linc demanded.

"David Rhodes isn't married."

Linc glanced over his shoulder. "How do you know?"

"Mary Jo told me."

Ned and Mary Jo were close, and he was more apt to take a statement like that at face value.

"He probably lied about that along with everything else," Mel said, voicing Linc's own thoughts.

"He didn't," Ned insisted.

"How can you be so sure?"

"I checked him out on the internet," Ned continued with the same certainty. "It's a matter of public record. David Rhodes lives in California and he's been married and divorced twice. Both his marriages and divorces are listed with California's Department of Records."

Funny Ned had only mentioned this now. Maybe he had other information that would be helpful.

"You mean to say he's been married more than once?" Mel asked.

Ned nodded. "Yeah, according to what I read, he's been

married twice. I doubt Mary Jo knows about the second time, though."

That was interesting and Linc wished he'd heard it earlier. "Did you find out anything else while you were doing this background search?" he asked. He eased onto the off ramp; as he'd expected, the highway was far less crowded.

"His first ex-wife, who now lives in Florida, has had problems collecting child support."

Linc shook his head. "Does that surprise anyone?"

"Nope," Mel said.

"How many children does he have?" Linc asked next.

"Just one. A girl."

"Does Mary Jo know this?" Mel asked. "About him being a deadbeat?"

"I didn't tell her," Ned admitted, adding, "I couldn't see any reason to upset her more than she already is."

"Good idea," Mel said. He leaned forward and looked up at the darkening sky. "Snow's starting again. The radio said there's going to be at least three inches."

"Snow," Linc groaned.

"Snow," Ned repeated excitedly. "That'll make a lot of little kids happy."

Mel agreed quickly. "Yeah, we'll have a white Christmas."

"Are either of *you* little kids?" Linc snapped. His nerves were frayed and he'd appreciate it if his brothers took a more mature outlook.

"I guess I'm still a kid at heart," Ned said, exhaling a sigh.

Considering Linc's current frame of mind, it was a brave admission. With a slow breath, Linc made a concerted effort to relax. He was worried about Mary Jo; he couldn't help it. He'd wanted the best for her and felt that he'd failed both his sister and his parents.

To some extent he blamed himself for what had happened. Maybe he'd been too strict with her after she turned eighteen. But to his way of thinking, she was under his protection as long as she lived in the family home.

Not once had she introduced him to David Rhodes. Linc was convinced that if he'd met the other man, it would've taken him all of two seconds to peg David for a phony.

"What are you gonna say when we find her?" Ned asked.

Linc hadn't worked out the specifics. "Let's not worry about that now. Main thing is, we're going to put her in the truck and bring her home."

"What if she doesn't want to come with us?"

"Why wouldn't she? We're her family and it's Christmas Eve. Mary Jo belongs with us. Besides, that baby could show up anytime."

Mel seemed distinctly queasy at the prospect.

Thinking back, Linc knew he should have realized she was pregnant a lot earlier than he had. In fact, he hadn't recognized the signs at all; she'd *told* him and after that, of course, they were easy to see.

Not until the day Mary Jo rushed past him in the hallway and practically shoved him into the wall so she could get to the toilet in time to throw up did he have the slightest suspicion that anything was wrong. Even then he'd assumed she had a bad case of the flu.

Boy, had he been wrong. She had the flu, all right, only it was the nine-month variety.

It just hadn't occurred to him that she'd do something so dumb. An affair with the guy was bad enough, but to take that kind of chance...

Frowning, Linc glanced in his rearview mirror at his youngest brother. He was beginning to wonder about Ned. He'd never seemed as shocked as he or Mel had, and Mary Jo had always confided in him.

"How long have you known?" he asked casually.

Ned met Linc's gaze in the rearview mirror, his expression trapped. "Known what?"

"That Mary Jo was going to have a baby."

Ned looked away quickly and shrugged.

"She told you as soon as she found out, didn't she?"

Ned cleared his throat. "She might have."

"How early was that?" Linc asked, unwilling to let his brother sidestep the question.

"Early," Ned admitted. "I knew before David."

"You knew *that* early?" Mel shouted. "Why'd she tell you and not me?"

"Because you'd tell Linc," Ned told him. "She wanted to keep the baby a secret as long as she could."

Linc couldn't figure that one out. It wasn't like she'd be able to hide the pregnancy forever. And why hadn't she trusted him the way she did Ned? Although he prided himself on being stoic, that hurt.

Mel tapped his fingertips against the console. "Did she tell you how David Rhodes reacted to the news?"

Ned nodded. "She said he seemed pleased."

"Sure, why not?" Linc said, rolling his eyes. "The pregnancy wasn't going to inconvenience *him* any."

"I think that's why he could string Mary Jo along all this time," Ned suggested.

"You're probably right."

"I warned her, you know." Ned's look was thoughtful.

"When?"

"When she first started seeing him."

"You knew about David even before Mary Jo got pregnant?" Linc couldn't believe his ears. Apparently Mary Jo had shared all this information with Ned, who'd remained tight-lipped about most of it. If he wasn't so curious to uncover what his brother had learned, Linc might've been downright angry.

"So?" Mel said. "How'd she meet him?"

Ned leaned toward the front seat. "Rhodes works for the same insurance company. He's at corporate headquarters in San Francisco. Something to do with finances."

His sister worked in the accounting department, so that explained it, he supposed. "She should've come to work at our office the way I wanted," Linc said, and not for the first time. That was what he'd suggested when, against his wishes, Mary Jo had dropped out of college.

From her reaction, one would think he'd proposed slave labor. He never had understood her objections. He'd been willing to pay her top wages, as well as vacation and sick leave, and the work wasn't exactly strenuous.

She'd turned him down flat. Mary Jo wouldn't even consider working for Three Wyse Men Automotive. Linc regretted not being more forceful in light of what had happened. She might be almost twenty-four, but she needed his protection.

As they approached the Narrows Bridge, Linc's mood began to lighten somewhat. Yeah, Mary Jo needed him, and he assumed she'd be willing to admit that now. Not just him, either. She needed all three of her brothers.

Ned's idea that they bring gifts had been smart, a good way to placate her and prove how much she meant to them. Women, in his experience anyway, responded well to gifts.

Except that was probably the same technique David Rhodes had used.

"Did he buy her gifts?" Linc asked, frowning.

Ned understood his question, because he answered right away. "If you mean Rhodes, then yes, he got her a few."

"Such as?"

"Flowers a couple of times."

"Flowers!" Mel said.

"In the beginning, at any rate, and then after she was pregnant he bought her earrings."

Linc sat up straighter. "What kind?"

Ned snickered. "He said they were diamonds but one of them came loose so I dropped it off at Fred's for her. While he had it, I asked him to check it out."

Fred's was a local jewelry store the Wyse family had used for years. "Fake, right?"

"As phony as David Rhodes himself."

Mel twisted around and looked at Ned. "You didn't tell Mary Jo, did you?"

Ned shook his head. "I didn't want to add to her heartache."

"Maybe she already knows." His sister might be gullible but she wasn't stupid.

"I think she considered pawning it." Ned lowered his voice. "She didn't, so she might've guessed...."

The mere thought of his sister walking into a pawnshop with her pathetic bauble produced a stab of actual pain. "If she needed money, why didn't she come to me?" Linc demanded.

"You'll have to ask her that yourself."

"I plan to." Linc wasn't about to let this slide. "What does she need money for, anyway?"

"She wants her own place, you know."

No one needed to remind Linc of that. Mary Jo herself did a fine job of informing him at every opportunity. But it wasn't going to happen now. With a baby on the way, she wouldn't be leaving the family home anytime soon.

Linc liked that idea. He could keep an eye on her and on the baby, too. Even if he got married, which was by no means a sure thing, the house was big enough for all of them. His nephew would need a strong male influence, and he fully intended to provide that influence.

"How much farther?" Mel asked.

His brother was like a kid squirming in the front seat, asking "Are we there yet?" every five minutes.

"Hey, look," Ned said, pointing at the sky. "It's really coming down now."

"Did you think I hadn't noticed?" Linc didn't have much trouble driving in bad weather; it was all the *other* drivers who caused the problem. Snow in the Seattle area was infrequent and a lot of folks didn't know how to handle it.

"Hey," Mel said as they approached the first exit for Cedar Cove. "We're here."

"Right." Not having any more specific indication of where they should go, Linc took the exit.

"Where to now?" Mel asked.

Linc could've said, "Your guess is as good as mine." But he figured his guess was better. "We'll do what Mary Jo did," he said. "We'll chase down David's family. That's where she's going to be."

Mel nodded. "Whoever said the Wyse Men needed a star to guide them obviously never met the three of us."

Eight

Olivia couldn't wait to see her husband. For one thing, she wanted to tell him about her stepbrother, get his advice.

David Rhodes...that...that—she couldn't think of a word that adequately described how loathsome he was. She wanted him exposed. Humiliated, embarrassed, *punished*. Only the fact that Ben would be humiliated and embarrassed, too, gave her pause.

When Olivia pulled into her driveway on Lighthouse Road she was delighted to see that Jack was already home from the newspaper office. Impatiently, she grabbed the grocery bag of last-minute items and made her way into the house, using the entrance off the kitchen.

"Jack!" she called out as soon as she was inside.

"What's wrong?" Her husband met her in the kitchen and stopped short. "Someone's made *you* mad."

Olivia finished unwinding the muffler from around her neck. "Why do you say that?" she asked, not realizing she'd been so obvious.

"Your eyes are shooting sparks. So, what'd I do this time?"

"It's not you, silly." She hung her coat on the hook

along with the bright red scarf her mother had knit for her. She stuffed the matching hat and gloves in the pockets, then kissed Jack's cheek.

As she filled the electric teakettle and turned it on, Jack began to put the groceries away.

"Are you ready to talk about it?" he asked cautiously.

"It's David."

"Rhodes?"

"The very one. The man is lower than pond scum."

"That's not news."

Early in her mother's marriage to Ben, his son had tried to bilk Charlotte out of several thousand dollars. He'd used a ruse about needing some surgery his medical insurance wouldn't cover, and if not for Justine's intervention, Charlotte would have given him the money. David Rhodes was shameless, and he'd dishonored his father's name.

"Is he in town?" Jack asked. He took two mugs from the cupboard and set them on the counter; Olivia tossed a couple of Earl Grey teabags in the pot.

"No, or at least not as far as I'm aware. And frankly it's a good thing he isn't."

Jack chuckled. "I couldn't agree with you more, and I haven't got a clue what he's done to upset you now."

"He got a young girl pregnant."

Jack's eyebrows rose toward his hairline. "And you know this how?"

"I met her."

"Today?"

"Not more than two hours ago. She's young, probably twenty years younger than he is, and innocent. Or she was until David got hold of her. I swear that man should be shot!"

"Olivia!" He seemed shocked by her words. "That doesn't sound like you."

"Okay, that might be drastic. I'm just so furious I can hardly stand it."

Jack grinned.

Olivia glared at her husband. "You find this entertaining, do you?"

"Well, not about the young lady but I will admit it's a pleasant change to see color in your cheeks and your eyes sparkling, even if it's with outrage." He reached for her and brought her close enough to kiss her lips, allowing his own to linger. When he released her, he pressed his forehead to hers and whispered, "It's an even greater pleasure to know all this indignation isn't directed at me."

"I've never been anywhere near this upset with you, Jack Griffin."

"I beg to differ."

"When?"

"I remember one time," Jack said, "when I thought you were going to kick me out."

"I would *never* have done that." Her arms circled his waist. They'd found ways to make their marriage work, ways to compromise between his nature—he was a slob, not to put too fine a point on it—and hers.

Olivia liked order. Their bathroom dilemma was a perfect example. She'd been driven to the brink of fury by the piles of damp towels, the spattered mirror, the uncapped toothpaste. The solution? They had their own bathrooms now. She'd kept the one off the master bedroom and he had the guest bath. Jack could be as sloppy as he wanted, as long as he closed the door and Olivia didn't have to see his mess.

"You're lucky I love you so much," Jack whispered.

"And why's that?" she asked, leaning back to look him in the eye.

"Because you'd be lost without me."

"Jack..."

The kettle started to boil, its piercing whistle enough to set the dogs in the next block howling. She tried to break free, but Jack held her fast. "Admit it," he insisted. "You're crazy about me."

"All right, all right, I'm crazy about you."

"And you'd be lost without me. Wouldn't you?"

"Jack!"

Chortling like a schoolboy, he let her go and she grabbed the kettle, relieved by the sudden cessation of that high-pitched shrieking.

Pouring the boiling water into the teapot, she covered it with a cozy and left the tea to steep. Then she opened the cookie jar and chose two of the decorated sugar cookies she'd baked a few days earlier with her grandson—a tree shape and a star. The afternoon had worn her out physically but she treasured every moment she'd spent in the kitchen with Leif.

Just as she was about to pour their tea, the phone rang.

"Want me to get that?" Jack called from the other room.

A glance at Caller ID told her it was Grace.

"I will," she told him. "Merry Christmas," she said into the receiver.

"Merry Christmas to you, too," her friend said in return. "I thought I'd check in and let you know how everything's going."

"So what's the update?"

"Everything's fine."

"Mary Jo's resting?"

"She was asleep the last time I looked, which was about five minutes ago. The girl must be exhausted. She told me she didn't get much sleep last night."

"She's in the apartment then, or at the house?"

"The apartment. Cliff's daughter and her family are already here, so…"

Olivia wasn't entirely comfortable with the idea of leaving Mary Jo alone, but it was probably for the best. This way she could relax undisturbed.

"There's something strange.…"

"What?" Olivia asked.

"Well, for no reason I can understand, I decided to do a bit of housekeeping in the apartment yesterday. Cal's been gone a few weeks now, and I put clean sheets on the bed and fresh towels in the bathroom. It's as if…as if I was waiting for Mary Jo."

That was a little too mystical for Olivia. "I'm so glad this is working out," she said.

"She's an animal-lover, too."

That didn't surprise Olivia. She sensed that Mary Jo had a gentleness about her, a soft heart, an interest in others.

"The minute I brought her into the barn, she wanted to see all the Nativity animals."

"You kept her away from that camel, didn't you?"

"I kept us both away," Grace was quick to tell her. "That beast is going to have to chew on someone else's arm."

"Yeah, David's would be ideal," Olivia said.

Grace laughed, but sobered almost immediately. "Listen, Mary Jo has a concern I'd like to talk to you about."

"Sure."

"She's got three older brothers who are most likely on their way into town, looking for her, as we speak."

"Does she *want* to be found?" Olivia asked.

"I think she does, only she wants to talk to Ben and Charlotte before her brothers do."

"She's not trying to protect David, is she?"

"I doubt it. What she's afraid of is that her brothers might try to insist that David marry her and she doesn't want to. At this point, she's accepted that she's better off without him."

"Smart decision."

"Yes, but it came at quite a price, didn't it?"

"True. A lesson with lifelong consequences."

"We all seem to learn our lessons the hard way," Grace said.

"I know I did." Her children, too, Olivia mused. Justine and James. As always, especially around the holidays, her mind wandered to Jordan, the son she'd lost that summer day all those years ago. Justine's twin.

"What time are Maryellen and Kelly coming by?" she asked Grace, changing the subject. Although Mary Jo would be staying in the barn, perhaps she should bring her over for dinner. Give her a chance to feel welcomed by Ben's second family. Cliff's daughter, Lisa, her husband and their little girl, April, were out doing some last-minute shopping, apparently, and not due back until late afternoon.

"My girls should be here around six."

"You're going straight to church after dinner?"

"That's the plan," Grace told her. "I was going to invite Mary Jo to join us."

"For dinner or Christmas Eve service?"

"Both, actually, but I'm having second thoughts."

"Why? And about what?"

"Oh, about inviting Mary Jo to dinner. I'm afraid it might be too much for her. We'll have five grandkids running around. You know how much racket children can make, and double that on Christmas Eve."

"Is there anything I can do for her?" Olivia asked. "Should I invite her to have dinner here?"

"I'm not sure. I'll talk to her when she wakes up and then I'll phone you."

"Thanks. And tell her not to worry about her brothers."

"I'll do that."

"See you tonight."

"Tonight," Olivia echoed.

After setting down the phone, Olivia poured the tea and placed both mugs on the table, followed by the plate of cookies, and called Jack into the kitchen again.

His eyes widened in overstated surprise. "Cookies? For me? You shouldn't have."

"I can still put them back."

"Oh, no, you don't." He grabbed the star-shaped cookie and bit off one point. "What's this in honor of?"

"I had pie with lunch. So I'm trying to be fair."

Knowing her disciplined eating habits, Jack did a double take. "You ate pie? At *lunch?*"

"Goldie made me do it."

"Goldie," he repeated. "You mean Will took you to the Pancake Palace?"

"It's where I wanted to go."

Jack sat down, scooped up the tree cookie and bit into that, too. "You're a cheap date."

"Not necessarily."

He ignored that remark. "Did you enjoy lunch with Will?" he asked, then sipped his tea. Jack was familiar with their sometimes tumultuous relationship.

"I did, although I'm a little worried." Olivia crossed her legs and held the mug in the palm of her hand. "He's interested in Shirley Bliss, a local artist."

"She's not married, is she?"

Olivia shook her head. "A widow."

Jack shrugged. "Then it's okay if he wants to see her."

"I agree. It's just that I don't know if I can trust my brother. It pains me to admit that, but still…" She left the rest unsaid. Jack knew her brother and his flaws as well as she did. "I want him to be successful here," she said earnestly. "He's starting over, and at this stage of his life that can't be easy."

"I don't imagine it will be," Jack agreed. "By the way, who was that on the phone?"

"Grace. She called to update me on Mary Jo."

"Problems?"

"Not really, but she said we need to keep an eye out for three irate brothers who might show up looking for her."

"A vigilante posse?"

"Not exactly." But now that Olivia thought about it, it might not be so bad if Mary Jo's brothers stumbled onto David Rhodes instead. "If her brothers find anyone, it should be David."

"There'd certainly be justice in that, but David's not going to let himself be found. And I think we should be focusing on the young woman, don't you?"

His tone was gentle, but Olivia felt chastened. "Yes— and her baby."

Nine

Mary Jo woke feeling confused. She sat up in bed and gazed around at the sparsely decorated room before she remembered where she was. Grace Harding had brought her home and was letting her spend the night in this apartment above the barn. It was such a kind thing to do. She was a stranger, after all, a stranger with problems who'd appeared out of nowhere on Christmas Eve.

Stretching her arms high above her head, Mary Jo yawned loudly. She was still tired, despite her nap. Her watch told her she'd been asleep for almost two hours. Two hours!

Other than in her first trimester, she hadn't required a lot of extra rest during her pregnancy, but that had changed in the past few weeks. Of course some of it could be attributed to David and his lies. Wondering what she should believe and whether he'd meant *any* of what he'd said had kept her awake many a night. Consequently she was tired during the day; while she was still working she'd nap during her lunch break.

Forcing her eyes shut, Mary Jo made an effort to cast David from her mind. She quickly gave up. Tossing aside the covers, she climbed out of bed, put on her shoes and left the apartment. The stairway led to the interior of the barn.

As soon as she stepped into the barn, several animals stuck their heads out of the stalls to study her curiously. The first she saw was a lovely horse. Grace had introduced her as Funny Face.

"Hello there, girl." Mary Jo walked slowly toward the stall door. "Remember me?" The mare nodded in what seemed to be an encouraging manner, and Mary Jo ran her hand down the horse's unusually marked face. The mare had a white ring around one eye and it was easy to see why the Hardings had named her Funny Face. Her dark, intelligent eyes made Mary Jo think of an old story she recalled from childhood—that animals can talk for a few hours after midnight on Christmas Eve—and she wondered what Funny Face would say. Probably something very wise.

The camel seemed curious, too, and thrust her long curved neck out of the stall, peering at Mary Jo through wide eyes, fringed with lush, curling lashes. Mary Jo had been warned to keep her distance. "Oh, no, you don't," she said, waving her index finger. "You're not going to lure me over there with those big brown eyes. Don't give me that innocent look, either. I've heard all about you."

After visiting a few placid sheep, another couple of horses and a donkey with a sweet disposition, Mary Jo walked out of the barn. She hurried toward the house through a light snowfall, wishing she'd remembered her coat. Even before she arrived, the front door opened and an attractive older gentleman held the screen.

"You must be Mary Jo," he said and thrust out his hand in greeting. "Cliff Harding."

"Hello, Mr. Harding," she said with a smile. She was

about to thank him for his hospitality when he interrupted.

"Call me Cliff, okay? And come in, come in."

"All right, Cliff. Thank you."

Mary Jo entered the house and was greeted by the smell of roasting turkey and sage and apple pie.

"You're awake!" Grace declared as she came out of the kitchen. She wore an apron and had smudges of flour on her cheeks.

"I'm shocked I slept for so long."

"You obviously needed it," Grace commented, leading her into the kitchen. "I see you've met my husband."

"Yes." Mary Jo smiled again. Rubbing her palms nervously together, she looked from one to the other. "I really can't thank you enough for everything you've done for me."

"Oh, nonsense. It's the least we could do."

"I'm a stranger and you took me in without question and, well...I didn't think that kind of thing happened in this day and age."

That observation made Grace frown. "Really? It does here in Cedar Cove. I guess it's just how people act in small towns. We tend to be more trusting."

"I had a similar experience when I first moved here," Cliff said. "I wasn't accustomed to people going out of their way for someone they didn't know. I didn't believe it could be genuine. Charlotte Jefferson—now Charlotte Rhodes—disabused me of *that* notion."

Despite everything, Mary Jo looked forward to meeting David's stepmother. The conversation would be difficult, but knowing that Charlotte was as kind as everyone else she'd met so far made all the difference.

"Really, Mary Jo," Grace continued. "All you needed was a friend and a helping hand. Anyone here would've done the same. Olivia wanted you to stay with her, too."

"Everyone's been so wonderful." Thinking about the willingness of these people to take her in brought a lump to her throat. She bent, with some effort, to stroke the smooth head of a golden retriever who lay on a rug near the stove.

"That's Buttercup," Grace said fondly as the dog thumped her tail but didn't stand up. "She's getting old, like the rest of us."

"Coffee?" Cliff walked over to the coffeemaker. "I'll make some decaf. Are you interested?" he asked, motioning in Mary Jo's direction with the pot.

"I'd love some. If it isn't any trouble."

"None whatsoever. I'm having a cup, too." Grace set out three mugs, then suddenly asked, "You didn't eat any lunch, did you?"

"No, but I'm not hungry."

"You might not be, but that baby of yours is," Grace said as if she had a direct line of communication to the unborn child. Without asking further, she walked to the refrigerator and poked her head inside. Adjusting various containers and bottles and packages, she took out a plastic-covered bowl.

"I don't want to cause you any extra work," Mary Jo protested.

"The work's already done. Cliff made the most delicious clam chowder," Grace said. "I'll heat you up some."

Now that Grace mentioned it, Mary Jo realized she really could use something to eat; she was feeling light-headed again. "Cliff cooks?" Her brothers were practically helpless around the kitchen and it always surprised her to find a man who enjoyed cooking.

"I am a man of many talents," Grace's husband answered with a smile. "I was a bachelor for years before I met Grace."

"If I didn't prepare meals, my brothers would survive on fast food and frozen entrées," she said, grinning. Thankfully her mother had taught her quite a bit before her death. The brothers had relied on Mary Jo for meals ever since.

The thought of Linc, Mel and Ned made her anxious. She'd meant to call, but then she'd fallen asleep and now… they could be anywhere. They'd be furious and frightened. She felt a blast of guilt; her brothers might be misguided but they loved her.

"If you'll excuse me a moment," she said urgently. "I need to make a phone call."

"Of course," Grace told her. "Would you like to use the house phone?"

She shook her head. "No, I have my cell up in the apartment. It'll only take a few minutes."

"You might have a problem with coverage. Try it and see. By the time you return, the coffee and soup will be ready."

Mary Jo went back to the barn and up the stairs to the small apartment. She was breathless when she reached the top and paused to gulp in some air. Her pulse was racing. This had never happened before. Trying to stay calm, she walked into the bedroom where she'd left her purse.

Sitting on the bed, she got out her cell. She tried the family home first. But the call didn't connect, and when Mary Jo glanced at the screen, she saw there wasn't any coverage in this area. Well, that settled that.

She did feel bad but there was no help for it. She'd ask to make a long-distance call on the Hardings' phone, and she'd try Linc's cell, as well as the house. She collected her coat and gloves and hurried back to the house, careful not to slip in the snow.

A few minutes later, she was in the kitchen. As Grace had promised, the coffee and a bowl of soup were waiting for her on the table.

Mary Jo hesitated. She really hated to ask, hated to feel even more beholden. "If you don't mind, I'd appreciate using your phone."

"Of course."

"It's long distance, I'm afraid. I'd be happy to pay the charges. You could let me know—"

"Nonsense," Grace countered. "One phone call isn't going to make a bit of difference to our bill."

"Thank you." Still wearing her coat, Mary Jo went over to the wall phone, then remembered that Linc's number was programmed into her cell. Speed dial made it unnecessary to memorize numbers these days, she thought ruefully.

She'd have to go back to the apartment a second time. Well, there was no help for that, either. "I'll need to get my cell phone," she said.

"I can have Cliff get it for you," Grace offered. "I'm not sure you should be climbing those stairs too often."

"Oh, no, I'm fine," Mary Jo assured her. She walked across the yard, grateful the snow had tapered off, and back up the steep flight of stairs, pausing as she had before to inhale deeply and calm her racing heart. Taking another breath, she went in search of her cell.

On the off chance the phone might work in a different location, Mary Jo stood on the Hardings' porch and tried again. And again she received the same message. No coverage.

Cell phone in hand, she returned to the kitchen.

"I'll make the call as quickly as I can," she told Grace, lifting the receiver.

"You talk as long as you need," Grace said. "And here, let me take your coat."

She found Linc's contact information in her cell phone directory and dialed his number. After a few seconds, the call connected and went straight to voice mail. Linc, it appeared, had decided to turn off his cell. Mary Jo wasn't sure what to make of that. Maybe he didn't *want* her to contact him, she thought with sudden panic. Maybe he was so angry he never wanted to hear from her again. When she tried to leave a message, she discovered that his voice mail was full. She sighed. It was just like Linc not to listen to his messages. He probably had no idea how many he'd accumulated.

"My brother has his cell off," Mary Jo said with a defeated shrug.

"He might be in a no-coverage zone," Grace explained. "We don't get good reception here at the ranch. Is it worth trying his house?"

Mary Jo doubted it, but she punched in the numbers. As she'd expected, no answer there, either. Her oldest brother's deep voice came on, reciting the phone number. Then, in his usual peremptory fashion, he said, "We're not here. Leave a message." Mary Jo closed her eyes.

"It's me," she began shakily, half afraid Linc would break in and start yelling at her. Grace had stepped out of the kitchen to give her privacy, a courtesy she appreciated.

"I'm in Cedar Cove," she said. "I'll be home sometime Christmas Day after I speak to David's parents. Probably later in the evening. Please don't try to find me. I'm with…friends. Don't worry about me. I know what I'm doing." With that she replaced the receiver.

She saw that Grace had moved into the dining room, setting the table. "Thank you," Mary Jo told her.

"You're very welcome. Is your soup still hot?"

Mary Jo had forgotten about that. "I'll check."

"If not, let me know and I'll reheat it in the microwave."

"I'm sure it'll be fine," she murmured. Even if it was stone-cold, she wouldn't have said so, not after everything Grace had done for her.

But as Mary Jo tried her first spoonful, she realized the temperature was perfect. She finished the entire bowl, then ate all the crackers and drank her decaf coffee after adding a splash of cream. As she brought her dishes to the sink, Grace returned to the kitchen. "My daughters will be here at six," she said, looking at the clock. "And my daughter-in-law and her family should be back soon. We're having dinner together and then we're leaving for the Christmas Eve service at our church."

"How nice." Mary Jo had missed attending church. She and her brothers just seemed to stop going after her parents' funeral. She still went occasionally but hadn't in quite a while, and her brothers didn't go at all.

"Would you like to join us?"

The invitation was so genuine that for a moment Mary Jo seriously considered it. "Thank you for the offer, but I don't think I should."

"Why not?" Grace pressed. "We'd love to have you."

"Thank you," Mary Jo said again, "but I should probably stay quiet and rest, like the EMT suggested."

Grace nodded. "Yes, you should take his advice, although we'd love it if you'd at least have dinner with us."

The invitation moved her so much that Mary Jo felt tears spring to her eyes. Not only had Grace and her husband taken her into their home, they wanted to include her in their holiday celebration.

"I can't believe you'd want me here with your family," she said.

"Why wouldn't we?" Grace asked. She seemed astonished by the comment. "You're our guest."

"But it's Christmas and you'll have your...your family here." She found it hard to speak.

"Yes, and they'll be delighted to meet you."

"But this isn't a time for strangers."

"Now, just a minute," Grace said. "Don't you remember the original Christmas story?"

"Of course I do." Mary Jo had heard it all her life.

"Mary and Joseph didn't have anywhere to stay, either, and strangers offered them a place," Grace reminded her. "A stable," she added with a smile.

"But I doubt those generous folks asked them to join the family for dinner," Mary Jo teased.

"That part we don't know because the Bible doesn't say, but I have to believe that anyone who'd lend their stable to those young travelers would see to their other needs, as well." Grace's warm smile wrapped its way around Mary Jo's heart. "Join us for part of the evening, okay? I'd love it if you met the girls, and I know they'd enjoy meeting you."

Mary Jo didn't immediately respond. Although she would've liked to meet Grace's family, she wasn't feeling quite right. "May I think about it?"

"Of course," Grace said. "You do whatever you need to do."

Leaning forward in the chair, Mary Jo supported her lower back with both hands, trying to ease the persistent ache. Sitting had become difficult in the last few weeks. It was as if the baby had latched his or her foot around one of her ribs and intended to hang on. Mary Jo was beginning to wonder if she'd ever find a comfortable position again.

"Can I help you with anything?" she asked.

Grace surveyed the kitchen. "No, I've got everything under control. I thought I'd sit down with you for a few minutes."

Mary Jo nodded. "Yes, please. I'd like that."

"So would I," the other woman said. "Here, let me get us some fresh coffee. And what about some Christmas shortbread to go with it?"

Ten

At the fire station, Mack McAfee sat by himself in the kitchen, downing yet another cup of coffee. The only call so far that day had been for the young pregnant woman who'd had the dizzy spell at the library. For some reason, she'd stayed in his mind ever since.

Because he wasn't married, Mack had volunteered to work Christmas Eve and part of Christmas Day, allowing one of the other firefighters to spend the time with family. Unfortunately, his mother was none too happy that he'd agreed to work over the holidays.

Mack's parents lived in Cedar Cove and his sister had, too, until she'd left several months ago, her heart broken by that cowpoke who used to work for Cliff Harding. Linnette had taken off with no plan or destination and ended up in some Podunk town in North Dakota. She seemed to love her new home out there in the middle of nowhere. Mack didn't understand it, but then it wasn't his life.

He was happy for Linnette, knowing she'd found her niche. She'd always said she wanted to live and work in a small rural town. As an experienced physician assistant, Linnette had a lot to offer a community like Buffalo Valley, North Dakota.

Gloria, Mack's oldest sister, had been given up for adoption as an infant; their relationship had only come to light in the past few years. Mack was just beginning to know her and so far he'd discovered that they had a surprising amount in common, despite their very different upbringings. She'd promised to stop by the house and spend part of Christmas with their parents, but she, too, was on the duty roster for tonight.

When Gloria had first moved into the area—with the goal of reconnecting with her birth family—she'd worked for the Bremerton police. Since then, however, she'd taken a job with the sheriff's department in Cedar Cove.

Mack's cell phone, attached to his waistband, chirped. He reached for it, not bothering to look at the screen. He already knew who was calling.

"Hi, Mom."

"Merry Christmas." Her cheerful greeting was strained and not entirely convincing.

"Thanks. Same to you and Dad."

"How's everything?"

His mother was at loose ends. Not having any of her children with her during the holidays was hard for her. "It's been pretty quiet here this afternoon," he said.

Corrie allowed an audible sigh to escape. "I wish you hadn't volunteered to work on Christmas."

This wasn't the first time his mother had brought it up. But as the firefighter most recently hired, he would've been assigned this shift anyway.

"It'll be lonely with just your father and me." Her voice fell and Mack sighed, wishing he could tell her what she wanted to hear.

"It'll be a wonderful Christmas," he said, sounding as positive as he could.

"I'm sure it'll be fine," she agreed in a listless voice.

"I decided to cook a ham this year instead of turkey. It's far less work and we had a turkey at Thanksgiving. Of course, I'm going to bake your father's favorite potato casserole and that green bean dish everyone likes."

Mack didn't understand why his mother felt she had to review her dinner menu with him, but he let her chatter on, knowing it made her feel better.

"I was thinking," she said, abruptly changing the subject.

"Yes, Mom?"

"You should get married."

If Mack had been swallowing a drink at the time he would've choked. "I beg your pardon?"

"You're settling down here in Cedar Cove?"

He noticed that she'd made it a question. "Well, I wouldn't go that far."

"I would," she said. "You have a steady job." She didn't add that this was perhaps his tenth career change in the last six years. Mack was easily bored and tended to jump from job to job. He'd worked part-time for the post office, done construction, delivered for UPS and held half a dozen other short-term jobs since dropping out of college. He'd also renovated a run-down house and sold it for a tidy profit.

Mack's restlessness had contributed to the often acrimonious relationship he'd had with his father. Roy McAfee hadn't approved of Mack's need for change. He felt Mack was irresponsible and hadn't taken his life seriously enough. In some ways Mack supposed his father was right. Still, his new job with the fire department seemed to suit him perfectly, giving him the variety, the excitement and the camaraderie he craved. It also gave him a greater sense of purpose than anything else he'd done.

He and his dad got along better these days. Roy had

actually apologized for his attitude toward Mack, which had come as a real shock. It had made a big difference in their relationship, though, and for that Mack was grateful.

"You think I should be *married*," he repeated, as though it was a foreign word whose meaning eluded him.

"You're twenty-eight."

"I know how old I am, Mom."

"It's time," she said simply.

"Really?" He found his mother's decree almost humorous.

"Have you met anyone special?" she asked.

"Mom!" he protested. Yet the picture of Mary Jo Wyse shot instantly into his mind. He knew from the conversation he'd overheard at the library that she was pregnant and single and that David Rhodes was her baby's father. He'd also heard a reference to Charlotte and Ben Rhodes. He was familiar with them, but completely in the dark about David.

"I'm not trying to pressure you," his mother said. "It's just that it would be nice to have grandchildren one day."

Mack chuckled. "If you want, I'll get to work on that first thing."

"Mack," she chastised, "you know what I mean."

He did but still enjoyed teasing her. While she was on the phone, he decided to take the opportunity to find out what he could about the father of Mary Jo's baby. "Can you tell me anything about David Rhodes?" he asked.

"David Rhodes," his mother said slowly. "Is he related to Ben Rhodes?"

"His son, I believe."

"Let me go ask your father."

"That's okay, Mom, don't bother. It's no big deal."

"Why'd you ask, then?"

"Oh, someone mentioned him, that's all." Mack was reluctant to bring up Mary Jo; for one thing, it'd been a chance encounter and he wasn't likely to see her again. Clearly she wasn't from here.

"Mack. Tell me."

"I treated a young woman at the library this morning."

"The pregnant girl?" Her voice rose excitedly.

Word sure spread fast in a small town, something Mack wasn't used to yet. "How do you know about Mary Jo?" he asked.

"Mary Jo," his mother said wistfully. "What a nice name."

She had a nice face to go with it, too, Mack mused and then caught himself. He had no business thinking about her. None whatsoever.

"I met Shirley Bliss in the grocery store earlier," his mother went on to say. "The last thing I wanted to do was make a dash to the store. You know how busy they get the day before a big holiday."

Actually, he didn't, not from experience, but it seemed logical enough.

"Anyway, I ran out of evaporated milk. I needed it for the green Jell-O salad I make every Christmas."

Mack remembered that salad well; it was one of his favorites. His mother had insisted on making it, he noted, even though Mack wouldn't be joining the family for dinner.

"I could've used regular milk, I suppose, but I was afraid it wouldn't taste the same. I don't like to use substitutes if it can be avoided."

"Shirley Bliss, Mom," he reminded her.

"Oh, yes. Shirley. I saw her at the store. She was with her daughter, Tanni."

"O-k-a-y." Mack dragged out the word, hoping she'd get to the point.

"That's a lovely name, isn't it?" his mother asked. "Her given name is Tannith."

"Tanni's the one who told you about Mary Jo?" he asked, bringing her back to the discussion.

"No, Shirley did." She hesitated. "Well, on second thought, it was Tanni's boyfriend, Shaw, who told her, so I guess in a manner of speaking it *was* her daughter."

"And how did Shaw hear?" he pressed, losing track of all these names.

"Apparently Mary Jo came into Mocha Mama's this morning and was asking him a lot of questions."

"Oh."

"And he suggested she ask Grace Harding about David Rhodes."

"I see." Well, he was beginning to, anyway.

"Shirley said Shaw told her that Mary Jo looked like she was about to deliver that baby any minute."

"She's due in two weeks."

"My goodness! Do you think David Rhodes is the baby's father?" his mother breathed, as if she'd suddenly made the connection. "It makes sense, doesn't it?"

He already knew as much but preferred not to contribute to the gossip obviously making the rounds. "Did Shirley happen to say where Mary Jo is right now?" Maybe someone should check up on her. Mack had recommended she rest for the remainder of the day but he didn't like the idea of her being alone.

"No," his mother said. "She'll be fine, won't she?"

"I assume so.…"

"Good."

"Where's Dad?" Mack asked.

His mother laughed softly. "Where do you think he is?"

It didn't take a private eye—which his father was—to know the answer to that. "Shopping," Mack said with a grin.

"Right. Your father's so efficient about everything else, yet he leaves gift-buying until the last possible minute."

"I remember that one year when the only store open was the pharmacy," he recalled. "He bought you a jigsaw puzzle of the Tower of London, two romance novels and some nail polish remover."

"And he was so proud of himself," Corrie said fondly.

"We all had a good time putting that puzzle together, didn't we?" It'd been one of their better Christmases, and the family still did jigsaw puzzles every holiday. A small family tradition had come about as a result of that particular Christmas and his father's last-minute gift.

"You'll call in the morning?" his mother asked.

"I will," Mack promised. "And I'll stop by the house as soon as I'm relieved. It'll be late tomorrow afternoon. Save me some leftovers, okay?"

"Of course," his mother said. "Gloria's schedule is the reverse of yours, so she's coming over in the morning." Corrie sounded slightly more cheerful as she said, "At least we'll see you both for a little while."

After a few words of farewell, Mack snapped his cell phone shut and clipped it back on his waistband.

He'd no sooner started getting everything ready for that night's dinner than Brandon Hutton sauntered into the kitchen. "You got company."

"Me?" Mack couldn't imagine who'd come looking for him. He was new in town and didn't know many people yet.

"Some guy and a woman," Brandon elaborated.

"Did they give you a name?" Mack asked.

"Sorry, no."

Mack walked toward the front of the building and as he neared he heard voices—one of them unmistakably his sister's.

"Linnette!" he said, bursting into the room.

"Mack." She threw herself into his arms for a fierce hug.

"What are you doing here?" he asked. The last he'd heard she was in Buffalo Valley and intended to stay there for the holidays.

She slipped one arm around his waist. "It's a surprise. Pete suggested it and offered to drive me, so here I am."

Mack turned to the other man. In a phone conversation the month before, Linnette had told him she'd met a farmer and that they were seeing each other. "Mack McAfee," he said, thrusting out his hand.

Pete's handshake was firm. "Pleased to meet you, Mack."

"Happy to meet you, too." He turned back to his sister. "Mom doesn't know?"

Linnette giggled. "She doesn't have a clue. Dad, either. It's going to be a total shock to both of them."

"When did you arrive?"

"About five minutes ago. We decided to come and see you first, then we're going to the house."

"Dad's out doing his Christmas shopping."

Linnette laughed and looked at Pete. "What did I tell you?"

"That he'd be shopping," Pete said laconically.

"Mom's busy cooking, I'll bet." This comment was directed at Mack.

"My favorite salad," he informed her. "Even though I won't be there, she's making it for me. I'm already looking forward to the leftovers. Oh, and she's doing a ham this year."

Linnette laughed again. "She discussed her Christmas menu with you?"

"In minute detail."

"Poor Mom," Linnette said.

"I wish I could see the expression on her face when you walk in the door."

"I love that we're going to surprise her." Linnette's wide grin was perhaps the best Christmas gift he could have received. His sister, happy again.

Mack hadn't seen her smile like this in…well, a year anyway.

"Call me later and let me know how long it takes Mom to stop crying."

"I will," Linnette said.

His sister and Pete left for the house, and Mack returned to the firehouse kitchen, where he was assigned cooking duty that evening. He resumed chopping onions for the vat of chili he planned to make—how was that for Christmas Eve dinner? He caught himself wishing he could be at his parents' place tonight, after all. Although he'd just met Pete, Mack sensed that he was a solid, hard-working, no-nonsense man. Exactly what Linnette needed, and someone Mack wanted to know better.

It seemed that Linnette had found the kind of person *she* needed, but had he? Mack shook his head.

And yet, he couldn't forget Mary Jo Wyse.

Which wasn't remotely logical, considering that their relationship consisted mostly of him taking her blood pressure.

And yet…

Eleven

Linc drove down Harbor Street, peering out at both sides of the street. Fortunately, the snow had let up—Ned was probably disappointed by that. He wasn't sure what he was searching for, other than some clue as to where he might locate his runaway sister. He'd give anything to see that long brown coat, that colorful striped scarf....

"Nice town," Ned commented, looking around.

Linc hadn't noticed. His mind was on Mary Jo.

"They seem to go all out with the Christmas decorations," Mel added.

Ned poked his head between the two of them and braced his arms against the back of their seats. "Lots of lights, too."

"There's only one that I can see," Linc said, concentrating on the road ahead. His brothers were so easily distracted, he thought irritably.

They exchanged knowing glances.

"What?" Linc barked. He recognized that look. In fact, he'd already seen it several times today.

"In case you weren't aware of it, there are lights on every lamppost all through town," Ned pointed out slowly, as if he was speaking to a child. "The street is decorated with Christmas lights. And that clock tower, too, with the Christmas tree in front of it."

"I was talking about traffic signals," Linc said.

"Oh, signals. Yeah, you're right about that." As Linc drove through the downtown area, there'd been just that one traffic light. Actually, he was going back to it. He made a sharp U-turn.

"Where are you going?" Mel asked, clutching the handle above the passenger window.

"Back to the light—the traffic light, I mean."

"Why?" Ned ventured with some hesitation.

Linc's mood had improved since they'd arrived in Cedar Cove. The traffic was almost nonexistent and his sister was here. Somewhere.

He tried to think like Mary Jo. Where could she be? It had started to get dark, although it was barely four in the afternoon. Twilight had already settled over the snowy landscape.

"Practically everything in town is closed for the day," Mel said, pressing his face against the passenger window like an anxious child.

"Stands to reason. It's Christmas Eve." Ned sounded as if he was stating something neither Linc nor Mel had discovered yet.

Linc waited for the light before making a sharp left-hand turn. The road ended at a small traffic circle that went around a totem pole. The building to the right with the large mural was the library, and there was a large, mostly vacant parking lot situated to his left. Directly in front of him was a marina and a large docked boat.

The sign read Passenger Ferry.

Linc immediately went through the traffic circle and pulled into the parking lot.

"Why are we stopping here?" Mel asked in surprise. "Not that I'm complaining. I could use a pit stop."

"Yeah, me, too," Ned chimed in. "Let's go, okay?"

"Come on," Mel said. "I wanna hit the men's room."

"How did Mary Jo get to Cedar Cove?" he asked them both, ignoring their entreaties. "The ferry, right? Isn't that what we figured?"

"Yeah, she must've taken it to Bremerton," Mel agreed. "And then she rode the foot ferry across from Bremerton to Cedar Cove." He pointed to the boat docked at the end of the pier.

Linc playfully ruffled his brother's hair. "Give the man a cigar."

Mel jerked his head aside. "Hey, don't do that." He combed his fingers through his hair to restore it to order.

Linc swung open the truck door and climbed out.

"Where you goin' now?" Mel asked, opening his own door.

"It's not for us to question why," Ned intoned and clambered out, too.

Linc sighed. "I'm going to ask if anyone saw a pregnant girl on the dock this morning."

"Good idea," Ned said enthusiastically. "Meanwhile, we'll visit that men's room over there."

"Fine," Linc grumbled, scanning the street as he waited for them. Unfortunately he hadn't found anyone to question in the vicinity of the dock. The only nearby place that seemed to be doing business was a pub—imaginatively called the Cedar Cove Tavern.

"I Saw Mommy Kissing Santa Claus" blasted out the door the instant Linc opened it. A pool table dominated one side of the establishment; a man was leaning over it, pool cue in hand, while another stood by watching. They looked over their shoulders when the three brothers came inside.

Linc walked up to the bar.

The bartender, who had a full head of white hair and was wearing a Santa hat, ambled over to him. "What can I get you boys?"

"Coke for me." Linc was driving, so he wasn't interested in anything alcoholic. Besides, he'd need a clear head once he tracked down his obstinate younger sister.

"I'll have a beer," Mel said. He propped his elbows on the bar as though settling in for a long winter's night.

"Coke," Ned ordered, sliding onto the stool on Linc's other side.

The bartender served them speedily.

Linc slapped a twenty-dollar bill on the scarred wooden bar. "You seen a pregnant woman around today?" he asked. "Someone from out of town?"

The man frowned. "Can't say I have."

"She's *real* pregnant." For emphasis Mel held both hands in front of his stomach.

"Then I definitely didn't," Santa informed them.

"She arrived by foot ferry," Ned told him. "Probably sometime midmorning."

"Sorry," Santa Claus said. "I didn't start my shift until three." He rested his bulk against the counter and called out, "Anyone here see a pregnant gal come off the foot ferry this morning?"

The two men playing pool shook their heads. The other patrons stopped their conversation, glanced at Linc and his brothers, then went back to whatever they were discussing.

"Doesn't look like anyone else did either," the bartender told them.

The brothers huddled over their drinks. "What we gotta do," Mel said, "is figure out what her agenda would be."

"She came to find David's parents," Ned reminded them. "*That's* her agenda."

"True." Okay, they both had a point. Turning back to the bartender, Linc caught his attention. "You know any people named Rhodes in the area?"

Santa nodded as he wiped a beer mug. "Several."

"This is an older couple. They have a son named David."

The bartender frowned. "Oh, I know David. He stiffed me on a sixty-dollar tab."

Yeah, they were talking about the same guy, all right. "What about his parents?"

"Ben and Charlotte." Santa folded his arms across his chest. "Really decent folks. I don't have anything good to say about their son, though."

"Where do they live?"

"I'm not sure."

Looking around, Linc saw a pay phone near the restrooms. "I'll check if Ben Rhodes is in the phone book," he said, leaving his stool.

"Sounds like a plan," Santa muttered.

Linc removed the phone book from a small shelf. The entire directory was only half an inch thick. The Seattle phone book had a bigger section just of government agencies than the combined Cedar Cove White *and* Yellow Pages. He quickly found the listing for Ben and Charlotte Rhodes, then copied down the phone number and address.

"Got it," he announced triumphantly.

"Should we call?"

"Nope."

"Why not?" Mel asked. He walked back to the bar and downed the last of his beer.

"I don't want to give Mary Jo a heads-up that we're in town. I think the best thing to do is take her by surprise."

Ned nodded, although he seemed a bit uncertain.

Linc thanked the bartender, got some general directions and collected his change. He left a generous tip; it was Christmas Eve, after all. Then he marched toward the door, his brothers scrambling after him.

In the parking lot again, Linc climbed into the truck and started the engine. He'd noticed that Harbor Street angled up the hill. He guessed David's parents' street wasn't far from this main thoroughfare. Trusting his instincts, he returned to the traffic signal, took a left and followed the road until it intersected with Pelican Court.

Within five minutes of leaving the tavern, Linc was parked on Eagle Crest Avenue, outside Ben and Charlotte Rhodes's house.

The porch light was on, and there appeared to be a light on inside, too. The house was a solid two-story dwelling, about the same age as the one he shared with his brothers in Seattle. White Christmas lights were strung along the roofline and the bushes were lighted, too. There was a manger scene on the front lawn.

"This is a neat town," Mel said. "Did you see they have an art gallery? We passed it a couple of minutes ago."

"When did you get so interested in art?" Linc asked.

"I like art."

"Since when?"

"Since now. You want to make something of it?"

"No," Linc said, puzzled by Mel's defensiveness.

Linc walked up the steps leading to the front door while his brothers stood out on the lawn. Mel amused himself by rearranging the large plastic figures in the Nativity scene.

Linc felt smug. If Mary Jo thought she'd outsmarted him, she had a lesson to learn. He didn't want to be self-righteous, but he was going to teach his little sister that she wasn't nearly as clever as she seemed to think. He also wanted Mary Jo to understand that he had her best interests at heart—now and always.

He leaned hard against the doorbell, then waited several minutes and when nothing happened, he pressed the bell a second time.

"Want me to scope out the backyard?" Ned called from the lawn.

"Sure."

His youngest brother took off and disappeared around the side of the house.

Mel trailed after Ned, while Linc stood guard on the porch. Since no one was bothering to answer—although there seemed to be people home—he stepped over to the picture window and glanced inside through the half-closed blinds.

A cat hissed at him from the windowsill on the other side. Or at least he assumed it was hissing, since its teeth were bared and its ears laid back. Startled, he took a deep breath and stepped away. Although there was a window between them, the cat glared at him maliciously, its intentions clear.

"Nice kitty, nice kitty," Linc remarked, although he knew the animal couldn't hear his attempt to be friendly. This cat was anything but. Linc didn't doubt for a moment that if he were to get inside the house, "nice kitty" would dig all his claws into him within seconds.

Linc hurried to the other side of the porch and leaned over the side, but that didn't provide him with any further information.

A minute or two later, his brothers were back. "The house is locked up. Door wouldn't budge."

This wasn't going the way Linc had planned. "Okay, so maybe they aren't home."

"Then where *are* they?" Mel demanded.

"How am I supposed to know?" Linc asked, growing irritated.

"You're the one with all the answers."

"Hey, hey," Ned said, coming to stand between his brothers. "Let's skip the sarcasm. We're looking for Mary Jo, remember?"

"Where is she?" Mel asked.

"I haven't got a clue," Ned returned calmly. "But someone must."

"Maybe we should ask a neighbor," Mel said.

"Be my guest." Linc motioned widely with his arm.

"Okay, I will. I'll try…that one." Mel marched down the steps, strode across the street and walked up to the front door. He pounded on it. Even from this distance Linc could hear his knock.

An older woman with pink rollers in her hair pulled aside the drape and peeked out.

"I just saw someone," Ned yelled. "There's someone inside."

Linc had seen her, too.

"Why isn't she answering the door?" Mel asked loudly, as if the two of them had some secret insight into this stranger.

"Would *you* answer if King Kong was trying to get in *your* front door?" Linc asked. Apparently Mel hadn't figured out that most people responded better to more sensitive treatment.

"Okay, fine," Mel shouted after several long minutes. "Be that way, lady."

"She just doesn't want to answer the door," Ned shouted back.

Mel ignored that and proceeded to the next house.

"Knock more quietly this time," Linc instructed.

Mel ignored that, too. Walking to the door, he pushed the buzzer, then turned and glanced over his shoulder.

This house seemed friendlier, Linc thought. A large ever-green wreath hung on the door and lights sparkled from the porch columns.

Again no one answered.

Losing patience, Mel looked in the front window, fram-ing his face with both hands. After peering inside for sev-eral seconds, he straightened and called out, "No one's home here."

"You want me to try?" Ned asked Linc. Mel wasn't exactly making friends in the neighborhood.

"Do you think it'll do any good?"

"Not really," Ned admitted.

A piercing blare of sirens sounded in the distance, dis-rupting the tranquility of the neighborhood.

Mel hurried back across the street. "Everyone seems to be gone. Except for the lady with those pink things in her hair."

Despite their efforts, they obviously weren't getting anywhere. "Now what?" Ned muttered.

"You got any ideas?" Linc asked his two brothers, yelling to be heard over the sirens.

"Nope," Mel said with a shrug.

"Me, neither," Linc said, not hiding his discourage-ment.

They sauntered back to the truck and climbed inside. Linc started the engine and was about to drive away from the curb when two sheriff's vehicles shot into the street and boxed him in.

The officers leaped out of their cars and pulled their weapons. "Get out of the truck with your hands up!"

Twelve

Mary Jo hadn't intended to spill her heart out to Grace, but the older woman was so warm, so sympathetic. Before long, she'd related the whole sorry tale of how she'd met and fallen in love with David Rhodes. By the time Mary Jo finished, there was a pile of used tissues on the table.

"You aren't the only one who's ever loved unwisely, my dear," Grace assured her.

"I just feel really stupid."

"Because you trusted a man unworthy of your love?" Grace asked, shaking her head. "The one who needs to be ashamed is David Rhodes."

"He isn't, though."

"No," Grace agreed. "But let me repeat a wise old saying that has served me well through the years."

"What's that?" Mary Jo asked. She dabbed tears from the corners of her eyes and blew her nose.

"Time wounds all heels," Grace said with a knowing smile. "It will with David, too."

Mary Jo laughed. "I guess the reverse is true, as well. I'll get over David and his lies…" Her voice trailed off. "Is everyone in Cedar Cove as nice as you and Cliff?" she asked a moment later.

The question seemed to surprise Grace. "I'd like to think so."

"Olivia—Ms. Griffin—certainly is." Mary Jo sighed and looked down at her hands. "That firefighter—what's his name again?"

"Mack McAfee. He's new to town."

What Mary Jo particularly remembered was that he had the gentlest touch and the most reassuring voice. She could still hear it if she closed her eyes. The way he'd knelt at her side and the protectiveness of his manner had calmed her, physically and emotionally.

"His parents live in town," Grace was explaining. "Roy McAfee is a retired Seattle detective turned private investigator, and his wife, Corrie, works in his office."

"Really." She recalled seeing Mr. McAfee's sign on Harbor Street. What a fascinating profession. She suspected Mack's father got some really interesting cases. Maybe not, though, especially in such a small town. Maybe she was just influenced by the mystery novels she loved and the shows she watched on television.

"I suppose I should change clothes before dinner," Grace said, rising from her chair with seeming reluctance. "I've enjoyed sitting here chatting with you."

"Me, too," Mary Jo told her. It'd been the most relaxing part of her day—except, of course, for her nap.

"I'll be back in a few minutes."

Mary Jo took that as her signal to leave. "I'll go to the apartment."

"Are you sure? I know Mack said you should rest but like I said, Cliff and I would be delighted if you joined our family for dinner."

"Where is Cliff?" she asked, glancing over one shoulder, assuming he must be somewhere within sight.

"He's out with his horses. They're his first love." Grace smiled as she said it.

Mary Jo had noticed the way Cliff regarded his wife. He plainly adored Grace and it was equally obvious that she felt the same about him. Mary Jo gathered they'd only been married a year or two. The wedding picture on the piano looked recent, and it was clear that their adult children were from earlier marriages.

Then, without letting herself consider the appropriateness of her question, Mary Jo said, "About what you said a few minutes ago... Have *you* ever loved unwisely?"

Grace sat down again. She didn't speak for a moment. "I did," she finally said. "I married young and then, after many years together, I was widowed. I'd just started dating again. It was a whole new world to me."

"Were you seeing Cliff?"

"Yes. He'd been divorced for years and dating was a new experience for him, too. I'd been married to Dan for over thirty years, and when another man—besides Cliff— paid attention to me, I was flattered. It was someone I'd had a crush on in high school."

"Did Cliff know about him?"

"Not at first. You see, this other man lived in another city and we emailed back and forth, and he became my obsession." Grace's mouth tightened. "I knew all along that he was married and yet I allowed our internet romance to continue. He said he was getting a divorce."

"It was a lie?"

"Oh, yes, but I believed him because I wanted to. And then I learned the truth."

"Did Cliff find out about this other man?"

Regret flashed in her eyes. "Yes—and as soon as he did, he broke off our relationship."

"Oh, no! You nearly lost him?"

"As I said, I'd learned the truth about Will by then and was crushed to lose Cliff over him. I was angry with myself for being so gullible and naive. I'd lost a wonderful man because of my foolishness. For a long time I could hardly look at my own face in the mirror."

"That's how I feel now," she whispered. *Will,* she thought. She'd heard that name before….

"It does get better, Mary Jo, I promise you that. Will, the man I was…involved with, did eventually lose his wife. She divorced him and, while I believe he had genuine feelings for me, it was too late. I wanted nothing more to do with him. So you see, he was really the one who lost out in all this."

"Cliff forgave you?"

"Yes, but it took time. I was determined never to give him cause to doubt me again. We were married soon after that and I can honestly say I've never been happier."

"It shows."

"Cliff is everything I could want in a husband."

The door off the kitchen opened just then, and Cliff came in, brushing snow from his jacket. He hung it on a peg by the door, then removed his boots. "When I left, you two were sitting right where you are now, talking away."

Grace smiled at him. "I was about to change my clothes," she said. "Keep Mary Jo entertained until I get back, will you?"

"Sure thing."

Grace hurried out, and Cliff claimed the chair next to Mary Jo. As he did, he eyed the crumpled tissues. "Looks like you two had a good heart-to-heart."

"We did," she said and then with a sigh told him, "I've been very foolish."

"I'm sure Grace told you we've all made mistakes in

our lives. The challenge is to learn from those mistakes so we don't repeat them."

"I don't intend to get myself into this predicament ever again," Mary Jo said fervently. "It's just that…" She hesitated, uncertain how much to tell him about her brothers. "I feel like my family's smothering me. I have three older brothers and they all seem to think they know what's best for me and my baby."

"They love you," he said simply.

She nodded. "That's what makes it so difficult. With my parents gone, they feel *they* should be the ones directing my life."

"And naturally you take exception to that."

"Well, yes. But when I tried to live my life my *own* way and prove how adult I was, look what happened." She pressed both hands over her stomach, staring down at it. "I made a mistake, a lot of mistakes, but I discovered something…interesting after I found out I was pregnant."

"What's that?" Cliff asked. He stretched his long legs out in front of him and leaned back, holding his coffee mug. She noticed that his hand-knit socks had a whimsical pattern of Christmas bells, at odds with his no-nonsense jeans and shirt.

"Well, at first," she began, "as you can imagine, I was terribly upset. I was scared, didn't know what to do, but after a while I began to feel really excited. There was a new life inside me. A whole, separate human being with his or her own personality. This tiny person's going to be part David, part me—and all himself. Or herself," she added, refusing to accept her brothers' certainty that the baby was a boy.

Cliff smiled. "Pregnancy is amazing, isn't it? I can't pretend to know what a woman experiences, but as a man

I can tell you that we feel utter astonishment and pride—and a kind of humbling, too."

"I think David might've felt like that in the beginning," Mary Jo whispered. He really had seemed happy. Very quickly, however, that happiness had been compromised. By fear, perhaps, or resentment. She wanted to believe he'd loved her as much as he was capable of loving anyone. She now realized that his capacity for feeling, for empathy, was limited. Severely limited. Barely a month after she learned she was pregnant with his baby, David had become emotionally distant. He continued to call and to see her when he was in town but those calls and visits came less and less frequently, and the instant she started asking questions about their future, he closed himself off.

"It's not all that different with my horses," Cliff was saying.

His words broke into her reverie. "I beg your pardon?" What did he mean? They hadn't been talking about horses, had they?

"I've bred a number of horses through the years and with every pregnancy I feel such a sense of hopefulness. Which is foolish, perhaps, since even the best breeding prospects don't always turn out the way you expect. Still…"

"I met Funny Face today."

Cliff's eyes brightened when she mentioned the mare. "She's my sweetheart," he said.

"She seems very special." Mary Jo remembered the moment of connection she'd felt with this horse.

"She is," Cliff said. "She's gentle and affectionate—a dream with the grandchildren. But as far as breeding prospects go, she was a disappointment."

"No." Mary Jo found that hard to believe.

"She's smaller than we thought she'd be and she doesn't have the heart of a show horse."

"But you kept her."

"I wouldn't dream of selling Funny Face. Even though she didn't turn out like Cal and I expected, we still considered her a gift."

Mary Jo released a long sigh. "That's how I feel about my baby. I didn't plan to get pregnant and I know David certainly didn't want it, yet despite all the problems and the heartache, I've come to see this child as a gift."

"He definitely is."

"He?" She grinned. "Now you're beginning to sound like my brothers. They're convinced the baby's a boy."

"I was using *he* in a generic way," Cliff said. "Would you prefer a girl?"

"I...I don't know." She shrugged lightly. "There's nothing I can do about it, so I'll just leave it up to God." She was somewhat surprised by her own response. It wasn't something she would've said as little as six months ago.

During her pregnancy, she'd begun to reconsider her relationship with God. When she was involved with David, she'd avoided thinking about anything spiritual. In fact, she'd avoided thinking, period. The spiritual dimension of her life had shrunk, become almost nonexistent after her parents' death.

That had changed in the past few months. She thought often of the night she'd knelt by her bed, weeping and desperate, and poured out her despair, her fears and her hopes. It was nothing less than a conversation with God. That was probably as good a definition of prayer as any, she mused. Afterward, she'd experienced a feeling of peace. She liked to imagine her mother had been in the room that night, too.

"You've got everything you need?"

She realized Cliff had spoken. "I'm sorry, what did you say?" She hated to keep asking Cliff to repeat himself, but her mind refused to stay focused.

"I was asking if you have everything you need for the baby."

"Oh, yes… Thanks to my friends and my brothers." Mary Jo was grateful for her brothers' generosity to her and the baby. Their excitement at the idea of a nephew—or niece, as she kept telling them—had heartened her, even as their overzealous interference dismayed her.

Linc, who tended to be the practical one, had immediately gone up to the attic and brought down the crib that had once belonged to Mary Jo. He'd decided it wasn't good enough for her baby and purchased a new one.

Mary Jo had been overwhelmed by his thoughtfulness. She'd tried to thank him but Linc had brushed aside her gratitude as though it embarrassed him.

Mel was looking forward to having a young boy around—or a girl, as she'd reminded him, too—to coach in sports. She'd come home from work one day this month to find a tiny pair of running shoes and knew they'd come from Mel.

And Ned. Her wonderful brother Ned had insisted on getting her a car seat and high chair.

Mary Jo had knitted various blankets and booties, and her friends from the office had seen to her layette in what must have been one of the largest baby showers ever organized at the insurance company. Other than her best friend, Casey, no one had any inkling who the father was, and if they speculated, they certainly never asked. Regardless, their affection for Mary Jo was obvious and it made a difference in her life.

Just as Grace returned, Mary Jo heard the sound of a car door closing. The front door opened a moment later and a girl of about five ran inside. "Grandma! Grandma!" she cried. "I'm an angel tonight! I'm an angel tonight!"

Grace knelt down, clasping the child's hands. "You're going to be an angel in the Christmas pageant?"

The little girl's head bobbed up and down. "In church tonight."

Grace hugged her granddaughter. "Oh, Katie, you'll be the best angel ever."

The girl beamed with pride. Noticing Mary Jo, she skipped over to her. "Hi, I'm Katie."

"Hi, Katie. I'm Mary Jo."

"You're going to have a baby, aren't you?"

"Yes, I am."

The door opened again and a young couple came in. The man carried a toddler, while the woman held a large quilted diaper bag.

"Merry Christmas, Mom," Grace's daughter said, kissing her mother's cheek. She turned to Mary Jo. "Hello, I'm Maryellen. And I'm so glad you're going to be joining us," she said, smiling broadly.

Mary Jo smiled back. She'd never expected this kind of welcome, this genuine acceptance. Tonight would be one of the most memorable Christmas Eves of her life.

If only her back would stop aching....

Thirteen

"**O**fficer, let me explain," Linc said, trying his hardest to stay calm. His brothers stood on either side of him, arms raised high in the air. The deputy, whose badge identified him as Pierpont, appeared to have a nervous trigger finger.

The second officer was in his car, talking into the radio.

"Step away from the vehicle," Deputy Pierpont instructed, keeping his weapon trained on them.

The three brothers each moved forward one giant step.

"What were you doing on private property?" Pierpont bellowed as if he'd caught them red-handed inside the bank vault at Fort Knox.

"We're looking for our sister," Mel blurted out. "She ran away this morning. We've got to find her."

"She's about to have a baby," Linc said, feeling some clarification was required.

"Then why are you *here?*" the deputy asked, his tone none too friendly.

"Because," Linc said, fast losing patience, "this is where we *thought* she'd be."

The second officer approached them. His badge said he was Deputy Rogers. "We had two separate phone calls from neighbors who claimed three men were breaking into this house."

"We weren't breaking in!" Mel turned to his brothers to confirm the truth.

"I looked in the window," Linc confessed, shaking his head. "I didn't realize that was a crime."

Pierpont snickered. "So we got a Peeping Tom on our hands."

"There's no one at home!" Linc shouted. "There was nothing to peep at except a crazed cat."

"I tried to open the back door," Mel said in a low voice.

"Why'd you do that?" Rogers asked.

"Well, because…" Mel glanced at Linc.

As far as Linc was concerned, Mel was the one who'd opened his big mouth; he could talk his own way out of this.

"Go on," Rogers prodded. "I'd be interested to know why you tried to get into this house when your brother told us you were searching for your sister *and* that you knew there was no one here."

"Okay, okay," Mel said hurriedly. "I probably shouldn't have tried the door, but I suspected Mary Jo was inside and I wanted to see if that elderly couple was at home or just hiding from us."

"*I'd* hide if the three of you came pounding on my door." Again this was from Deputy Rogers.

"What did I tell you, Jim?" Pierpont said. Mel's comment seemed to verify everything the officers already believed. "Why don't we all go down to the sheriff's office so we can sort this out."

"Not without my attorney," Linc said in a firm voice. He wasn't going to let some deputy fresh out of the academy railroad him. "We didn't break any law. We came to the Rhodes residence in good faith. All we want…all we care about is locating our little sister, who's pregnant and alone and in a strange town."

At that point another car pulled up to the curb, and a middle-aged man stepped out, dressed in street clothes.

"Now you're really in for it," Pierpont said. "This is Sheriff Troy Davis."

As soon as Sheriff Davis walked toward them, Linc felt relieved. Troy Davis was obviously a seasoned officer and looked like a man he could reason with.

The sheriff frowned at the young deputies. "What's the problem here?"

They both started talking at once.

"We got a call from dispatch," Pierpont began.

"Two calls," Rogers amended.

"From neighbors, reporting suspicious behavior," Pierpont continued.

"The middle one here admits he was trying to open the back door."

Mel leaned forward. "Just checking to see if it was locked."

Linc groaned and turned to his brother. "Why don't you keep your trap shut before we end up spending Christmas in jail."

To his credit, Mel did seem chagrined. "Sorry, Linc. I wanted to help."

Linc appealed directly to the sheriff. "I understand we might have looked suspicious, peeking in windows, Sheriff Davis, but I assure you we were merely trying to figure out if the Rhodes family was at home."

"Are you family or friends of Ben and Charlotte's?" the man asked, studying them through narrowed eyes.

"Not exactly friends."

"Our sister knows Ben's son," Ned told them.

Mel nodded emphatically. "Knows him in the Biblical sense, if you catch my drift."

Linc wanted to kick Mel but, with all the law enforcement surrounding them, he didn't dare. They'd probably arrest him for assault. "Our sister's having David Rhodes's baby," he felt obliged to explain.

"Any day now," Mel threw in.

"And she disappeared," Ned added.

"If we're guilty of anything," Linc said, gesturing with his hands, "it's being anxious to locate our sister. Like I said, she's alone in a strange town and without family or friends."

"Did you check their identification?" the sheriff asked.

"We hadn't gotten around to that yet," Deputy Rogers replied.

"You'll see we're telling the truth," Linc asserted. "None of us have police records."

With the sheriff and his deputies watching carefully, Linc, Mel and Ned handed him their identification.

The sheriff glanced at all three pieces, then passed them to Pierpont. The young man swaggered over to his patrol car, apparently to check for any warrants or arrest records. He was back a couple of minutes later and returned their ID.

"They don't have records." He seemed almost disappointed, Linc thought.

The sheriff nodded. "What's your sister's name?"

"Mary Jo Wyse," Linc answered. "Can you tell us where we might find the Rhodes family? All we want to do is talk to them."

"Unfortunately Ben and Charlotte are out of the country," the sheriff said.

"You mean they aren't even in town?" Mel asked,

sounding outraged. He turned to Linc. "What are we going to do *now?*"

"I don't know." Mary Jo must have discovered this information about the Rhodes family on her own. The only thing left for her to do was head back to Seattle. She wouldn't have any other options, which meant this entire venture through dismal traffic, falling snow and wretched conditions had been a complete waste of time.

"She's probably home by now and wondering where the three of us are," Linc muttered.

"Maybe." Ned shook his head. "But I doubt it."

"What do you mean, you doubt it?"

"Mary Jo can be stubborn, you know, and she was pretty upset last night."

"We should phone the house and see if she's there," Linc said, although he had a sneaking suspicion that Ned was right. Mary Jo wouldn't give up that easily.

"Sounds like a good idea to me," Sheriff Davis inserted.

Linc reached for his cell phone and called home. Five long rings later, voice mail kicked in. If his sister *had* gone back to Seattle, she apparently wasn't at the house.

"She's not there," Linc informed his brothers.

"What did I tell you?" Ned sighed. "I know Mary Jo, and she isn't going to turn tail after one setback."

This was more than a simple setback, in Linc's opinion. This was major.

"Have you tried her cell phone?" the sheriff suggested next.

"Yeah, we did. A few times. No answer," Linc said tersely.

"Try again."

"I'll do that now." Linc took out his phone again and realized he didn't know her number nor had he programmed it into his directory.

He cleared his throat. "Ah, Ned, could you give me the number for her cell?"

His youngest brother grabbed the phone from him and punched in Mary Jo's number, then handed it back.

Linc waited impatiently for the call to connect. After what seemed like minutes, the phone automatically went to voice mail. "She's not answering that, either."

"Maybe her cell battery's dead," the sheriff said. "It could be she's out of range, too."

Actually, Linc was curious as to why the sheriff himself had responded to dispatch. One would think the man had better things to do—like dealing with *real* criminals or spending the evening with his family. "Listen, Sheriff, is Cedar Cove so hard up for crime that the sheriff responds personally to a possible break-in?"

Troy Davis grinned. "I was on my way to my daughter's house for dinner when I heard the call."

"So you decided to come out here and see what's going on."

"Something like that."

Linc liked the sheriff. He seemed a levelheaded guy, whereas his deputies were overzealous newbies, hoping for a bit of excitement. He'd bet they were bored out of their minds in a quiet little town like Cedar Cove. The call about this supposed break-in had sent these two into a giddy state of importance.

"The only essential thing here is finding our sister," Linc reiterated to the sheriff.

"The problem is, we don't know *where* to find her," Ned put in.

The sheriff rubbed the side of his face. "Did you ask around town?"

No one at the pub had been able to help. "Not really. We asked the guys at some tavern, but they didn't seem aware of much except how full their glasses were."

The sheriff grinned and seemed to appreciate Linc's wry sense of humor.

"She's *very* pregnant," Ned felt obliged to remind everyone. "It isn't like someone wouldn't notice her."

"Yeah." Mel once more thrust his arms out in front of him and bloated his cheeks for emphasis.

Linc made an effort not to groan.

"Wait," Deputy Pierpont said thoughtfully. "Seems to me I heard something about a pregnant woman earlier."

That got Linc's attention. "Where?" he asked urgently. "When?"

"I got a friend who's a firefighter and he mentioned it."

"What did he say?"

Deputy Pierpont shrugged. "Don't remember. His name's Hutton. You could go to the fire station and ask."

"Will do." Linc stepped forward and shook hands with the sheriff and then, for good measure and goodwill, with each of the deputies. "Thanks for all your help."

Troy Davis nodded. "You tell your sister she shouldn't have worried you like this."

"Oh, I'll tell her," Linc promised. He had quite a few other things he planned to say to her, too.

After receiving directions to the fire station, they jumped back in the truck. Finally they were getting somewhere, Linc told himself with a feeling of satisfaction. It was just a matter of time before they caught up with her.

It didn't take them long to locate the fire station.

Rather than repeat their earlier mistakes—or what Linc considered mistakes—he said, "Let me do the talking, understand?"

"Okay," Ned agreed.

"Mel?"

"Oh, all right."

They walked into the station house and asked to speak to the duty chief, who eyed them cautiously.

Linc got immediately to the point. "I understand that earlier today you responded to an incident involving a young pregnant woman. A firefighter named Hutton was mentioned in connection with this call. Is that correct?"

When the chief didn't reply, Linc added, "If so, we believe that's our sister."

The man raised his eyebrows, as if determined not to give out any information.

"She needs her family, chief."

There must've been some emotion in Linc's voice, some emotion he didn't even know he'd revealed, because the man hesitated, then excused himself. He returned a few minutes later, followed by a second man.

"This is Mack McAfee. He's one of the EMTs who took the call."

"You saw Mary Jo?" Linc asked. He extended his hand, and Mack shook it in a friendly fashion.

"I did."

Linc's relief was so great he nearly collapsed into a nearby chair. "That's great!"

"She's okay, isn't she?" Ned said anxiously. "She hasn't gone into labor or anything?"

"No, no, she had a dizzy spell."

"Dizzy?" Linc repeated and cast a startled look at his brothers.

"Does that mean what I think it means?" Mel asked.

Linc felt sick to his stomach. "I was twelve when Mary Jo was born and I remember it like it was yesterday. Mom got real dizzy that morning and by noon Mary Jo had arrived."

"That's not generally a sign of oncoming labor," Mack reassured him.

"It is in our family. Dad told me it was that way with each and every pregnancy. According to him, Mom had very quick deliveries and they all started with a dizzy spell. He barely made it to the hospital in time with Mary Jo. In fact—"

"She was born while Dad was parking the car," Mel said. "He dropped Mom off at the emergency door and then he went to look for a parking space."

That tale had been told around the kitchen table for years. Once their father had parked the car and made his way back to the hospital, he was met by the doctor, who congratulated him on the birth of his baby girl.

"Do you know where she is?" Linc asked with renewed urgency.

"You might talk to Grace Harding," Mack said.

"Who's Grace Harding?"

"The librarian." Mack paused for a moment. "Mary Jo was at the library when I treated her."

"The library?" That didn't make any sense to Linc. Why had Mary Jo gone to the library?

"What was she doing there?" Mel asked.

"That isn't as important as where she is now," Linc said. "Mack, do you have any idea where she might've gone after she left the library?" He remembered seeing it earlier. The building with the mural.

Mack shook his head. "She didn't say, although I told her to put her feet up and rest for a few hours."

"She must've gotten a hotel room." They should have realized that earlier. Of course! If Mr. and Mrs. Rhodes were out of town, that was exactly what Mary Jo would have done.

"I don't think so," Mack said. "I thought I'd check on her myself and discovered she isn't at any of the motels in town."

"Why not?"

"No rooms available."

"Where would she go?"

"My guess," Mack said slowly, "is to Grace Harding's house."

"Why her place?"

"Because it seems like the kind of thing Mrs. Harding would do. I have the Hardings' phone number. I could call if you'd like."

Linc couldn't believe their good fortune. "Please."

The firefighter was gone for what seemed like a long time. He returned wearing a grin. "You can talk to her yourself if you want."

Linc bolted to his feet, eager to hear the sound of his sister's voice. He'd been upset earlier—angry, worried, close to panic—but all he felt now was relief.

"She's at the Harding ranch in Olalla."

The three brothers exchanged smiling glances. "Is she all right?"

"She said she's feeling great, but she also said she's ready to go home if you're willing to come and get her."

"Wonderful." Linc couldn't have wished for anything more.

"I'll give you directions to the Harding place. She's on the phone now if you'd like to chat."

Linc grinned, following Mack to the office, his brothers on his heels.

This was finally working out. They'd get Mary Jo home where she belonged.

Fourteen

"No, please," Mary Jo said, looking at Grace and her family. "I want you to go to the Christmas Eve service, just like you planned."

"Are you positive?" Grace seemed uncertain about leaving her behind.

Mary Jo had bowed to their entreaties and been their guest for a truly wonderful dinner, but she had no intention of imposing on them any further that evening.

"I am." There was no reason for them to stay home because of her, either. This crazy adventure of hers was over; she'd admitted defeat. Her brothers were on their way and she'd be back in Seattle in a couple of hours.

"I'd like to meet those young men," Grace said. "But it sounds as if they'll get here while we're at church."

"You will meet them," Mary Jo promised. "Sometime after Christmas." In one short afternoon, she'd become strongly attached to both Grace Harding and Cliff. Her two daughters, her daughter-in-law, their husbands and the grandchildren had made Mary Jo feel like part of the family. They'd welcomed her without question, opened their hearts and their home to her, given her a place to sleep, a meal, the comfort of their company. In this day and age, Mary Jo knew that kind of unconditional friendship wasn't the norm. This was a special family and she planned to keep in touch with them.

While the fathers loaded up the kids and Cliff brought his car around, Grace lingered.

"You have our phone number?" she asked as they stood by the front door.

"Oh, yes. Cell numbers, too." Mary Jo patted her pants pocket. Grace had carefully written out all the numbers for her.

"You'll call us soon."

Mary Jo nodded. Grace was like the mother she'd lost—loving, protective, accepting. And now that she was becoming a mother herself, she valued her memory even more profoundly. It was Grace who'd reminded Mary Jo of everything her mother had been to her, of everything *she* wanted to be to her own child. Even though her baby wasn't born yet, she felt blessed. She was grateful for everything her pregnancy had brought her. A new maturity, the knowledge that she could rise to the occasion, that she had the strength to cope. This brand-new friendship. And, of course, the baby to come.

"If your brothers are hungry when they get here, there are plenty of leftovers," Grace was saying. "Tell them to help themselves."

"Thank you."

Cliff parked the car closer to the house and got out to open the passenger door. Still Grace lingered. "Don't hesitate to phone if you need *anything,* understand?"

"I won't—and thank you." Wearing her coat like a cloak, Mary Jo walked outside with her into the clear, beautiful night. Snow outlined the branches of trees, and the air was crisp.

"Wait in the house," Grace said.

"I'll be fine in the apartment. It's comfortable there."

The two women hugged and Grace slid into the car next to her husband. Maryellen, Kelly and Lisa, with their families, had already left for the church.

Grace lowered the window. "Thank you for being so patient with Tyler," she said, giving her an apologetic look.

Mary Jo smiled, completely enchanted with the six-year-old who'd received a drum for Christmas and had pounded away on it incessantly.

"He's a talented little boy." In fact, she loved all of Grace and Cliff's grandchildren.

"Now go inside before you get cold," Grace scolded.

But Mary Jo remained in the yard until the car lights faded from sight. Then, pulling her coat more snugly around her, she strolled toward the barn. Several of the participants in the live Nativity scene were inside a corral attached to the barn and she went there first.

"Hello, donkey," she said. "Merry Christmas to you."

As if he understood that she was talking to him, the donkey walked toward her until he was within petting range. Mary Jo stroked his velvety nose, then walked into the barn.

"Hello, everyone."

At the sound of her voice, Funny Face stuck her head over the stall door.

"Hi there," Mary Jo greeted the mare. "I hear you're very special to Cliff," she said. Funny Face nickered loudly in response.

Apparently curious about what was causing all the commotion, the camel poked her head out, too. "Sorry, camel," Mary Jo called, "but your reputation has preceded you and I'm not giving you a chance to bite *my* arm."

After several minutes of chatting with the other horses, Mary Jo washed her hands at a sink in the barn and headed up the stairs to the apartment. About halfway up, her back started to ache again. She pressed one hand against it and continued climbing, holding on to the railing with the other.

When she reached the apartment, she paused in the middle of removing her coat as she felt a powerful tightening across her stomach.

Was this labor?

She suspected it must be, but everything she'd heard and read stated that contractions began gradually. What she'd just experienced was intense and had lasted several long, painful seconds. Another contraction came almost right away.

Mary Jo checked her watch this time. Three minutes later there was a third contraction of equal severity.

Only three minutes.

At the class she'd attended, she'd learned that it wasn't uncommon for labor pains to start at fifteen-minute intervals. Perhaps hers had started earlier and she hadn't noticed. That didn't seem possible, though. How could she be in labor and not know it? Except…there were all those family stories about her mother and how a dizzy spell always signaled the onset of labor. A dizzy spell like the one she'd had at the library…

The next pain caught her unawares and she grabbed her stomach and doubled over.

"*That* got my attention," she announced to the empty room.

Not sure what to do next, Mary Jo paced, deliberating on the best course of action. Her brothers were due any moment. If she told them she was in labor the second they arrived, they'd panic. One thing Mary Jo knew: she did *not* want her three brothers delivering this baby.

None of them had any experience or even the slightest idea of what to do. Linc would probably order the baby to wait until they could get to a hospital. Knowing Mel and his queasy stomach, he'd fall over in a dead faint, while Ned would walk around declaring that this was just perfect. He was going to be an uncle to a baby born on Christmas Eve—or Christmas Day, depending on how long this labor business was going to take.

Three minutes later, another pain struck and again Mary Jo bent double with the strength of it. She exhaled slowly and timed it, staring at her watch. This contraction lasted thirty seconds. Half a minute. It wasn't supposed to happen this fast! Labor was supposed to go on for hours and hours.

Mary Jo didn't know what to do or who to call. Her mind was spinning, her thoughts scrambling in a dozen different directions at once. She considered phoning Grace. If she was going to give birth here, at the ranch, she wanted a woman with her—and she couldn't think of anyone she'd rather have than Grace Harding. But Grace had left just a few minutes before and the only way to reach her was by cell phone. Unfortunately, as she'd learned earlier, coverage in this area was sporadic at best. And she hated to interfere with the Hardings' Christmas plans.

The second person she thought of was Mack McAfee. He'd been so kind, and he was a trained medical technician. He was calm and logical, which was exactly what she needed. He'd called—when was it? Half an hour ago—and urged her to go home with her brothers. There'd be plenty of time to talk to Ben and Charlotte Rhodes after the baby's birth. Her brothers wouldn't have the opportunity to confront David or his father now, anyway, and she'd manage, somehow or other, to prevent it in the future, too. While she was speaking with Linc, she'd realized how desperate her brothers had been to find her. Mary Jo hadn't meant to worry them like this.

If Linc or Mel or even Ned had reasoned with her like Mack had, she would've listened. Too late to worry about any of that now...

Mary Jo went back down the stairs to the barn. She didn't want to dial 9-1-1 and cause alarm the way she had with her dizzy spell at the library earlier, so she decided to call the fire station directly.

The barn phone was the same number as the house. Sure enough, when she picked up the receiver she saw that Caller ID displayed the number of the last call received—the firehouse. Mary Jo pushed the redial button.

On the second ring, someone picked up. "Kitsap County Fire District."

Relief washed over her at the sound of Mack's voice. "Mack?"

There was a slight hesitation. "Mary Jo? Is that you?"

"Ye-es."

"What's wrong?"

"I... Grace and her family left for the Christmas Eve service about ten minutes ago. I didn't go because my brothers are on their way here."

"They haven't arrived yet?" He seemed surprised.

"Not yet."

Mack groaned. "I'll bet they're lost."

Mary Jo didn't doubt that for an instant.

"I'm sure they'll be there anytime," he said.

"I hate to bother you," she whispered and gasped at the severity of the next contraction.

"Mary Jo!"

Closing her eyes, she mentally counted until the pain subsided.

"What's wrong?" he asked urgently.

"I'm afraid I've gone into labor."

Mack didn't miss a beat. "Then I should get out there so I can transport you to the birthing center."

At the rate this was progressing, he'd better not lose any time. "Thank you," she said simply.

He must have sensed her fear, because he asked, "How far apart are the contractions?"

"Three minutes. I've been timing them."

"That's good."

"I didn't take all the birthing classes… I wish I had, but David said he'd take them with me and it never happened. I went once but that was just last week and—"

"You'll do fine. If you want, I'll stay with you."

"You?"

"I'm not a bad coach."

"You'd be a wonderful coach, but you have to remember I've only had the one class."

"Listen, instead of talking about it over the phone, why don't I hop in the aid car and drive over."

"Ri-ight." At the strength of the last contraction, Mary Jo was beginning to think this was an excellent idea.

"Where are you?"

"In the barn at the moment." She gave a small laugh.

"Why is that funny?"

"I'm with the animals from the live Nativity scene."

Mack laughed then, too. "That seems appropriate under the circumstances, but I want you to go to the house and wait for me there."

"I'd rather go back to the apartment if you don't mind." It was hard to explain but the place felt like home to her now, at least for this one night.

"Fine. Just don't lock the door. I'll be there soon, so hold on, okay?"

She didn't have any choice but to hold on. "Okay. But, Mack?"

"Yes?"

"Please hurry."

"You got it. I'm leaving now."

"No sirens, please," she begged, and Mack chuckled as if she'd made some mildly amusing joke.

Walking seemed to help, and instead of following Mack's instructions, she paced the length of the barn once, twice, three times.

She noticed that the camel was watching her every move. "Don't be such a know-it-all," she said. She'd swear the creature was laughing at her. "This isn't supposed to be happening yet."

A sheep walked up to the gate, bleating loudly, and Mary Jo wagged her index finger. "I don't want to hear from you, either."

All the horses in their stalls studied her with interest, but the only one who looked at her with anything that resembled compassion was Funny Face.

"Wish me well, Funny Face," Mary Jo whispered as she started back up the stairs. "I need all the good wishes I can get."

Absorbed in the cycle of pain and then relief, followed by pain again, Mary Jo lost track of time. Finally she heard a vehicle pull into the yard. A moment later, Mack entered the apartment, a second man behind him. They were both breathless; they must have run up the stairs.

Mary Jo was so grateful to see him she nearly burst

into tears. Clutching her belly, she walked over to Mack and said hoarsely, "I'm so glad you came."

"How's it going?"

"Not…good."

"Any sign of your brothers?"

She shook her head.

Mack glanced over his shoulder at the second EMT. "This is Brandon Hutton. Remember him from this morning?"

"Hi." Mary Jo raised her hand and wiggled her fingers.

"How far apart are the pains now?"

"Still three minutes, but they're lasting much longer."

Mack turned to the other man. "I think we'd better check her before we transport."

"I agree."

This was all so embarrassing, but Mary Jo would rather be dealing with Mack than any of her brothers. Mack would be impersonal about it, professional. And, most important of all, he knew what he was doing.

Taking her by the hand, Mack led her into the bedroom. He pulled back the sheets, then covered the bed with towels. Mary Jo lay down on the mattress and closed her eyes.

"Okay," Mack announced when he'd finished. "You're fully dilated. You're about to enter the second phase of labor."

"What does that mean?"

"Basically, it means we don't have time to take you to the hospital."

"Then who's going to deliver my baby?" she asked, fighting her tears.

"It looks like that'll be me," he said calmly.

Mary Jo held out her hand to him and Mack grabbed it in both of his.

"Everything's going to be fine," he said with such confidence she couldn't help believing him. "You can do this. And I'll be with you every step of the way."

Fifteen

"Admit it," Mel taunted, "we're lost."

"I said as much thirty minutes ago." Linc spoke through tightly clenched teeth. He didn't need his brother to tell him what he already knew.

"We should've gotten the Hardings' phone number," Ned commented from the backseat.

That was obvious. "You might've mentioned it at the time," Linc snapped. They'd been driving around for almost an hour and he had no idea where they were. Mack McAfee had drawn them a map but it hadn't helped; somehow they'd gone in the wrong direction and were now completely and utterly lost.

To further complicate matters, a fog had settled in over the area. It seemed they'd run the gamut of Pacific Northwest winter weather, and all within the last eight hours. There'd been sleet and snow, rain and cold. Currently they were driving through a fog so thick he could hardly see the road.

"Read me the directions again," he said.

Mel flipped on the interior light, which nearly blinded Linc. "Hey, turn that off!"

"I thought you wanted me to read these notes."

"You don't need the light," Ned told him. "I've got them memorized."

"So where are we?" Mel asked.

"You're asking *me?*" Linc muttered in frustration.

"Okay, okay." Mel sighed deeply. "Fighting isn't going to help us find Mary Jo."

"You're right." Linc pulled over to the side of the road and shifted to face his brothers. "Either of you have any other ideas?"

"We could go to the firehouse and start over," Mel said.

"Once we're there, we could get the Hardings' phone number," Ned added. "We could call and let Mary Jo know we're on our way."

Linc closed his eyes. "Fine. But have either of you geniuses figured out *how* to get back to the firehouse?"

"Ah…" Mel glanced at Ned, who shrugged his shoulders.

"I guess we can't do that, because we're lost."

"Exactly," Linc said. "Any *other* ideas?" He was feeling more helpless and frustrated by the second.

"We could always ask someone," Ned suggested next.

"Who are we supposed to ask?" Mel cried. "We haven't seen another car in over half an hour."

"There was a place down this road," Ned said in a tentative voice.

Linc stared at him. "Where?"

"You're sure about that?" Mel didn't seem to believe him, and Linc wasn't convinced, either.

"It's there, trust me." Ned's expression, however, did little to inspire Linc's confidence.

"I remember the name," his youngest brother said indignantly. "It was called King's."

"What kind of place was it?"

Ned apparently needed time to consider this.

"A tavern?" Linc asked.

Ned shook his head.

"A gas-and-go?" Mel offered.

"Could've been. There were a bunch of broken-down cars out front."

Linc didn't recall any such place. "How come I didn't see it?" he asked.

"'Cause you were driving."

That actually made sense. Concentrating on maneuvering down these back roads in the fog, it was all he could do to make sure his truck didn't end up in a ditch.

"I think I saw it, too," Mel said a moment later. "The building's set off the road, isn't it?"

Ned perked up. "Yes!"

"With tires edging the driveway?"

"That's the one!"

"Do we have a prayer of finding it again?" Linc asked his brothers.

Ned and Mel exchanged looks. "I think so," Ned told him.

"Good." Linc put the pickup back in gear. "Which way?"

"Turn around," Ned told him.

Linc started down the road, then thought to ask, "Are you sure this King's place is open?"

"Looked like it to me."

"Yeah," Mel concurred. "There were plenty of lights. Not Christmas lights, though. Regular lights."

Linc drove in silence for several minutes. Both his brothers were focused on finding this joint. Just when the entire trip seemed futile, Linc crested a hill and emerged out of the fog, which made a tremendous difference in visibility. Instantly he breathed easier.

"There!" Ned shouted, pointing down the roadway.

Linc squinted and, sure enough, he saw the place his brothers had been yapping about. Maybe there was some hope, after all.

Linc had no idea how his sister had ended up in the boondocks. He wished she'd stayed in town, but, oh, no, not Mary Jo.

As they neared the building, Linc noticed a sign that said King's. Linc could see what his brother meant; it was hard to tell exactly what type of business this was. The sign certainly didn't give any indication. True, there were beat-up old cars out front, so one might assume it was some sort of junk or salvage yard. The building itself was in ill repair; at the very least, it needed a coat of paint. There wasn't a single Christmas decoration in sight.

However, the Open sign in the window was lit.

Linc walked up to the door, peered in and saw a small restaurant, basically a counter with a few stools, and a convenience store. He went inside and strolled up to the counter, taking a seat. Mel and Ned joined him.

A large overweight man wearing a stained white T-shirt and a white apron waddled over to their end of the counter as if he'd been sitting there all day, waiting for them.

"Merry Christmas," Linc said, reaching for the menu.

"Yeah, whatever."

This guy was in a charming mood.

"Whaddaya want?" the cook asked.

"Coffee for me," Linc said.

"What's the special?" Mel asked, looking at a sign on the wall that said, *Ask About Our Daily Special.*

"Meat loaf, mashed potatoes, corn."

"If you want to order food, it's gotta be takeout," Linc told his brothers, although now that the subject had come up, Linc realized he was hungry, too. Famished, in fact.

"We do takeout," the cook said, filling Linc's mug with coffee that had obviously been in the pot far too long. It was black and thick and resembled liquid tar more than coffee.

"Is that fresh?" Linc risked asking.

"Sure is. Made it yesterday."

Linc pushed the mug away. "We'll take three meat loaf sandwiches to go," he said, making a snap decision.

"You want the mashed potatoes with that?"

"Can I have potato chips instead?" Ned inquired.

"I guess."

"Say," Linc said, leaning back on the stool. "Do you happen to know where the Harding ranch is?"

The cook scowled at him. "Who's askin'?"

Linc didn't want to get into long explanations. "A friend."

Cook nodded. "Cliff's a...neighbor."

"He is?" Maybe they were closer than Linc had thought.

"Raises the best horses around these parts." The cook sounded somewhat grudging as he said this.

Linc knew car engines inside out but didn't have a clue about horses, and he had no idea how to respond.

Fortunately he didn't have to. "You fellows interested in buying one of Cliff's horses?" the old curmudgeon asked.

"Not really." Linc hoped that wasn't disappointing news. "We're, uh, supposed to be meeting our sister, who's staying at the Harding place."

"We *had* directions," Mel explained.

"But we sort of got turned around."

"In other words, we're lost," Linc said.

"Lemme make you those sandwiches."

"What about giving us directions?"

King, or whatever his name was, sighed as if this was asking too much. "I could—for a price."

Linc slapped a ten-dollar bill on the counter.

The grouch eyed the money and shrugged. "That might get you there. Then again, it might not."

Linc threw in another ten. "This is all you're getting."

"Fine." He pocketed the money and slouched off toward the kitchen. "I'll be back with your order."

Ten minutes later, he returned with a large white bag packed with sandwiches, potato chips and canned sodas. Linc decided not to ask how old the meat loaf was. He paid the tab and didn't complain about the price, which seemed seriously inflated.

"About those directions?" Linc asked.

Ned took out the map the firefighter had drawn and spread it on the linoleum counter. The route from Cedar Cove to the Harding place looked pretty direct, and Linc didn't know how he'd managed to get so confused.

"The King's gonna set you straight," the grouch told them.

"Good, because we are *lost,*" Mel said, dragging out the last word.

"Big-time lost," Ned added.

This was a point that did not need further emphasis. Linc would've preferred his brothers keep their mouths shut, but that wasn't likely to happen.

"Okay, you're here," King informed them, drawing a circle around their current location. He highlighted the street names at the closest intersection. "You're near the corner of Burley and Glenwood."

"Got it," Linc said.

"You need to head east."

"East," Linc repeated.

"Go down about two miles and you cross the highway via the overpass."

"Okay, got that."

The grouch turned the directions around and circled the Harding ranch. "This is where Cliff and Grace Harding live."

"Okay."

"So, all you do after you cross the highway is go east. Keep going until you see the water, then turn left. The Harding place will be about three-quarters of a mile down the road on the left-hand side."

"Thanks," Linc said. Those directions seemed easy enough for anyone to follow. Even the three of them.

The grouch frowned at him, and Linc assumed he was hinting for more money, which he wasn't about to get. Grabbing their sandwiches, Linc handed the bag to his youngest brother and they piled out the door.

"Merry Christmas," Ned called over his shoulder. Apparently he hadn't grasped yet that this man wasn't doing any kind of celebrating.

The grouch's frown darkened. "Yeah, whatever."

Linc waited until they were back in the vehicle before he commented. "Miserable old guy."

"A regular Scrooge," Mel said.

Ned tore open the sack and passed one sandwich to Linc and another to Mel. Linc bit into his. The old grouch made a good meat loaf sandwich, surprisingly enough, and right now that compensated for a lot.

The three of them wolfed down the food and nearly missed the sign for the highway overpass.

"Hey, you two, I'm driving," Linc said, swallowing the last bite. "Pay attention, will you?"

"Sorry." Ned stared out at the road.

"He said to drive until we can see the water," Linc reminded them.

"It's dark," Mel protested. "How are we supposed to see water?"

"We'll know when we find it," Ned put in.

Linc rolled his eyes. "I hope you're right, that's all I can say."

Linc couldn't tell how far they'd driven, but the water never came into view. "Did we miss something?" he asked his brothers.

"Keep going," Mel insisted. "He didn't say *when* we'd see the water."

"He didn't," Linc agreed, but he had a bad feeling about this. The road wasn't straight ahead the way the grouch had drawn it on the map. It twisted and turned until Linc was, once again, so confused he no longer knew if he was going east or west.

"You don't think that King guy would've intentionally given us the wrong directions, do you?"

"Why would he do that?" Mel asked. "You paid him twenty bucks."

Linc remembered the look on the other man's face. He'd wanted more. "Maybe it wasn't enough."

"Maybe Mr. Scrooge back there needs three visitors tonight," Ned suggested. "If you know what I mean."

"He had three visitors—us."

"Yeah, and I think he was trying to con us," Linc muttered.

"I guess he succeeded," Mel said, just as Ned asked, "But why? What's the point?"

"The point is that he's trying to make us miserable," Linc said. "As miserable as he is, the old coot."

The three of them fell into a glum silence. It sure didn't feel like any Christmas Eve they'd ever had before.

Sixteen

By the time Grace and Cliff arrived at church for the Christmas Eve service, both her daughters and their husbands were already seated. So were Lisa, Rich and April. Maryellen held Drake, who slept peacefully in his mother's arms. Katie, as well as Tyler, were with the other local children getting ready for the big Christmas pageant.

Katie was excited about being an angel, although Tyler, who'd been assigned the role of a shepherd, didn't show much enthusiasm for his stage debut. If he displayed any emotion at all, it was disappointment that he couldn't bring his drum. Kelly had explained to him that the shepherds of the day played the flute, not drums, because drums would frighten the sheep. The explanation satisfied Tyler, who was of a logical disposition, but it didn't please him.

Grace and Cliff located a pew directly behind her daughters and Lisa. As they slipped in, Grace whispered that she'd prefer to sit closest to the aisle, craving the best possible view of her grandchildren's performances. Once they were seated, Cliff reached for her hand, entwining their fingers.

Maryellen turned around and whispered, "Is every-thing all right with Mary Jo?"

"I think so." Grace still didn't feel comfortable about leaving her alone. But Mary Jo had been adamant that Grace join her family, so she had. Now, however, she wished she'd stayed behind.

Cliff squeezed her hand as the white-robed choir sang Christmas hymns, accompanied by the organist. "O Come All Ye Faithful" had never sounded more beautiful.

Olivia and Jack, carrying his Santa hat, came down the aisle and slid into the pew across from Grace and Cliff. Justine and Seth accompanied them. From a conversation with Justine earlier in the week, Grace knew Leif had gotten the coveted role of one of the three Wise Men.

As soon as Olivia saw Grace, she edged out of her pew and went to see her friend. Olivia had wrapped a red silk scarf around her shoulders, over her black wool coat. De-spite everything she'd endured, she remained the picture of dignity and elegance.

She leaned toward Grace. "How's Mary Jo?" she asked in a whisper.

Grace shrugged. "I left her at the house by herself, and now I wish I hadn't. Oh," she added, "apparently her brothers are in town…."

"Problems?"

Grace quickly shook her head. "Mary Jo actually seemed relieved to hear from them."

"Is she going home to Seattle with her family, then?" Olivia stepped sideways in the aisle to make room for a group of people trying to get past.

Grace nodded.

"How did they find out she was with you?" Olivia asked.

"They tracked her down through Mack McAfee. He

phoned the house and talked to her. Then Mary Jo spoke with her oldest brother and decided it would be best to go back to Seattle." Grace had been with her at the time and was struck by the way Mary Jo's spirits had lifted. Whether that was because of her brothers or because of Mack… Grace tended to think it was the latter.

"Mack appeared to have a calming effect on her when I saw them at the library," Olivia said, echoing Grace's thoughts.

"I noticed it after she got off the phone, too. I gather he suggested she should go home with her brothers."

"I'm glad," Olivia said. "For her own sake and theirs. And for Mom and Ben's…" She paused. "As necessary as it is for them to know about this baby, I'd rather it didn't happen the second they got home."

"Her real fear was that her brothers were going to burst onto the scene and demand that David do the so-called honorable thing."

"David and the word *honor* don't belong in the same sentence," Olivia said wryly.

"Mary Jo's brothers were arriving any minute. I'd like to have met them. Or at least talked to them." Grace would've phoned the house, but by now Mary Jo should be well on her way to Seattle.

Olivia straightened. "We'll catch up after the service," she said and returned to the opposite pew, beside Jack.

No sooner had Olivia sat down than Pastor Flemming stepped up to the podium. He seemed to be…at peace. Relaxed, yet full of energy and optimism. The worry lines were gone from his face. Grace knew this had been a difficult year for the pastor and his wife, and she was glad their problems had been resolved.

"Merry Christmas," he said, his voice booming across the church.

"Merry Christmas," the congregation chanted.

"Before the children come out for the pageant, I'd like us all to look at the Christmas story again. For those of us who've grown up in the church, it's become a familiar part of our lives. This evening, however, I want you to forget that you're sitting on this side of history. Go back to the day the angel came to tell Mary she was about to conceive a child."

He opened his Bible and read the well-known passages from the Book of Luke. "I want us to fully appreciate Mary's faith," he said, looking up. "The angel came to her and said she'd conceive a child by the Holy Spirit and she was to name him Jesus, which in those days was a common name." He paused and gazed out at his congregation.

"Can you understand Mary's confusion? What the angel told her was the equivalent of saying to a young woman in our times that she's going to give birth to God's son and she should name him Bob."

The congregation smiled and a few people laughed outright.

"Remember, too," Pastor Flemming continued, "that although Mary was engaged to Joseph, she remained with her family. This meant she had to tell her parents she was with child. That couldn't have been easy.

"What do you think her mother and father thought? What if one of our daughters came to us and said she was pregnant? What if she claimed an angel had told her that the child had been conceived by the work of the Holy Spirit?" Again he paused, as if inviting everyone to join him in contemplating this scenario.

Pastor Flemming grinned. "Although I have two sons and no daughters, I know what *I'd* think. I'd assume that a teenage girl—or her boyfriend—would say anything to explain how this had happened."

Most people in the congregation smiled and agreed with nodding heads. Grace cringed a little, remembering as vividly as ever the day she'd told her parents she was pregnant. She remembered their disappointment, their anger and, ultimately, their support. Then she thought of Mary Jo and turned to exchange a quick glance with Olivia.

"And yet," the pastor went on, "this child, the very son of God, was growing inside her womb. Mary revealed remarkable faith, but then so did her family and Joseph, the young man to whom she was engaged."

Something briefly distracted the pastor and he looked to his left. "I can see the children are ready and eager to begin their performance, so I won't take up any more time. I do want to say this one thing, however. As a boy, taking part in a Christmas pageant just like this, I was given the role of a shepherd standing guard over his sheep when the angel came to announce the birth of the Christ Child. When I grew up, I chose, in a sense, the very same job—that of a shepherd. Every one of you is a member of my flock and I care for you deeply. Merry Christmas."

"Merry Christmas," the congregation echoed.

As he stepped down from the podium, the children took their positions on the makeshift stage. Grace moved to the end of her pew to get a better view of the proceedings. Katie stood proudly in place, her gold wings jutting out from her small shoulders and her halo sitting crookedly atop her head. She couldn't have looked more angelic if she'd tried.

Tyler had borrowed one of Cliff's walking sticks to use as a staff. He was obviously still annoyed to be without his precious drum, glaring at the congregation as if to inform them that he was doing this under protest. Grace had to smother a laugh.

Oh, how Dan would've loved seeing his grandchildren tonight. Their grandson was like his grandfather in so many ways. A momentary sadness came over her and not wanting anyone to sense her thoughts, Grace looked away. She didn't often think about Dan anymore. She'd loved her first husband, had two daughters with him, and through the years they'd achieved a comfortable life together.

But Dan had never been the same after Vietnam. For a lot of years, Grace had blamed herself and her own failings for his unhappiness. Dan knew that and had done his best to make things right in the letter he wrote her before his death.

Christmas Eve, however, wasn't a night for troubled memories. The grandchildren Dan would never know were onstage, giving the performances of their young lives.

Out of the corner of her eye, Grace noticed Angel, the church secretary, rushing down the side aisle and toward the front. She went to the first pew, where Pastor Flemming sat with his wife, Emily.

Angel whispered something in his ear and the pastor nodded. He left with her. Apparently there was some sort of emergency.

"Look, there's a star in the East," Leif Gunderson, Olivia's grandson, shouted. As one of the three Wise Men, he pointed at the church ceiling.

"Let us follow the star," the second of the Wise Men called out.

It wasn't until Cliff tapped her arm that she realized Angel was trying to get her attention. She stood in the side aisle and motioned with her finger for Grace to come out.

"What's that about?" Cliff asked as she picked up her purse.

"I don't know. I'll tell you as soon as I find out."

He nodded.

Grace hurried down the center aisle to the foyer, reaching it just as Angel did. "What's going on?" she asked.

"It's a miracle I was even in the office," Angel said.

This confused Grace. "What do you mean?"

"For the phone call," she explained. "I went to get a pair of scissors. Mrs. Murphy, the first-grade Sunday School teacher, needed scissors and I thought there was a pair in my desk."

"The phone call," Grace reminded her.

"Oh, yes, sorry. It was from some young firefighter."

"Mack McAfee?" Grace blurted out.

"No, no, Brandon Hutton. At any rate, he wanted to speak to the pastor."

"Has there been an accident?"

"No... I don't know. I think it would be best if you talked to Pastor Flemming yourself. He asked me to get you."

Dave Flemming was on the phone, a worried expression on his face. When he saw Grace, he held out the receiver. "You'd better take this."

Grace dismissed her first fear, that there'd been an accident. Everyone she loved, everyone who was important to her here in Cedar Cove, was inside the church.

"This is Grace Harding," she said into the receiver, her voice quavering slightly.

"Ms. Harding, this is EMT Hutton from the Kitsap County Fire District. We received a distress call from a young woman who's currently at your home."

Grace gasped. "Mary Jo? She's still at the house? Is she all right?"

"I believe so, ma'am. However, she's in labor and asking for you."

"Won't you be transporting her to the hospital? Shouldn't I meet you there?" Grace would notify Cliff and they could go together.

From the moment she'd left the house, some instinct had told her she should've stayed with Mary Jo. Some inner knowledge that said Mary Jo would be having her baby not in two weeks but *now*. Tonight.

"We won't be transporting her, Ms. Harding."

"Good heavens, why not?" Grace demanded, wondering if it was a jurisdictional matter. If so, she'd get Olivia involved.

"It appears Ms. Wyse is going to give birth imminently. We don't have time to transport her."

"She's not alone, is she?"

"No, ma'am. EMT McAfee is with her."

Mack. Thank goodness. "What about her brothers?" she asked. Surely they'd arrived by now.

"There's no one else here, ma'am."

Grace's heart started to pound. "I'll get there as soon as possible."

"One last thing," Officer Hutton added. "Do you normally keep camels in your barn?"

"No. But be warned. She bites."

"She's already attempted to take a piece out of me. I managed to avoid it, though."

"Good."

She set down the receiver and turned to Pastor Flemming. "A young woman who's staying with us has gone into labor."

"So I understand."

"I'll collect my husband and get going." Grace hated to miss the pageant but there was nothing she could do about it.

Returning to the pew, she explained to Cliff what was happening. Maryellen twisted around and Grace told her, too.

"She doesn't have anything for the baby, does she?" Maryellen asked.

Grace hadn't even thought of that. She had blankets and a few other supplies for her grandchildren, but the disposable diapers would be far too big.

"Jon and I will stop by the house and get some things for Mary Jo and the baby and drop them off. I'm sure I still have a package of newborn-size diapers, too."

Grace touched her daughter's shoulder, grateful for Maryellen's quick thinking.

"We'll bring Lisa, Rich and April back to the house," Kelly whispered. "I wouldn't miss this for the world."

"Me, neither," Lisa said. "There couldn't be a more ideal way to celebrate Christmas!"

Seventeen

"You're doing great," Mack assured Mary Jo.

"No, I'm not," she cried, exhaling a harsh breath. Giving birth was hard, harder than she'd ever envisioned and the pain…the pain was indescribable.

The second EMT came back into the bedroom. "I talked to your friend and she's on her way."

"Thank God." It was difficult for Mary Jo to speak in the middle of a contraction. The pain was so intense and she panted, imitating Mack who'd shown her a breathing exercise to help deal with it.

Mack held her hand and she squeezed as tight as she could, so tight she was afraid she might be hurting him. If that was the case, he didn't let on.

"Get a cool damp washcloth," Mack instructed the other man.

"Got it." As though thankful for something to do, Brandon Hutton shot out of the room and down the hallway to the bathroom.

"I'm going to check you again," Mack told her.

"No!" She clung to his hand, gripping it even tighter. "I need you here. Beside me."

"Mary Jo, I have to see what position the baby's in."

"Okay, okay." She closed her eyes. Sweat poured off her forehead. Now she knew why giving birth was called *labor*. This was the hardest thing she'd ever done. Unfortunately there wasn't time to go to any more classes, or to finish reading the books she'd started…. She'd thought she had two more weeks. If only she hadn't waited for David, or believed him when he said he wanted to attend the classes with her. *This* was what she got for trusting him.

Suddenly liquid gushed from between her legs. "What was that?" she cried.

"Your water just broke."

"Oh." She'd forgotten about that. She had a vague recollection of other women's stories about their water breaking.

"That's good, isn't it?" she asked. What she hoped was that it meant her baby was almost ready to be born and this agony would come to an end.

"It's good," he told her.

"It'll be better now, right?"

Mack hesitated.

"What's wrong?" she demanded. "Tell me."

"Your labor may intensify."

This had to be a cruel joke. "Intensify." She couldn't imagine how the pains could get any stronger than they were now. "What do you mean…intensify?"

"The contractions will probably last longer…."

"Oh, no," she moaned.

Although she'd discovered this was Mack's first birth, he knew so much more than she did. He'd at least studied it and obviously paid attention during class. Mack had joked that he was getting on-the-job training—and so was she, but that part didn't seem so amusing anymore.

"The baby's fully in the birth canal. It won't be long

now, Mary Jo. Just a few more pains and you'll have your baby."

"Thank God." Mary Jo didn't know how much more of this she could take.

"Rest between contractions," Mack advised.

Brandon Hutton returned with a damp washcloth. Mack took it from him and wiped her face. The cool cloth against her heated skin felt wonderfully refreshing.

At the approach of another pain, she screamed, "Mack! Mack!"

Instantly he was at her side, his hand holding hers. Her fingers tightened around his.

"Count," she begged.

"One, two, three…"

The numbers droned on and she concentrated on listening to the even cadence of Mack's voice, knowing that by the time he reached fifty, the contraction would ease.

Halfway through, she started to pant. And then felt the instinctive urge to bear down. Arching her back, Mary Jo pushed with every ounce of her strength.

When the pain passed, she was too exhausted to speak.

Mack wiped her forehead again and brushed the damp hair from her face.

"Water," she mumbled.

"Got it!" Brandon Hutton tore out of the room, like a man on a quest.

Recovering from the pain, she breathed deeply, her chest heaving. She opened her eyes and looked up at Mack. His gaze was tender.

"How much longer?" she asked, her voice barely a whisper.

"Soon."

"I can't stand much more of this…I just can't."

Tears welled in her eyes and rolled down the sides of her face.

Mack dabbed at her cheeks. As their eyes met, he gave her an encouraging smile. "You can do it," he said. "You're almost there."

"I'm glad you're with me."

"I wouldn't want to be anywhere else," he told her. They continued to hold hands.

Brandon came back with the water. "Here," he said.

Mack took the glass and held it for Mary Jo, supporting her head. "Just a sip or two," he cautioned.

She nodded and savored each tiny sip.

The sound of a car door slamming echoed in the distance.

"Grace," Mary Jo said, grateful the other woman had finally come home.

"I'll bring her up." Brandon disappeared from the room.

Another pain approached. "No…no…" she whimpered, gathering her resolve to get through this next contraction. She closed her eyes and clung to Mack, thanking God once more that she wasn't alone. That Mack was with her…

Mack automatically began to count. Again she felt the urge to push. Gritting her teeth, she bore down, grunting loudly for the first time, straining her entire body.

"Mary Jo." Grace's serene voice broke through the haze of pain. "I came as soon as I heard."

The contraction eased and Mary Jo collapsed onto the mattress, sweat blinding her eyes.

"The baby's in the birth canal," Mack told her friend.

"What would you like me to do?" Grace asked.

"Hold on to her hand and count off the seconds when the contractions come."

"No...don't leave me." Mary Jo couldn't do this without Mack at her side.

"I need to deliver the baby," he explained, his words so gentle they felt like a warm caress. "Grace will help you."

"I'm here," Grace said.

"Okay." Reluctantly Mary Jo freed Mack's hand.

Grace slipped into his spot. "I don't want to hurt you," Mary Jo said.

"How would you do that?" Grace asked, clasping her hand.

Somehow she found the strength to smile. "I squeeze hard."

"You aren't going to hurt me," Grace said reassuringly. "You squeeze as hard as you need to and don't worry about me." She reached for the damp cloth and wiped Mary Jo's flushed and heated face.

"I...don't have anything for the baby," she whispered. That thought suddenly struck Mary Jo and nearly devastated her. Her baby wasn't even born yet, and already she was a terrible mother. Already she'd failed her child.

"That's all been taken care of."

"But...I don't even have a blanket."

"Maryellen and Jon are stopping at their house for diapers and baby blankets and clothes for a newborn."

"But..."

"Maryellen still has all of Drake's clothes, so that should be the least of your worries, okay?"

"Okay." A weight lifted from her heart.

Another pain approached. Mary Jo could feel herself pushing the infant from her womb. She gritted her teeth, bearing down with all her strength.

Grace, her voice strong and confident, counted off the seconds. Again, when the pain was over, Mary Jo collapsed on the bed.

In the silence that followed, Mary Jo could hear the sound of her own harsh breathing. Then in the distance she heard the laughter of children.

"The kids..."

"The grandchildren are outside with Cliff," Grace said.

"Laughing?"

"Do you want me to tell Cliff to keep them quiet?"

"No...no. It's...joyful." This was the way it should be on Christmas Eve. Hearing their happiness gave her hope. Her baby, no matter what the future held, would be born surrounded by people who were generous and kind.

Giving birth in a barn, the stalls below filled with beasts, children running and laughing outside, celebrating the season, hadn't been part of Mary Jo's plan. And yet—it was perfect.

So perfect.

This was a thousand times better than being alone with strangers in a hospital. None of her brothers would've been comfortable staying with her through labor. Maybe Ned, but even her youngest brother, as much as he loved her, wouldn't have done well seeing her in all this pain.

Mack had been with her from the first, and now Grace.

"Thank you," she whispered to them both.

"No, Mary Jo, thank *you*," Grace whispered back. "We're so honored to be helping you."

"I'm glad you're with me." She smiled tremulously at Grace, then Mack. How she wished she'd fallen in love with him instead of David. Mack was everything a man should be....

Another pain came, and she locked her eyes with his for as long as she could until the contraction became too strong. She surrendered to it, whimpering softly.

"The head's almost there," Mack said when the pain finally released her. "Your baby has lots of brown hair."

"Oh..."

"Another pain or two and this will be over," Grace promised.

"Thank God, thank God," Mary Jo said fervently.

"You're going to be a good mother," Grace told her.

Mary Jo wanted to believe that. Needed to believe it. All night, she'd been tortured with doubts and, worse, with guilt about arriving at this moment totally unprepared.

"I *want* to be a good mother."

"You already are," Mack said.

"I love my baby."

"I know." Grace whisked the damp hair from her brow.

Mary Jo was drenched in sweat, her face streaked with tears. "I'm never going through this again," she gasped, looking at Grace. "I can't believe my mother gave birth four times."

"All women think that," Grace said. "I know I did. While I was in labor with Maryellen, I told Dan that if this baby wasn't the son he wanted, he was out of luck because I wasn't having another one."

"You did, though."

"As soon as you hold your baby in your arms, nothing else matters. You forget the pain."

Footsteps clattered up the stairs. "Mom?"

It was Maryellen, Grace's daughter.

"In here," Grace called out.

Maryellen hurried into the room, then paused when she saw Mary Jo and smiled tearfully. Her arms were heaped with baby clothes.

A pain overtook Mary Jo. Again it was Mack she

looked to, Mack who held her gaze, lending her his strength.

She was grateful that Grace was at her side, but most of the time it had been Mack who'd guided and encouraged her. He had a way of comforting her that no one else seemed to have, not even Grace.

"You're doing so well," Mack said to her. "We have a shoulder...."

Mary Jo sobbed quietly. It was almost over. The baby was leaving her body. She could feel it now, feel the child slipping free and then the loud, fierce cry that resounded in the room.

Her relief was instantaneous.

She'd done it! Despite everything, she'd done it.

With her last reserves of strength, Mary Jo rose up on one elbow.

Mack held the child in his arms and Brandon had a towel ready. Mack turned to her and she saw, to her astonishment, that there were tears in his eyes.

"You have a daughter, Mary Jo."

"A daughter," she whispered.

"A beautiful baby girl."

Her own tears came then, streaming from her eyes with an intensity of emotion that surprised her. She hadn't given much thought to the sex of this child, hadn't really cared. Her brothers were the ones who'd insisted she'd have a son.

They'd been wrong.

"A daughter," she whispered again. "I have a daughter."

Eighteen

"The natives are getting restless," Jon Bowman reported to Grace when she came down from the apartment. After watching the birth of Mary Jo's baby, Grace felt ecstatic. She couldn't describe all the emotions tumbling through her. Joy. Excitement. Awe. Each one held fast to her heart.

Katie, April and Tyler raced around the yard, screaming at the top of their lungs, chasing one another, gleeful and happy. Jon went to quiet them, but Grace stopped him.

"Let them play," she told her son-in-law. "They aren't hurting anything out here."

"Kelly and Lisa are inside making hot cocoa," Cliff said, joining Grace. "And Paul's looking after Emma." He slid his arm around her waist. "Everything all right up there?" He nodded toward the barn.

"Everything's wonderful. Mary Jo had a baby girl."

"That's marvelous!" Cliff kissed her cheek. "I bet you never guessed you'd be delivering a baby on Christmas Eve."

Grace had to agree; it was the last thing she'd expected. She was thankful Mary Jo hadn't been stuck in some hotel room alone. These might not have been the best of circumstances, but she'd ended up with people who genuinely cared for her and her baby.

Grace didn't know Roy and Corrie McAfee's son well, but Mack had proved himself ten times over. He was a capable, compassionate young man, and he'd been an immeasurable help to Mary Jo. In fact, Grace doubted *anyone* could have done more.

After he'd delivered that baby girl, Mack had cradled the infant in his arms and gazed down on her with tears shining in his eyes. An onlooker might have thought he was the child's father.

The other EMT actually had to ask him to let go of the baby so he could wash her. After that, Grace had wrapped the crying baby in a swaddling blanket and handed her to Mary Jo.

The two EMTs were finishing up with Mary Jo and would be transporting her and the baby to the closest birthing center. Maryellen had stayed to discuss breastfeeding and to encourage and, if need be, assist the new mother.

Grace had felt it was time to check on the rest of her family.

"It's certainly been a full and busy night," Cliff said.

"Fuller than either of us could've imagined," Grace murmured.

A car pulled into the yard. "Isn't that Jack's?" Cliff asked, squinting into the lights.

"Yes—it's Olivia and Jack." Grace should've known Olivia wouldn't just go home after Christmas Eve services. She'd briefly told Olivia what was happening before she'd hurried out of the church, fearing she'd caused enough of a distraction as it was.

Jack parked next to Cliff's vehicle. Before he'd even

turned off the engine, Olivia had opened her door. "How's everything?" she asked anxiously as she stepped out of the car.

"We have a baby girl."

Olivia brought her hands together and pressed them to her heart. "I'm so *pleased*. And Mary Jo?"

"Was incredible."

"You delivered the baby?"

"Not exactly. But I was there."

Being with Mary Jo had brought back so many memories of her own children's births. Memories that were clear and vivid. The wonder of seeing that beautiful, perfectly formed child. The elation. The feeling of womanly power. She remembered it all.

"If not you, then who?" Olivia asked.

"Mack McAfee. The other EMT, Brandon, was there, too, but it was Mack who stayed with Mary Jo, who helped her through the worst of it. By the time I arrived, the baby was ready to be born."

"I'm sure she was happy to see you."

Mary Jo had been, but she hadn't really needed Grace; she and Mack had worked together with a sense of ease and mutual trust.

Grace almost felt as if she'd intruded on something very private. The communication between Mack and Mary Jo had been—she hesitated to use this word—*spiritual*. It was focused entirely on the birth, on what each needed to do to get that baby born. Grace felt moved to tears, even now, as she thought about it.

"Grandma, listen!" Tyler shouted. He pounded on his drum, making an excruciating racket.

Grace covered her ears. "Gently, Tyler, gently."

Tyler frowned as he looked up at her. "I was playing my best for you."

"Remember the song about the little drummer boy?" Olivia asked him.

Tyler nodded eagerly. "It's my favorite."

"It says in the song that he went pa-rum-pum-pum-pum, right?"

Tyler nodded again.

"It doesn't say he beat the drum like crazy until Baby Jesus's mother put her hands over her ears and asked him to go next door and play."

Tyler laughed. "No."

"Okay, try it more slowly now," Grace said.

Tyler did, tapping on the drum in a soft rhythm that was pleasing to the ear.

"Lovely," Grace told her grandson.

"Can I play for the ox and the lamb?" he asked.

"In the song they kept time, remember?"

Grinning, Tyler raced away to show his cousins what he'd learned and to serenade the animals.

"Come in for a cup of coffee," Cliff suggested to Olivia and Jack.

"We should head home," Jack said. His arm rested protectively on Olivia's shoulders.

"I just wanted to make sure everything turned out well," Olivia explained. "Do you think I could see Mary Jo and the baby for a few minutes?"

"I don't see why not," Grace said with a smile.

The two women left the men outside while Grace led the way up to the small apartment. Brandon Hutton sat on the top step with his medical equipment, filling out paperwork. He shifted aside and they skirted around him.

"Mary Jo?" Grace asked, standing in the doorway to the bedroom. "Would it be okay if Olivia came in to see the baby?"

"Of course. That would be fine," Mary Jo said.

When they walked into the bedroom, they found Mary Jo sitting up, holding her baby in her arms.

"Oh, my," Olivia whispered as she reached the bed. "She's so tiny."

"She didn't feel so tiny a little while ago." Mary Jo looked up with a comical expression. "I felt like I was giving birth to an elephant."

"It was worth it, though," Olivia said and ran her finger over the baby's head. "She's just gorgeous."

"I never would've believed how much you can love such a tiny baby." Mary Jo's voice was full of wonder. "I thought my heart would burst with love when Mack put her in my arms."

"Do you have a name for her?" Grace asked.

"Not yet. I had one picked out, but now I'm not sure."

"She's a special baby born on a special night."

"I was thinking the same thing," Mary Jo said, kissing the newborn's forehead. Her gaze fell lovingly on the child. "When I was first pregnant…I was so embarrassed and afraid, I prayed God would just let me die. And now…now I see her as an incredible gift."

Grace had felt that way when she discovered she was pregnant with Maryellen all those years ago. It was shortly before her high school graduation; she'd been dating Dan Sherman and their relationship had always been on-again, off-again. She'd dreaded telling him she was pregnant, even more than she'd dreaded telling her parents.

For weeks she'd kept her secret, embarrassed and ashamed. But like Mary Jo, she'd learned to see the pregnancy as an unexpected gift, and the moment Maryellen was placed in her arms, Grace had experienced an overwhelming surge of love. The birth hadn't been easy, they never really were, but as soon as she saw her daughter, Grace had recognized that every minute of that pain had been worth the outcome.

"If you need anything," Olivia was saying to Mary Jo, "make sure you give me a call."

"Thank you. That's so kind."

Olivia turned to Mack, who hovered in the background. "Are you taking her to the birthing center in Silverdale?"

He nodded. "We'll be leaving in about ten minutes."

"Then I won't keep you," Olivia said. "I'll stop by sometime tomorrow afternoon," she promised Mary Jo.

"Oh, please don't," Mary Jo said quickly. "It's Christmas—spend that time with your family. I'll get in touch soon. Anyway, I'll be with my own family." She looked up, her eyes widening.

"Mary Jo?" Grace asked in alarm. "What's wrong?"

"Oh, my goodness!"

"What is it?" Mack's voice was equally worried.

"My brothers," Mary Jo said. "They never showed up."

"That's true." The entire matter had slipped Grace's mind. "Mary Jo's brothers were due here—" she checked her watch "—three hours ago."

"Where could they be?" Mary Jo wailed.

Grace tried to reassure her. "They're probably lost. It's easy enough with all these back roads. They've never been in this area before, have they?"

Mary Jo shook her head.

"Don't worry. When they arrive, I'll tell them what happened and where to find you."

Mary Jo smiled down at the infant cradled in her arms. "They'll hardly believe I had the baby—but then it's hard for me to believe, too."

"I'll call you tomorrow," Olivia said.

"Thank you, but please…"

"Yes?"

"Don't tell your parents about the baby yet. Give them a chance to settle back into their routine before you let them know about David and me…and the baby."

"I won't say a word until you and I agree the time is right."

Mary Jo nodded.

Grace was impressed that Mary Jo wanted to spare Ben and Charlotte the unsavory news of David's betrayal until they were more prepared to accept it.

"I'll leave you now," Olivia told her. "But like I said, if you need *anything,* anytime, please call. You're practically family, you know."

Mary Jo thanked her softly. "You all feel like family to me.… Everyone's been so wonderful."

Grace walked down the stairs with Olivia. She was surprised to see Jack and Cliff still outside, huddled with the children.

"What's Cliff up to now?" Grace wondered aloud.

Jack glanced over. "You gotta see this!" he said, waving at Olivia. He sounded like a giddy child.

As soon as Grace saw the huge carton of fireworks Cliff had dragged out, she groaned. "Cliff!"

"I was saving them for New Year's Eve, but I can't think of a better night for celebrating, can you?"

"What about the horses?"

"They're all safe in their stalls. Don't worry about them."

"And Buttercup? She hates that kind of noise."

"She's locked in the house."

"Can we, Grandpa, can we?"

The children were jumping up and down, clapping their hands with enthusiasm.

"Why right now?" Grace asked.

Cliff sent her a look of pure innocence. "I was just casting about for a way to keep the grandkids entertained."

"Oh, all right." She sighed loudly, holding back a grin.

"Okay if we stay and watch?" Jack said.

Grace and Olivia glanced at each other. As they'd often had occasion to observe, most men were little boys at heart.

"If you must," Olivia murmured.

The front door opened and Kelly stepped out with her husband, Paul, who still held the baby. Grace's daughter balanced a large tray filled with mugs and Lisa followed with a tin of Christmas cookies.

"Anyone for hot chocolate?" Kelly asked.

"I'd love a cup," Olivia said.

"Me, too," Grace put in.

Paul gestured at the kids. "What's going on?"

"Fireworks in a few minutes," Grace told him.

"Wow! Great idea."

"Men," Olivia whispered under her breath, and then both Olivia and Grace broke into giggles, just like they had when they were schoolgirls.

Nineteen

"How did we get so lost—twice?" Linc groaned. The only thing left to do was return to Cedar Cove and start over. That *sounded* easy enough, except that he no longer knew how to find the town.

"That King did us wrong," Mel said.

"You think?" Linc asked sarcastically. He was past frustration, past impatience and past losing his cool. All he wanted was to track down his pregnant sister and bring her home. That shouldn't be such an impossible task, and yet...

"I'm never going back to King's," Ned said in disgust.

"Me, neither," Mel spat. "If I ever go back to Cedar Cove, which is unlikely."

Frankly, Linc was of the same mind, at least as far as King went. The man had blackmailed him into paying for directions and then completely misled him. True, the sandwiches weren't bad, but he'd overcharged for them. The old coot had an evil streak a mile wide. If he thought it was fun to misdirect them, then he had a perverse sense of humor, too. Perverse? Downright twisted!

"Let's find a phone that works," Ned suggested, not

for the first time. His brother had harped on that for the last half hour. Their cell phones were useless out here. But it wasn't as if there was a phone booth sitting on the side of the road just waiting for them to appear.

"Okay, you find one, Ned, and I'll be more than happy to pay for the call."

Ned didn't respond, which was definitely for the best.

"What we need is a sign," Mel said.

Linc bit off another sarcastic comment. They needed a sign, all right, and it had better be one from heaven. He could only imagine what Mary Jo must be thinking. By now his sister probably figured they'd abandoned her, yet nothing could be further from the truth.

"What's that?" Ned shouted, pointing into the distance.

"What's what?" Linc demanded.

"There," Mel said, leaning forward and gazing toward the sky.

Linc saw a flash of light. He pulled over to the side of the road and climbed out of the truck. He needed to stretch his legs, anyway, and the cold air would revive him. Sure enough, someone was setting off fireworks. The sky burst with a spectacular display of lights.

"Wow, that was a big one," Mel said, like a kid at a Fourth of July display.

His brothers didn't seem to appreciate the gravity of their situation. "Okay, it's nice, but how's that going to help us?"

"You said I should find a phone," Ned pointed out. "Whoever's setting off those fireworks must have a phone, don't you think?"

"Yeah, I guess," Linc agreed. He leaped back into the

truck, his brothers with him. "Guide me," he said and jerked the transmission into Drive.

"Turn right," Ned ordered.

"I can't!"

"Why not?"

"I'd be driving across someone's pasture, that's why." Obviously Linc was the only one with his eye on the road.

"Then turn as soon as you reach an intersection," Mel told him.

Linc had never liked taking instructions from his younger brothers. He gritted his teeth. As the oldest, he'd always shouldered responsibility for the others. He had no choice now, however—not that things had worked out all that well with *him* in charge.

At the first opportunity, Linc made a sharp right-hand turn, going around the corner so fast the truck teetered on two wheels. It came down with a bounce that made all three of them hit their heads on the ceiling. "Now what?"

"Pull over for a minute."

"Okay." Linc eased to a stop by the side of the road.

"There!" Mel had apparently seen another display in the heavens. "That star!"

"Which way?" Linc asked with a sigh.

"Go straight."

Linc shook his head. The road in front of him was anything but straight. It twisted and curved this way and that.

"Linc," Mel said, glaring at him. "Go!"

"I'm doing the best I can." He came to a straight patch in the road and floored the accelerator. If anyone had told him he'd be chasing around a series of dark roads, desperately seeking guidance from a fireworks display, he would've laughed scornfully. Him, Mr. Great Sense of Direction? Lost? He sighed again.

"We're getting close," Mel said.

"Okay, stop!" Ned yelled.

Linc slammed on the brakes. The three of them jerked forward and just as abruptly were hurled back. If not for the seat belts, they would've been thrown headfirst into the windshield.

"Hey!" Mel roared.

"Maybe don't stop *quite* so suddenly," Ned added in a voice that was considerably less hostile.

"Sorry."

"Wait, wait, wait." Mel cocked his head toward the sky. "Okay, continue down this road." Mercifully it was flat and straight.

"Here," Ned said a minute later.

Once more Linc slammed on the brakes, only this time his brothers were prepared and had braced themselves.

"Look!" Ned shouted. "This is it. We're here!"

Linc didn't know what he was talking about. "We're where?"

"The Harding ranch," Mel answered.

Then Linc saw. There, painted on the rural route box, was the name Cliff Harding. To his left was a pasture and a large barn.

"I think I see a camel," Linc said. He'd heard about people raising llamas before but not camels.

"Are you sure?" Ned mumbled. "Maybe it's just an ugly horse."

"A camel? No way," Mel insisted.

"I say it's a camel." Linc wondered if his brother's argumentative nature had something to do with being a middle child. Ned, as the youngest, was usually the reasonable one, the conciliator. Whereas he—

"A *camel?*" Mel repeated in an aggressive tone. "What would a camel be doing here?"

"Does it matter?" Ned broke in. "This is where Mary Jo's waiting for us."

"Right." Linc turned into the long driveway that led to the house and barn. The fireworks had stopped, but some kind of party seemed to be taking place, because the yard was filled with people. There was a bunch of little kids running around and the atmosphere was festive and excited.

"There's an aid car here." Ned gestured urgently in its direction.

"Do you think someone's hurt?" Mel asked.

"No," Linc said slowly, thoughtfully. This was what he'd feared from the first. The minute he'd heard about Mary Jo's dizzy spell he'd suspected she was about to give birth. "I think Mary Jo might have had her baby."

"But she isn't due for another two weeks," Mel said.

Ned opened the truck door. "Instead of discussing it, let's go find out."

A middle-aged woman approached as Linc got out of the truck. "You must be Mary Jo's brothers," she said. "I'm Grace Harding. Merry Christmas!"

The woman looked friendly, and Linc appreciated the pleasant greeting. "Merry Christmas to you, too. Sorry for the delay...."

"We got lost."

How helpful of Mel to point out the obvious.

"Some guy named King gave us the wrong directions."

"King's Gas and Grocery?" A man came up to them, extending his hand. "Cliff Harding."

"That's the one," Ned answered.

Cliff pinched his lips together, but didn't speak.

Linc shook hands with Grace's husband. "Linc Wyse," he said, introducing himself. "My brothers, Ned and Mel."

Hands were shaken and greetings exchanged all around.

"We were wondering if you were ever going to find the place," Cliff told them.

"If it hadn't been for the fireworks, we probably wouldn't have," Mel admitted.

Linc ignored him and glanced at the aid car. "Mary Jo?" He couldn't bring himself to finish the question.

Grace nodded. "She had the baby."

"A boy," Mel said confidently. "Right?" His eyes lit up with expectation.

"A girl."

"A girl?" Linc was shocked. "Mary Jo had a girl?"

"You sound disappointed," Grace said, studying him closely.

"Not…disappointed. Surprised."

Ned felt obliged to explain. "For some reason, we were all sure she was having a boy."

"Well, she didn't. You have a niece."

"We have a niece," Linc said to his brothers. Mel gave him a congratulatory slap on the back that nearly sent him reeling. He suddenly realized what this all meant. He was an *uncle*. He hadn't thought of himself in those terms until that very moment.

"The EMTs are bringing Mary Jo and the baby down now," Grace was saying.

"Can we see the baby?" Linc asked.

"And talk to Mary Jo?" Mel added.

Grace warmed them with a smile. "I'm sure you can."

A little boy raced up to her. "Grandma, Grandma, can I play my drum for the baby and Mary Jo?"

Grace crouched down so she was eye level with her grandson. "Of course, Tyler, but remember you have to play quietly so you won't disturb the baby."

"Okay!"

Two EMTs rolled Mary Jo toward the aid car on a gurney.

As soon as she saw her brothers, Mary Jo—holding the sleeping newborn in one arm—stretched out the other. "Linc, Mel, Ned…oh, my goodness, you're here!"

They hurried to her side.

"You had a girl," Mel said, staring down at the bundle in her arms.

"She looks just like you," Ned commented.

"No, she doesn't," Linc chimed in. "She looks like the Wyse family—like all of us."

"And like herself," Mary Jo said.

"I'm sorry we were so late," Ned apologized.

"Yeah, we got lost."

If Mel announced that to one more person, Linc might be tempted to slug him.

"Where are they taking you?" he asked.

"To the birthing center in Silverdale," one of the EMTs answered.

"You won't have any trouble finding it," Cliff assured them. "I'll draw you a map."

"No, thanks." Mel shuddered noticeably.

"We'd better follow the aid car," Linc said.

"Mary Jo, we brought you gifts."

"Thank you, Ned." Her face softened as she looked at the three of them. "That's so sweet."

"We're sorry about the things we said." Again this

came from Ned, who was more willing to acknowledge that he was wrong than either Mel or Linc.

"Yeah," Mel agreed.

Linc muttered something under his breath, hoping it would pass for an apology. He did feel bad about the way everything had gone and the pressure they'd put on Mary Jo. They hadn't meant to. Their intentions had been good, although he could see now that they'd gone too far. Still, he wasn't letting David Rhodes off the hook. The man had responsibilities and Linc was as determined as ever to see that he lived up to them.

"Linc, Mel, Ned, I want you to meet Mack McAfee," his sister said, her arm out to the EMT. "Oh, I forgot. You guys met earlier."

Linc nodded at the other man. So did Mel and Ned.

"Great to see you again," Mack said. "And congratulations on your brand-new niece. Oh, and this is my partner, Brandon Hutton."

Once more the brothers nodded.

"I couldn't have managed without them," Mary Jo said fervently.

Linc thanked them both. "Our family's much obliged to you for everything you've done."

"Just part of the job," Brandon said.

"It was an honor," Mack told them. "I have to tell you this was the best Christmas Eve of my life."

"And mine," Mary Jo said. She looked at Mack, and the two of them seemed to maintain eye contact for an extra-long moment.

"Now, Grandma?" Tyler stepped up to Grace, a small drum strapped over his shoulders.

"Now, Tyler."

The youngster set his sticks in motion. Pa-rum-pum-pum-pum, pa-rum-pum-pum-pum.

Linc glanced over at the barn and saw the ox and the lamb in the paddock. They seemed to be keeping time to the drum, bowing their heads with each slow beat.

Mary Jo was right. This was the best Christmas Eve of his life. Of *all* their lives.

Twenty

Mary Jo woke to find Mack McAfee standing in the doorway of her private hospital room. "Mack," she whispered. Her heart reacted to the sight of him, pounding extraordinarily hard. She hadn't been certain she'd ever see him again.

"How are you feeling?" he asked, walking into the room.

"Fine." Actually, she was sore and tired and eager to get home, to be with her family.

"I brought you something."

"You did?" She sat up in bed and self-consciously brushed her fingers through her hair.

Mack produced a bouquet of roses, which he'd been hiding behind his back. "For you, Mary Jo." He bowed ever so slightly.

"My goodness, where'd you get these on Christmas Day?"

He raised his eyebrows. "I have my ways."

"Mack."

"Oh, all right, I got them in the hospital gift shop."

"They're open?"

"Sort of… I saw someone I knew who had a key and she let me in."

Mary Jo brought the fragrant flowers to her nose and breathed in their fresh scent. The vase was lovely, too. "You shouldn't have, but I'm thrilled you did."

"I wasn't sure your brothers would remember to send flowers."

Her brothers. Just thinking about the three of them, all bumbling and excited, made her want to laugh. They'd practically shoved each other out of the way last night, fussing over her and the baby. They'd been full of tales about their misadventures in Cedar Cove and the people they'd met and their near-arrest. Mel had a few comments about a meat loaf sandwich, too—and then they'd all decided they were hungry again. Their gifts of the gold coin, the perfume and the incense lay on the bedside table.

When they'd arrived at the hospital, her brothers wouldn't let her out of their sight—until the physician came into the room to examine her and then they couldn't leave fast enough.

They'd returned for a few minutes an hour later—apparently well-fed—to wish her a final good-night, promising to come back Christmas Day. Then they'd all trooped out again.

"I stopped at the nursery to see…" Mack paused. "Do you have a name for her yet?"

Mary Jo nodded. "Noelle Grace."

"Noelle for the season and Grace after Grace Harding?"

Mary Jo smiled, nodding again.

"I like it," Mack said. "The name's just right. Elegant and appropriate."

His approval pleased her. She didn't want to think too closely about how much his opinion meant to her—or why. She understood that they'd shared something very special, something intimate, while she was in labor. But that didn't mean the bond they'd experienced would last, no matter how much she wanted it to. Mack had come into her life for a brief period of time. Soon she'd go back to Seattle with her family, and he'd go on living here, in Cedar Cove. It was unlikely that she'd see him again; there was no real reason to. The thought was a painful one.

"Noelle Grace was a joy to behold," Mack said with a grin.

"Was she asleep?"

"Nope, she was screaming her head off."

Mary Jo instantly felt guilty. "Oh, the staff should've woken me. It's probably her feeding time."

Mack pulled up a chair and sat down beside the bed. "Nope, she just needed her diaper changed and to be held a little."

"Did someone hold her?" The nursery was crowded with newborns and there were only a couple of nurses on duty.

"I did," Mack admitted, somewhat embarrassed.

"You?"

"I hope you don't mind."

"Of course I don't! I—I'm just surprised they'd let you."

"Yes, well…" Mack looked away and cleared his throat. "I might've led the nurse to believe that Noelle and I are… related."

Mary Jo burst out laughing. "Mack, you didn't!"

"I did. And I have to say that the minute I settled her in my arms, Noelle calmed down, stopped crying and looked straight up at me."

"You brought her into the world, after all." She probably didn't need to remind Mack of that; nevertheless, she wanted him to know she hadn't forgotten what he'd done for her.

The night before, she'd told her brothers that she would never have managed if not for Mack, and that was true. He'd been her salvation. She wanted to tell him all this, but the right words escaped her. Besides, she wasn't sure she could say what was in her heart without getting teary-eyed and emotional.

"I'm so glad you stopped by... I was going to write you and Brandon and thank you for everything."

"It's our job." Those had been Brandon's words, too, and in his case, she assumed they were true. But Mack... Dismissing her appreciation like that—it hurt. Not wanting him to see how his offhand comment had upset her, she stared down at the sheet, twisting it nervously.

Mack stood and reached for her hand, entwining their fingers.

"Let me explain," he said. "It *is* part of what we agreed to do when we took the job with the fire department." He paused for a moment. "But the call from you wasn't an ordinary one."

"How so?" she asked and looked up, meeting his eyes.

"I've never delivered a baby before."

"I know. Me, neither," she said and they smiled at each other.

"It was one of the highlights of my life, being there with you and Noelle."

"Mine, too—I mean, you being there."

"Thank you." His words were low and charged with intent. He leaned forward and braced his forehead against hers. "If it's okay with you..."

"What?" she asked breathlessly.

"I'd like to see Noelle sometime."

"See her?"

"See both of you."

"Both of us," she repeated, afraid she was beginning to sound like an echo.

"As long as it's okay with you," he said again.

She nodded, trying not to act too excited. "If you want."

"I want to very much."

"I'll be back in Seattle," she said.

"I don't mind the drive."

"Or you could take the ferry."

"Yes." Mack seemed just as eager to visit as she was to have him come by. "When?"

She wanted him there as soon as possible. "The doctor said he'd release Noelle and me this afternoon. My brothers are picking us up at three."

"Is tomorrow too soon?" he asked.

Mary Jo was convinced the happiness that flowed through her must have shone from her eyes. She didn't think she could hide it if she tried. "That would be good," she said shyly.

"Merry Christmas, Mary Jo."

"Merry Christmas, Mack."

Just then the nurse came in carrying Noelle. "It's lunchtime," she said cheerfully.

Mary Jo held out her arms for her baby, born on Christmas Eve in Cedar Cove, the town that had taken her in. A town whose people had sheltered her and accepted her. The town that, one day, she'd love to call home.

Home for her and Noelle.

* * * * *

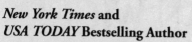

New York Times and
USA TODAY Bestselling Author

SHERRYL WOODS

Sherryl Woods brings the O'Brien family home
for a heartwarming Christmas....

After years apart, Mick and Megan O'Brien are finally
ready to make it official...again. Most of their grown
children couldn't be happier about their rekindled love
and impending marriage this holiday season. Only
Connor, the divorce attorney, is a holdout.

The last thing Megan wants to do is hurt her
family again. After all, is she really sure she
and Mick can make it this time around?
And when an unexpected delivery causes chaos,
it seems only a miracle can reunite this family.

Of course, it *is* Christmas—the season of miracles.

A Chesapeake Shores Christmas

Available wherever books are sold.

MIRA®

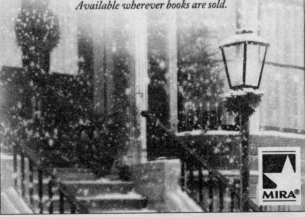

REQUEST YOUR
FREE BOOKS!

2 FREE NOVELS
FROM THE ROMANCE COLLECTION
PLUS 2 FREE GIFTS!

YES! Please send me 2 FREE novels from the Romance Collection and my 2 FREE gifts (gifts are worth about $10). After receiving them, if I don't wish to receive any more books, I can return the shipping statement marked "cancel." If I don't cancel, I will receive 4 brand-new novels every month and be billed just $5.74 per book in the U.S. or $6.24 per book in Canada. That's a saving of at least 28% off the cover price. It's quite a bargain! Shipping and handling is just 50¢ per book.* I understand that accepting the 2 free books and gifts places me under no obligation to buy anything. I can always return a shipment and cancel at any time. Even if I never buy another book, the two free books and gifts are mine to keep forever.

194/394 MDN E7NZ

Name _____ (PLEASE PRINT) _____

Address _____ Apt. # _____

City _____ State/Prov. _____ Zip/Postal Code _____

Signature (if under 18, a parent or guardian must sign)

Mail to **The Reader Service:**
IN U.S.A.: P.O. Box 1867, Buffalo, NY 14240-1867
IN CANADA: P.O. Box 609, Fort Erie, Ontario L2A 5X3

Not valid for current subscribers to the Romance Collection
or the Romance/Suspense Collection.

Want to try two free books from another line?
Call 1-800-873-8635 or visit www.morefreebooks.com.

* Terms and prices subject to change without notice. Prices do not include applicable taxes. N.Y. residents add applicable sales tax. Canadian residents will be charged applicable provincial taxes and GST. Offer not valid in Quebec. This offer is limited to one order per household. All orders subject to approval. Credit or debit balances in a customer's account(s) may be offset by any other outstanding balance owed by or to the customer. Please allow 4 to 6 weeks for delivery. Offer available while quantities last.

Your Privacy: Harlequin Books is committed to protecting your privacy. Our Privacy Policy is available online at www.eHarlequin.com or upon request from the Reader Service. From time to time we make our lists of customers available to reputable third parties who may have a product or service of interest to you. If you would prefer we not share your name and address, please check here. ☐

Help us get it right—We strive for accurate, respectful and relevant communications. To clarify or modify your communication preferences, visit us at www.ReaderService.com/consumerschoice.

MROM10R

DEBBIE MACOMBER

32798	ORCHARD VALLEY GROOMS	___ $7.99 U.S.	___ $9.99 CAN.
32783	THE MAN YOU'LL MARRY	___ $7.99 U.S.	___ $9.99 CAN.
32702	FAIRY TALE WEDDINGS	___ $7.99 U.S.	___ $9.99 CAN.
32767	SUMMER ON BLOSSOM STREET	___ $7.99 U.S.	___ $9.99 CAN.
32971	92 PACIFIC BOULEVARD	___ $7.99 U.S.	___ $9.99 CAN.
32679	MARRIED IN SEATTLE	___ $7.99 U.S.	___ $7.99 CAN.
32883	TWENTY WISHES	___ $7.99 U.S.	___ $9.99 CAN.
32602	THE MANNING GROOMS	___ $7.99 U.S.	___ $7.99 CAN.
32595	SMALL TOWN CHRISTMAS	___ $7.99 U.S.	___ $7.99 CAN.
32881	BACK ON BLOSSOM STREET	___ $7.99 U.S.	___ $9.99 CAN.
32569	ALWAYS DAKOTA	___ $7.99 U.S.	___ $7.99 CAN.
32474	THE MANNING BRIDES	___ $7.99 U.S.	___ $7.99 CAN.
32970	8 SANDPIPER WAY	___ $7.99 U.S.	___ $9.99 CAN.
32861	204 ROSEWOOD LANE	___ $7.99 U.S.	___ $9.99 CAN.
32882	THE SHOP ON BLOSSOM STREET	___ $7.99 U.S.	___ $9.99 CAN.
32880	A GOOD YARN	___ $7.99 U.S.	___ $9.99 CAN.
32968	6 RAINIER DRIVE	___ $7.99 U.S.	___ $9.99 CAN.
32862	50 HARBOR STREET	___ $7.99 U.S.	___ $9.99 CAN.
32911	THE MANNING SISTERS	___ $7.99 U.S.	___ $9.99 CAN.
32969	74 SEASIDE AVENUE	___ $7.99 U.S.	___ $9.99 CAN.
32511	DAKOTA BORN	___ $7.99 U.S.	___ $9.50 CAN.
32884	SUSANNAH'S GARDEN	___ $7.99 U.S.	___ $9.99 CAN.
32393	DAKOTA HOME	___ $7.99 U.S.	___ $9.50 CAN.
32892	READY FOR LOVE	___ $7.99 U.S.	___ $9.99 CAN.
32366	BE MY VALENTINE	___ $7.99 U.S.	___ $9.50 CAN.
32362	COUNTRY BRIDES	___ $7.99 U.S.	___ $9.50 CAN.
32967	44 CRANBERRY POINT	___ $7.99 U.S.	___ $9.99 CAN.
32028	CHANGING HABITS	___ $7.50 U.S.	___ $8.99 CAN.
32972	16 LIGHTHOUSE ROAD	___ $7.99 U.S.	___ $9.99 CAN.
32946	311 PELICAN COURT	___ $7.99 U.S.	___ $9.99 CAN.
66434	MONTANA	___ $6.99 U.S.	___ $7.99 CAN.

(limited quantities available)

TOTAL AMOUNT	$ _____
POSTAGE & HANDLING	$ _____
($1.00 for 1 book, 50¢ for each additional)	
APPLICABLE TAXES*	$ _____
TOTAL PAYABLE	$ _____

(check or money order—please do not send cash)

To order, complete this form and send it, along with a check or money order for the total above, payable to MIRA Books, to: **In the U.S.:** 3010 Walden Avenue, P.O. Box 9077, Buffalo, NY 14269-9077; **In Canada:** P.O. Box 636, Fort Erie, Ontario, L2A 5X3.

Name: _____

Address: _____ City: _____

State/Prov.: _____ Zip/Postal Code: _____

Account Number (if applicable): _____

075 CSAS

*New York residents remit applicable sales taxes.
*Canadian residents remit applicable GST and provincial taxes.

MIRA®

www.MIRABooks.com

MDM0910BL